**Other Mysteries
by
Martha Kemm Landes**

Framed Fur Murder

Pity the Garage Sale Addict

Pity the Movie Lover

Upcycled to Death

by

Martha Kemm Landes

Elemar Publishing

www.marthalandes.com

Pitymystery@gmail.com

Print ISBN: 978-1-956912-06-7
e-Book ISBN: 978-1-956912-07-4
Audiobook ISBN: 978-1-956912-08-1

Cover design by Samantha Galasso

First Edition

DEDICATION

This book is dedicated to the state of New Mexico and its beautiful blend of cultures. I feel fortunate to live in the Land of Enchantment with its mild weather, and stunning natural beauty.

Special thanks to my husband, Dan, who supports me even when I acquire and repurpose my own found items.

Upcycled to Death

Martha Kemm Landes

OUT OF THE BOX

MAP

see p. 17

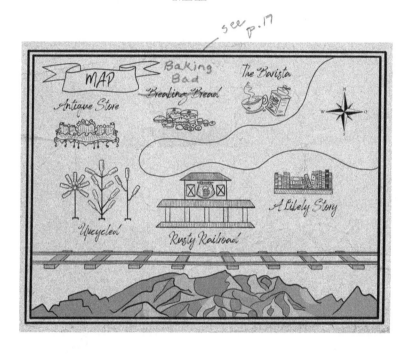

CHAPTER 1

"Well?" I mumbled with a mouthful of screws.

When I didn't hear a response, I wrenched my head down to see my best friend, who sat on the tailgate of my truck, gazing with a goofy expression at the brewery situated just across from us.

I tried again louder, "Jill, is it straight?" Although my speech was incomprehensible, she could have at least looked up. After all, I stood on a ladder, one hand holding a bicycle wheel over my head, and the other gripping a drill.

I took the longest screw from my lips and poked it through the spokes. With limited leverage, I managed to start the screw into the metal. Besides the whir of the drill, I was pretty sure I heard my muscles groan as I worked. My forehead dripped sweat as I tightened the last screw and secured the bike wheel in place. I lowered my arms and stepped down from my perch in relief.

The redhead announced nonchalantly, "Um if you want it to be in the middle of the door, you're off by several inches."

My scowl was wasted since Jill's gaze was again fixed across the parking lot. She added with a dreamy voice, "You're so lucky to be so close to those guys."

With no hardware in my mouth this time, I spoke clearly. "And I'm so lucky to have my best friend help me today. I could have fallen off the ladder, impaled myself with the screwdriver, and you wouldn't have even noticed."

She cocked her head and turned to me with glassy eyes. "But have you seen them? They're gorgeous!"

Rolling my eyes, I said, "No. But, then I'm not boy crazy like you." I stepped off the curb into the front parking space to give my handiwork a look. She was right. The sign was not centered, but wasn't symmetry overrated? I studied the scene and saw the solution. By curving the lettering around the left side of the tire, it would all be centered and perfect.

I took a deep satisfying breath and grinned uncontrollably. My decade-long dream was coming true. My very own shop, 'Upcycled', would open in a week. I was a real business owner and had a shop in the coolest area in all of Albuquerque. I shook my head in wonder, smiling at my quirky place.

When I remembered how much needed to be done before the doors opened for business, I snapped out of my reverie. While collecting the drill and hardware, I said, "Any chance you could stop staring at boys and come inside to help me?"

Jill's head lolled around on her shoulders as if she'd just had a satisfying massage. She stood slowly wearing a silly smile, folded the ladder, and started to haul it inside.

"Whoa there, Jill! You aren't carrying that. I don't want little Sophia popping out here in my shop."

She looked down at her enormous belly and in her usual perky manner announced, "We've got another three weeks before she's fully cooked and I doubt carrying a ladder will get her here today. But then again, if she's a true daughter of mine, she will make a grand entrance of some sort."

"Well, just in case, go in and sit on my stool." I grabbed the ladder from her and leaned it against the exterior of my shop then led her in and waited for her reaction to the new changes.

Jill's eyes widened as she scanned the space. "Hey, you got walls? It looks like an actual room now! Before I was kinda like, 'whatever!' when I saw this big tin can, but now it looks sweet!" She rubbed her manicured hand along the newly painted wall.

I scoffed, "Just because my store is in a shipping container doesn't mean it can't be nice." I did a Vanna White, pointing out the changes with my un-manicured hands, currently covered with green paint. I often use my fingernails as screwdrivers, so there was no point in ever polishing them.

I beamed. "I hired a guy to frame it out and sheetrock, then install the laminate floor. None of it was cheap, but he promised it will be water and airtight."

Jill did a surprisingly nimble, for her condition, tap dance on the vintage-looking black and white checked floor. "But is it sand tight?"

She had a valid point. New Mexico isn't called high desert for nothing. When the heavy winds blew, our second most abundant natural resource got in every crevice.

I shrugged. "Hope so. Oh, check this out!" Giddy with the anticipation of her reaction, I skipped halfway back and to the left side of the 40-foot shipping container and unlatched a corrugated metal panel on hinges, and pulled it toward me, revealing the great outdoors. I shouted, "Voila!"

She rushed across the empty floor to get a look. "A window! Maria, Now I can actually come to visit you!" She held her hand up to the side of her mouth as if it was a secret. "I wasn't going to tell you, but I figured I'd be too claustrophobic in here to hang out much."

That was a joke. Jill was a human boomerang – she always came back, no matter what. I gazed over her shoulder at the top of the gorgeous Sandia Mountains. The peaks were well defined on this beautiful, clear summer day.

A tear of happiness slid down my face, but I quickly brushed it off so she wouldn't see. I pulled my hair into a ponytail and cleared my throat then said, "It has a screen too. And there's another window upfront for a cross breeze." I walked backward a few steps not worrying about hitting anything since the shop was empty. "And did you notice this?" I pulled back a black and white curtain and uncovered a small storage area with the world's tiniest bathroom. Hardly able to contain my excitement, I pointed to a dorm-sized refrigerator.

"Cool!" she squealed. "You're all set now."

"Well, I kind of had to do it since I'll be here alone and can't leave the shop unattended when nature calls. Plus, I need a place for my crafting materials. I took a breath and shrugged. "So, I gave up my last 8 feet of space for this convenience. I'm so glad I got a 40-foot container instead of 20."

She laughed. "There is no way you could have gotten all your stuff in a place half this size. You probably should have added another one or two containers."

I bit the inside of my cheek, wondering if I should have gotten two. Oh well, maybe I could add on in the future, but this would have to work for now. "Jill, will you hold the ladder while I hang some ceiling lights?"

"Sure, after I use your potty – if I can fit in the little space." She made a face. "Someone is sitting right on my bladder."

I snickered as she rushed off holding her crotch. Jill, a mother! I still couldn't believe it. I figured my crazy friend would be the last one to settle down. After dating just about every boy in college and declaring them all lame, she swore she'd never tie the knot. But then, she met Kelly and the unique couple was born. It wouldn't be long before 'Jill Junior' would hit the stage with a bang. Not sure the world was ready for that.

She came out of the bathroom with a thumbs-up. "Flushes like a pro!"

While Jill held the ladder steady, I hoisted a lamp I'd made from a vintage globe up to the ceiling. She said, "That's cute, Maria. You are so creative! And how in the world did you do all this so fast?"

I snorted and almost choked. "Fast? It took me as long to plan this shop as it took you to grow Sophia."

"Oh, that's right! I told you I was pregnant the same day you got the lease on this place. I'll bet you were like a kid in a candy store designing this shop."

She knew me well. Creating got my juices flowing. I nodded. "Hey, Jill, if you ever start a business, let me help."

Her lip curled into an unnatural scowl. "That'll never happen. My professional fate was sealed at birth. Wait. You have outlets on the ceiling?" With Jill's head bent back as she looked up, her long curly red locks touched her jeans. Our hair looked to be the same length, but if her curls were straightened, she'd have an extra ten inches on my stick-straight hair.

I was hit with the memory of the day we met in first grade. The freckly redhead bounded into the classroom and sat in front of me and never has stopped talking. That whole year, I had to brush her long curls off my desk to see my work. She irritated me then and still does, but I wouldn't trade her for anything. I would love to have just one day with those bouncy ringlets.

"Yeah, the electrician thought outlets on the ceiling was an odd request, but I convinced him to put six up there. You see...if people actually buy my light fixtures, I can change them out in an instant. Hey, can you flip the light on?" Jill left her post to do so, and the glow through the globe illuminated the room and the dangling world. Perfect.

I stepped down to the floor and we commenced to hang teacup lights. Once they were up, I attempted to attach a trombone to the wall. Jill sat on the floor untangling an extension cord for me, chatting all the while. "So, I didn't hear how you ended up getting the turquoise container you wanted? Did you have to pay extra for this color, or…" she lifted an eyebrow, "maybe kill someone?"

"None of the above," I smiled. "The landlord, Larry, who by the way is a sleazy dude, arranged them for us. He said the brewery guys wanted six red containers."

She visibly melted again. "Ummm. Why so many?"

"Oh, they are stacking two smaller ones for upstairs seating and making a balcony. The bookstore owner wanted green. The antique store didn't care about the color and the bakery got the two short yellow units and the coffee shop wanted brown. I only needed one for my little shop and there was only one shipping container in turquoise, so I got it." I grinned because I couldn't help it. I handed Jill the trombone while I turned the screws and hooks into the wall.

"How did you think to use that trombone?"

"You know me. I can't throw anything away and I like to think outside the box...or in this case, outside the boxcar."

We chuckled at my lame joke but I still couldn't believe how lucky I was to lease a spot in 16 Boxes. As soon as I'd heard about the new trendy shipping container shopping center, I took it as a sign. It was time to take the giant leap from my online upcycle shop to a walk-in store. It just had to be profitable. It just had to.

Unlike most shipping container shopping centers that stack and attach all the shops, ours were spread out, each with its own parking and entrance. I was glad to have more room around my unit for now. If they were to expand and add even more containers, I would have to get used to closer neighbors.

I got the trombone from Jill and climbed back up to finagle it.

She said, "Well, I'm so proud of you for having the guts to go for your dream. You've had a tough time, girl, but are finally on your way. I'm sure it will be a financial…"

Jill stopped mid-sentence, probably thinking of the word she wanted to say. Attempting to attach the awkward instrument to the wall, I guessed the word to follow aloud, "Burden? Commitment?" I raised my eyebrows and guessed again, "Success?" When she stayed silent, I glanced down at her. Jill sat wearing that same stupid expression she had earlier, but this time her face was redder than her hair as she stared at the door.

I lifted my gaze to see two handsome guys in jeans and t-shirts standing inside my shop. So, this was Jill's distraction from earlier. Now I understood. The two men looked like they stepped out of a GQ magazine. One had dark hair and stubble and the other was clean-shaven with blond wavy hair. When I realized that I too was staring, I quickly blurted, "Can I help you?"

The one with dark hair said, "Need a hand with the horn?"

"Thanks, but I've just about got it." I was instantly self-conscious with my arms raised since my bare waist showed above my jeans. I turned back to the trombone and hung the slide brace on the last hook, then straightened the instrument and glanced back.

The taller man with lighter hair said, "Is it still playable? I mean, I was quite the trombonist in middle school." He crossed his arms and nodded. "I could serenade you with a slick version of Boogie Woogie Brass." He gave an irresistible wink.

I pictured the big guy as a gawky 13-year-old blatting on a trombone, but even that version of him was endearing. I shook my head and looked away. "I'm sorry. It was in pretty bad shape, so I put it out of its misery, and now it's a…" I flipped a switch causing the bell to emit a soft glow. "…lamp!"

Both guys smiled and nodded. The former trombone player said, "Sweet! I'm Joey and this is my brother, Jett. We're opening the Rusty Railroad Brewpub across the lot."

What a perfect name for a brewery located only a few blocks from a Railrunner station. The commuter train ran from south of Albuquerque to Santa Fe carrying workers and tourists daily.

I stepped down from the ladder, pulled down the hem of my t-shirt, and walked to the two, holding out my hand. "I'm Maria and this is my friend, Jill."

I shook Jett's hand, then Joey's. In addition to the vast difference in the brothers' looks, there was a big contrast in their grips. The appropriately-named Jett had jet-black hair and green eyes. Although his skin was smooth, he had a firm handshake. I determined he was confident and possibly a bit edgy. There was something a little dark about him.

In contrast, Joey's handshake was strong and rough, as though he'd spent a lot of time outdoors. His twinkly blue eyes oozed friendliness and humor.

Jett sighed. "Well, I'm glad that 'bone' is out of commission. I got my fill of Joey honking his horn years ago."

Joey rolled his eyes at his brother. "So, what kind of shop is this?" He looked around the nearly empty building, and nodded to the door, "We saw the bicycle wheel and thought you might sell bikes." He shook his head and squinted, "but the trombone and teacups don't exactly go with that theme."

I smiled as I nodded. "I can see why you thought that. I haven't finished the sign yet. My shop is called Upcycled, which still may be a little confusing. I sell items that I've repurposed…like that!" I pointed up to the globe light. "You'll have to come back to see more when I'm all set up." I crossed my arms, attempting to look casual, then leaned against the wall

Joey smiled. "Will do. So, does your friend speak?"

We all looked down curiously at my silent partner, still sitting on the floor, mouth agape. I smirked. "She usually never stops." This was true. In all the 25 years I'd known Jill, I generally watched and listened to her. It wasn't that I was shy, but with her huge personality, it was easier to hang back and let her fly.

Jill cleared her throat. "Um… Nice to meet you." She blushed and tried to stand up, but like a turtle trying to roll over from its back, she was stuck. I ran over and pulled her up.

"Thanks." She attempted to smooth her wild hair, then without taking a breath said, "Maria is very talented. She has an online store and sells most of her creations as soon as she posts them. I told her it was time to have a real brick and mortar store and she listened to me…except that this one isn't actually brick and mortar – more like bolts and steel." She stopped to breathe.

Joey chuckled at me "I see what you mean." He turned back to Jill. "And what do you do, Jill?"

"Besides posing as a whale? I sell grass." She giggled nervously and said quickly, "Just kidding, well not really kidding. I'm the bookkeeper for my family's synthetic turf company. If you want a good deal, just call 'The Grass Man' and ask for Jill."

"Well, thanks," Joey said, "With the lack of water in New Mexico, that's the way to go if you want green around here."

Jett added, "But we're both in temporary spaces now, so it will be a while before either of us needs landscaping."

Joey looked at me and got to the point of their visit, "We stopped by to invite you over to our place at seven tonight. We're having all the tenants in to get to know each other."

Jett shook his head. "All but the jerk in the antique store."

Joey said, "Jett? Really? Can't it wait?"

"Well, aren't you a little upset that he's trying to shut us down before we even open?" Jett's jaw clenched as he said, "I could just kill him."

I was a little taken aback by his sudden show of anger.

Joey rolled his eyes and used his hands to calm his brother. "He doesn't have grounds to do anything. There are no violations, no matter what he said." He turned to us and said with a much brighter voice, "We'll have beer and are ordering salad and pizza from Dion's."

"Yum," I said, then blinked a few times. "Wait. You already have your brew ready?"

Joey puffed, "I wish. Unfortunately, tonight we'll have to buy from the competition. But we'll be pouring our own in a few days. Then, you can try the good stuff," he said with a wink, then turned to my friend. "Jill, you should come too."

Jill made a tiny squeak when he mentioned her name and then she frowned. "I can't. I've gotta help my brother get ready for a business trip. And, I have to wait a while to have a beer anyway." She pointed down to her belly and flashed her famous Jilly smile.

I nodded to the guys, "Thanks for the invite. I would love to meet the new community. I've been so busy with my place I haven't met anyone, well except the landlord." I wrinkled my nose.

The guys nodded. Jett said, "That Larry is something else, isn't he?"

"You could say that."

The guys said their goodbyes and left, continuing their discussion of the antique store owner's threat. The instant the door closed, Jill sat on the stool and leaned back on the glass counter dramatically. "Didn't I tell you they were dreamy?"

I nodded. "Yes, and for once you were right." Then in a teasing voice, I added, "It might be hard to concentrate when I can see their brewery from my new window."

Jill jumped up and ran over to look out. "You can see their front door from here. Oh my!" She shook her head and said, "I may come to visit more than you want. And to think they are brothers. I just can't decide which one is hotter."

It truly was a tough decision. I nodded, but I had to call her out. "Jill, you do remember you're married, right? I mean the pregnancy hasn't gotten you all goofy has it?"

"Kelly says I can look at anyone I like. I just can't touch." She cocked her head, "Now you on the other hand..." She raised her eyebrows and waggled them at me.

I scoffed. "Ha! As if. I've pretty much given up on that. My last two blind dates were disastrous with one being such a mama's boy he called her to tell her about the date while we ate dinner. And you remember the other one."

Jill said, "Well, I'm pretty sure those guys aren't mama's boys and chances of either of them asking to smell your shoe on the first date are pretty unlikely."

"We can only hope."

"Give them a chance. It's been months since you've had a date, Maria. You're thirty for heaven's sake! Get out there."

"I'm too busy to date. Besides, the man I'm attracted to is fictitious. I'll never find someone who is creative and outdoorsy who reads books and appreciates the arts." I considered the handsome brothers. Could one of them fit my bill? Wait a minute. Why was I even thinking about them? I added, "Besides, Jett and Joey are probably both married anyway."

"Hmmm. It's interesting how you remembered their names. And FYI, neither of them wore a wedding ring."

Of course, Jill had checked out their ring status. She looked at her phone and sighed. "I guess I'd better leave. Want me to help carry in those boxes from your truck before I go?"

"No. I'll get them."

"Let me know what happens tonight." Jill grinned as she tucked her red curls behind her ears.

Jill truly glowed. I smiled at my happy, healthy pregnant friend and said, "Will do. And thanks. You're a pretty good helper when no men are around. Otherwise, you're worthless."

She shrugged and climbed awkwardly into her green Prius with the 'Grass Man' logo on the side. "You love me anyway. See you tomorrow." She shut the door and zipped out of the parking lot, kicking up gravel as she sped off.

As the dust settled, I noticed an old man coming out of the drab antique store across the lot. He struggled to carry a stack of books to his car.

I took a few steps toward him and shouted, "Sir, can I help you with those?"

He turned his head toward me, revealing bushy white hair and even bushier eyebrows. With surprising volume, he shouted, "No! Leave me alone!" He hobbled quickly to his silver Toyota Avalon and then glanced back at me with a scowl as though he thought I might attack him.

I stood frozen, my heart pounding with worry. What was that about? At 5'3" and 100 pounds, I couldn't be that scary. Maybe Jett was right and the old man was just mean.

CHAPTER 2

Back in my shop, while unloading my boxes, I tried to forget the encounter with the old antique store owner. Feeling unsettled, I put on headphones and listened to Wynton Marsalis. Jazz can fix anything.

With a deep cleansing breath, I looked around my shop and took in a visual inventory. Glass counter–check. Lights–check. What next? I couldn't display products until I had shelving and I hadn't even decided where to put the shelving yet.

I worked for a while designing a layout of my shop on graph paper. I then made tiny, cut-out paper versions of the furniture to scale. Moving the paper pieces around the diagram, it was easy to see how they might work best in the eight-foot-wide building without having to move heavy items from one place to another. Once I had concocted a plan, I looked up from my virtual store to my actual space and smiled. I had a plan.

A summer breeze blew from one window to the other, just as I had hoped it would. The evening temperature had cooled and was in the mid-70s. Lovely!

I jumped when my door opened. I should probably put a bell on the door so I wasn't startled every time a customer entered. I looked up at my visitor, but the glare from the bright sun blinded me. I blinked at the silhouette in the doorway. The figure was reminiscent of a villain entering an Old West saloon. He had slightly bowed legs and wore a cowboy hat.

Then came the recognizable whiny voice. "Hey, Missy Maria. Whatcha workin' on?"

I sighed. "Oh, Hi Larry." I gave a polite smile but immediately wished he would leave, even though I understood the landlord might stop by now and then to check on me. I said, "I'm just planning my layout."

He scuffed his boots as he sashayed over to me. I watched his feet as he approached, hoping he wouldn't scratch my new floor, but was distracted as soon as I smelled his gross odor, a combination of stale smoke, wintergreen chewing tobacco, and heavy aftershave. I almost gagged as he leaned over my shoulder to see my miniature shop.

"Darlin', if you need shelving, I know a guy who has deep discounts. I can hook you up." He moved in front of me and leaned his elbow on the counter bringing his face far too close to mine. He gave me a creepy wink.

I shook my head and leaned back. "That's OK. I've got it under control." I quickly stood and moved away from him and his smell. "But I'm glad you stopped by since I still don't have outdoor security lights on my building."

I watched the scrawny man blink his beady eyes. He looked like a lounge lizard version of Barney Fife, but that analogy didn't seem fair to Barney. This guy wasn't loveable or funny at all. And he reeked.

"Oh yeah." He said as he smacked his lips. "I'll get those installed as soon as I get my tools." He stood and stretched his arms overhead, sending a waft of B.O. my way, making my eyes tear up. He yawned. "Well, I better get movin'. Just wanted to see if you're doin' OK."

"I'm fine. Thanks." I nodded, trying not to breathe. He gave me another wink and slid out the door, whistling a tune. Yuck. So far, he was the only part of the new business that I didn't like. But I'll admit I chuckled when I realized the song he whistled was 'Maria' from "West Side Story."

I opened the door to air out the place. When I glanced at my phone, it was already after seven. Great. I was late to the gathering. I dug through a box and found the mirror that I had framed in old barn wood and studied the reflection. My ponytail was a mess so I pulled the band out, letting my thick black hair fall around my shoulders, and finger-combed it until smooth. Luckily, I had mascara and lip gloss in my purse and applied enough to look presentable.

For the past three years with an online business, nobody saw me while I worked, but now I would be visible to customers and other merchant, so I had to consider my appearance.

After one more glance in the mirror, I took a deep breath to gain confidence but gagged on Larry's lingering odor. I coughed as I locked the door, then tiptoed past the antique store, hoping the old man wouldn't see me and throw another fit.

When I passed the bakery, I was surprised to see how cheerful the shop was. I had been so focused on my place I hadn't even looked at the others being set up. Their yellow container had a bright red door painted with a cartoon character wearing a porkpie hat and sunglasses holding a box of cupcakes. The bookstore was on the far side of the brewery, so I would check it out later.

Orange cones surrounded the front of the brewpub, I assumed for incoming landscaping. I skirted around the cones and made my way up the steps to the porch, appropriately built with railroad ties. The strong smell of creosote cleansed my abused sinuses and I smiled at the rusted yellow railroad crossing sign hanging above the door. The vintage double R was a perfect, natural logo for Rusty Railroad Brewpub.

The sound of lively voices hit me as soon as I entered the pub. It sounded like the place was full, but only one of the ten or so rustic tables had occupants. The place was much larger than I expected, but I supposed four long containers placed side by side would seem huge compared to my single boxcar. Soft lighting from antique railroad lights made me feel at home right away.

Jett stood and yelled, "Come on in!" He motioned for me to join the others. I looked over at the group as I stepped closer. My eyes were drawn to an older lady with big gray hair and thick blue eye make-up. Next to her sat a posh-looking girl with dark hair in a blunt cut and deep red lipstick. Across the table from them sat two guys, one heavy and one thin, both a little older than me. The other two spots were taken by the brothers, Jett and Joey. Everyone smiled as I approached.

Joey said, "This is Maria, the beautiful upcycle girl."

I was taken aback by his introduction but managed to smile and say, "Hi everyone." I waved my hand across the table. "And you are?"

The woman with big hair spoke in a slow smooth drawl, "Honey, I'm Louise. I'm opening the bookstore made of green tin cans." Her thick Texas accent was adorable and she twinkled when she spoke. "Wanna know its name?" She didn't wait for me to respond. "'A Likely Story.' I wanted to call it, 'Get Under my Covers', but my daughter just had a fit."

It wasn't hard to tell this Louise was a hoot. I smiled at her.

The classy-looking girl with angular hair lifted her head, or maybe her nose, and said "I'm Victoria. The coffee shop is mine." Although she was probably my age, her appearance suggested she was too sophisticated to be my peer.

With an 'ooh la la' waggle of his head, Joey said, "It's called 'The Barista'."

I raised my eyebrows wondering why she would name the shop after herself.

He continued, "And this is Mike and Pat. They own the bakery."

I said to the friendly-looking guys, "Please limit the number of visits I make to see you. I have an addiction to pastry. What did you name your bakery?"

The larger man said almost apologetically, "It's called Baking Bad. You know, like Breaking Bad?"

The other nudged him. "It's a great name for a bakery in Albuquerque,"

Apparently, the name was a sore subject, but I sensed all was good when the larger man smiled and took his hand.

Louise piped up in her slow drawl. "I tried to watch that show, but it was just too danged gory. And they even filmed part of it at the house across the street from me. A character named Jesse was supposed to own it?"

I raised my eyebrows. Jesse was always my favorite on Breaking Bad.

Joey said, "You live by Jesse's house? I've driven by it many times. Nice neighborhood."

Louise shrugged. "Well, when the TV crews came, they took up the whole street. But…I got to be an extra in one episode." She put her hand up to tamp down our excitement. "Hold your horses. I just drove my truck into my driveway. I had to do it ten times before they were satisfied. But I made forty bucks!"

The bigger baker, the one named Mike, turned to Joey and Jett and changed the subject, "So, did you invite the Antique store owner tonight?"

The brothers looked at each other. Jett said, "Um, yes. We tried to, but Mr. Harrison was not very…"

Joey jumped in and finished the sentence, "receptive."

Jett scoffed. "That's an understatement. He shooed us off his property. I thought he might get a gun." He opened his mouth to say more, but Joey elbowed him.

I frowned. "You're not the only ones. He yelled at me today too."

Pat, the thinner baker, reached across the table and took the first slice of pizza, and said, "Well, he sure won't win many customers that way."

I looked around the pub. "I love the way you've decorated this place. If you want me to keep an eye out for more train paraphernalia, let me know. I live at junkyards and garage sales." Realizing that sounded odd, I added, "Looking for items to repurpose of course."

The group nodded. I chose a slice of pizza with bacon, green chile, and pine nuts and took a bite. Now that was a little slice of heaven. As I chewed, I became aware of a stocky man in his 40s, standing behind the bar gawking at me. His thick brown hair hung down to his chin as he wiped the bar top meticulously. When our eyes connected, he looked down and his face turned red.

Then, I noticed Louise staring at me too. What was with the staring? Did I have pizza on my face? I wiped my mouth just in case.

Louise cocked her head. "So, tell me, Maria. What nationality are you? I can't figure it out. Your hair is straight and black, but you have fair skin and eyes the color of Texas Bluebonnets."

All colors of eyes stared at me, waiting for a response. I should have expected curious looks about my curious looks since I have gotten them all my life. I started in, "Well, my dad was Norwegian, and my mom was Mexican. So, I'm Maria Olson, possibly the world's only Norwexican."

The group laughed, but Louise studied me with interest and said, "Was?"

I sighed. "Yes. Unfortunately, I lost them both years ago in a car accident."

The whole group looked somber. Jett's dark eyebrows almost touched. "That's terrible."

I nodded. "It was. I took a semester off from UNM. Then, I had to get back to work." I brightened. "And ten years later, I'm finally doing what I promised them I would do…opening a store."

Joey said with a sweet smile, "I'm sure they would be proud." The others agreed with nods.

"Any siblings, Dear?" Louise asked, her eyes still locked on mine.

I took a breath and thought about my sweet little sister and the struggles she had with Leukemia. Her death at such an early age was anything but fair. I blinked when I realized everyone still stared at me and answered, "No. No siblings."

Joey furrowed his eyebrows, then possibly sensing my discomfort, he stood and bounced to the kitchen and returned with a bucket of drinks on ice. "I believe it's time for a toast. Drinks all around!" He popped open a beer while everyone else grabbed a bottle. "Here's to this mixed bag of nuts, starting our new businesses. May it be the beginning of an exciting and profitable venture for us all!"

Mike held up a Coke and said, "Hear! Hear!"

I held out my Corona. "Skoll!" I clinked my bottle with his. For the second time today, a tear streaked down my face. My family should have been here to witness this.

The next morning, I was still glowing from meeting my awesome new work family. I headed to the shop early, stoked to get the shelving moved into their preplanned places. It was a beautiful day and I planned to use every minute filling the shop with my repurposed goodies.

"You've got some real muscles there, girl. I didn't think you and Kelly could carry that cabinet inside without recruiting your boyfriends." This came from Jill, who sat comfortably on my couch made from an old Ford truck's front seat. I could barely understand her since she crunched carrot sticks as she spoke.

I laughed. "For the last time, they're not my boyfriends. And, don't you remember when we were kids, how I pushed you and your wagon all the way up the arroyo? If I was that able-bodied at age eight, I'm likely to still be strong."

"Sure, I remember. I also remember the cast I wore on my arm for six weeks after you pushed me back down the arroyo."

I shrugged. "How was I to know you couldn't steer a wagon?" I winked at Jill.

Jill's hulking husband ran his fingers through his thick black hair and said in his characteristically flat tone, "I'll never let my kid play in a drainage ditch, or do half of what I did on the pueblo."

Kelly Standing Bear was an Albuquerque Police officer and a member of the Zia tribe. He had moved to Albuquerque when they got married. Jill was way too citified to live forty minutes away from town, but she loved to visit the pueblo and swore baby Sophia would learn her father's native language.

Jill raised an eyebrow seductively and said, "So, I married a bad boy? Do tell what you did on the pueblo, Kel."

He shook his head with no intention of answering, but he gave a little smirk at her reaction. He pulled the bubble wrap padding off my prized antique cash register. I was happy Kelly was off work so he could help me move the heavy items to the shop.

I studied the two, who couldn't be more different; Kelly the tall, dark silent type, and Jill, a redheaded tornado. When she first told me she found her perfect mate and his name was Kelly, I assumed he was an Irishman that would fit in the red-headed O'Brien family perfectly. Then when we met at a bar, I thought it must be a mistake. This guy was the biggest, most handsome Native American I'd ever seen. Turns out Jill's family had the same initial reaction. But, within seconds of seeing them together it was obvious, they were meant to be.

When my big friend set the heavy cash register on the glass cabinet, I cringed in hopes the glass would hold. It held. Then my heart skipped a beat when I saw the light from my trombone lamp illuminate the brass filigree cash register. The antique was more beautiful than I'd thought. At that moment, I decided not to sell the lamp after all.

A low rumble began to sound. As it grew louder, Jill's eyes widened. "What in the world?"

The rumble escalated to a roar, and I had to practically shout to be heard, "It's the Railrunner! The track is just behind my shop. I'm starting to get used to it!" I could feel the ferocious vibration and hoped my fragile items wouldn't shift or break on their shelves when the train went by. That was something I'd have to consider when displaying my handmade treasures.

Once the train passed, I carried a box over to Jill and sat beside her. We unwrapped jewelry made from pages of a book. I said, "I'm kind of on a book kick and want to start making clocks and purses out of them. I just need to get more used books."

Before Jill got a chance to react, Kelly said, "Oh No." I looked up, expecting to see a crack in the glass counter, but he said, "Please don't make a purse out of a book. Jill will have to have one, but hers would have to be that 'Shopaholics' book."

It was rare to hear Kelly make a joke. I chuckled but thought it was a great idea. "Well, I owe her a special purse for being my accountant anyway."

I turned to Jill. "And by the way, Mrs. Standing Bear, I'm paying you the going rate and no arguing!"

She waved a hand at me. "Maria, why don't you wait and see how business goes? You have some hefty new loans starting out, and then there's your house…"

There was no need for her to continue. We both knew the problems I'd had keeping my childhood home. My parents took out a second mortgage to pay for my sister's medical expenses and I have struggled to keep up with payments ever since the small inheritance ran out. This business was my last chance to keep the house.

Kelly said, "I think it's working." Dramatically, he pushed a lever and the drawer popped out making a resounding DING!

"Now that's the sound you want to hear all day, girl," Jill said. She turned to her husband. "Kel, we better get going. We still have a baby bed to assemble."

After hugging the two, I watched them leave in his truck. I carried the boxes and trash out to the group of dumpsters behind my building and tossed them in their respective bins.

As I glanced around the center, I wondered if the bookstore had any inexpensive books to use for my projects. I locked my door and headed across the gravel parking lot. As I passed the antique store, I paused. Why not check it out?

I was prepared to get thrown out of the antique store by the crotchety old man. Standing on the doorstep, I studied the drab décor. A small dull gray sign above the gray door on the gray building, It read simply, "Antiques". The shop was not at all inviting, but I knocked anyway.

After 30 seconds of silence, I started to turn away, but the door creaked open and there was the same white hair and eyebrows I'd seen before. They were even bushier up close. I braced myself for another row, but this time his blue Santa Claus eyes twinkled and he said with a lilt, "Well, hello there. We're not quite open yet, but we will be on Saturday at nine o'clock sharp."

I was almost as flabbergasted with this behavior as I had been when he'd yelled at me in the parking lot. Maybe his memory had failed due to his old age? I stammered, "Um. Hi. I'm Maria, I own the shop over there in the turquoise container." I pointed across the way. "I wondered if I could peek at your antique books. But, if you would rather, I can wait until you open."

I watched the older gentleman's face, ready for his cute smile to turn upside down when he realized I was the dastardly one who had offered to carry his boxes. But he smiled and said in a comforting voice, "Come right on in, Maria. It's wonderful to meet you."

I followed him into the dark shop and was temporarily blinded after being in the bright New Mexican sun. My underarms started to sweat, not from being alone in a dark room with a stranger who had been hostile to me yesterday, but from the sweltering heat in the store.

The more I thought about the man though, the more I wondered if I should have told someone where I was going. To add to my trepidation, the place smelled musty and had terrible lighting. The small window in the back didn't help much. I relaxed somewhat when I realized I could easily outrun the frail old man.

My eyes got used to the dim space as I walked slowly behind him. He shuffled across the wooden floor past an antique rocking horse, a group of copper pots, a large display of movie items, and over to two large bookshelves. I wasn't sure how, but his shop seemed as though it had been full of antiques forever, which was impossible since it was just as new as mine. I half expected to see cobwebs hanging from the shelves.

The man asked, "Are you interested in anything in particular?" He waited patiently for a reply.

"I probably should explain what I sell in my store." As if he were hard of hearing, I spoke slowly and used my hands to demonstrate. "I take old and discarded items and then repurpose them into interesting and useful products. Today, I'm looking for inexpensive old books to make clocks and purses."

"Now what in the world got you interested in doing that?"

"I don't know…I just like to look at things in different ways, and I hate to see good items tossed out. Seems like a waste."

He nodded. "I used to keep everything – never threw anything away, then found out I could make money selling my old stuff." He chuckled as he stopped in front of a bookshelf. "Here are some books that might interest you. You can have any on the bottom row for $3 each. The others are priced in the jackets."

"Oh good. Thank you." I was pleased to spot some covers on the bottom shelf that would be perfect for projects and knelt to look closer.

"Well, I'll leave you to browse. Let me know if you need anything." He shuffled off and sat down in a rocker a few feet away. How cliché – an old man in a rocker.

I wanted to ask him why he was so mean to me the other day but refrained. Perhaps he had a bad day, didn't take his meds, or wouldn't want to talk about it. Anyway, he was sure nice now.

I looked through the old books and chose four. I couldn't believe the old copy of Huckleberry Finn was such a good price.

We stood at the register, and I paid him cash. I asked, "So, what is your name?"

He stopped still and practically lost his balance as he put his wrinkled hand up and saluted. "Jonathan Harrison at your service, but people call me "Pops."

How adorable was that? I smiled. "Interesting nickname. Sounds like there is a story there."

He looked at his watch, handed me the receipt, then started slowly toward the door. "Oh, there is a story, but I'll have to tell you on another occasion. I must leave soon to meet my wife for dinner. You know us old folks. We like to eat early."

As we made our way to the door, I wondered how he would be able to leave this early every day. I asked, "Do you have someone to help you run the store?"

When he opened the door, the sunlight hit his face, accentuating his many wrinkles. He answered, "I've got family to assist me. Some are more helpful than others, but I certainly won't be alone." I slipped past him and stepped outside, shielding my eyes from the brightness. He gave a smile as warm as the sun and said, "Goodbye now, Maria."

When the door shut gently behind me, I stood baffled, amazed by his kindness. Maybe the guy suffered from mood swings. I felt guilty having complained about Mr. Harrison to the other shop owners last night and planned to tell them that he had been much nicer today.

Before moving on, I looked across at my place and tried to view it as a new customer might. Even though the finished Upcycled sign looked perfect, the curb appeal wasn't much better than the antique store's. It was too bland and needed something.

While the idea was fresh in my mind, I called Jill and said "Girl, can you send Jack or John over to put a few plants in by my shop. It needs to be spruced up ASAP. I don't care what they choose, as long as they can thrive with little to no water."

I could hear her shouting something on the other end of the line, then she came back and said, "The boys are free tomorrow after work and will bring you something special."

"Wow, now that's what I call service. Thanks, Momma Jill."

She said, "Soon, very soon!"

We hung up. It was so nice to have a friend with a landscaping company and handy brothers.

I caught sight of Louise shaking out a rug in front of her bookstore. That simple image conjured up a feeling of nostalgia as if I was transported back in time to a quaint 1950s neighborhood. I moseyed down towards her shop at the other end of the center enjoying the peaceful walk in my new neighborhood.

As I passed the brewpub, I noticed the caution cones had already been replaced with a beautifully landscaped walkway, complete with three tall yuccas. Wow, that must have cost them a fortune. The strange guy from the pub who had stared at me carried a bag of trash down the steps.

I spoke to him in a friendly voice, ala the 1950s, "It's a beautiful day, isn't it?"

He froze and looked down, greasy hair in his eyes. His face, which looked as though it could use a shave, turned a deep crimson.

I tried again, unshaken, "My name is Maria. What's yours?" I held out my hand to him, still trying for a friendly neighbor award.

He waited for a beat, then stuttered softly, "C C C Carl." He looked at my feet then raised his eyes to look at the books in my hand, but they never made it to my face. Without shaking my hand or saying another word, he turned and ambled behind their building. Whatever, Carl.

I continued to the bookstore. The flashy owner was attaching decals to the window. I said, "Hi, Louise. Remember me?"

She jumped a little and turned around to reveal a bedazzled Texas flag t-shirt and huge sparkly Texas-shaped earrings. I had to refrain from gawking at her outrageous outfit, heavy make-up, and over-sprayed hair.

Her huge smile was contagious. "Of course! You're that darling little Norwexican, Maria. I told my daughter all about you." Louise's hands were just flying with expression. "She said I shouldn't call you that, but I told her you said it first. Ain't that right?"

Smiling, I said, "Of Course. Call me whatever you want. May I take a look in your store?"

"Well, sure, honey. Just come on in and make yourself at home." She noticed the books I carried and asked, "Do you want to sell me some used books?"

I looked down at my hands and said, "Oh, no. I just bought these from the antique store. I'm going to make purses or clocks out of them." Then I asked, "You buy used books?"

"I sure do. But I don't pay much. I like to have a used book section for customers who are looking for a bargain."

"Wow. I had no idea. Then I'll look at new and used." What a gold mine. I was always looking for a good used bookstore and there are two within a block of my shop. Jackpot!

"Take your time, Darlin'. I'm just over here in my little corner trying to figure out this computer program to help me keep track of inventory." She put on big pink glasses with jeweled frames and frowned as she stared at her computer. What a funny lady.

I walked around the colorful neatly arranged shelves full of books and started to wonder if I was the only one not ready to open. A sign on the top of a bookshelf read, "The Butler Did It." Underneath was the mystery section. Cute. As I continued, I realized she had labeled all her genres in clever ways. I laughed as I read some of them, especially the label for the western section, "Smelly Men and Their Animals."

The loud Texan bellowed as if she were a character in one of those books, "Darlin' are you about ready to open? Only five days to showtime!"

"Not yet, but I'm getting there." I chuckled again when I saw the cookbook section titled, 'You Sure You Want to Eat That?'

When I reached, 'Been There, Read That,' I figured I'd found the used books. Hardbacks were only a dollar. I scanned the book jackets for just the right covers to become clocks. I formed a stack of books that had possibilities.

Her slow, mega-drawn-out words echoed throughout the room, "Did I hear ya right? You are gonna make a purse out of a book? I sure would like to see that."

"Well, I hope they turn out cute." I walked to her desk with my stack of six used books. I pulled $10 from my shorts pocket.

"You can just take them if you'll show me the first purse."

"But you won't make any money doing that," I protested.

She ducked her head down and looked up through hooded eyes and heavy blue eyeshadow, "I have an ulterior motive. I'm hoping for a discounted price on my book purse."

"Aha. You got it. Thanks, Louise. Come check out my shop. It's finally starting to shape up."

"I'll stop by tomorrow." She put my books in a darling paper bag printed with 'A Likely Story' and a cartoon drawing of Louise waving a Texas flag. I hadn't even thought of special bags. I couldn't afford to order any now, but typed 'bags' on my phone's to-do list along with 'improve curb appeal.'

That evening, inspired by the books I'd bought and by Louise's enthusiasm, I stopped by a craft store and bought the materials needed to make clocks and purses. I spent the evening working on several other easy-to-make projects, hoping they would be fast sellers.

CHAPTER 3

I woke up earlier than planned Monday and took time to eat a bowl of granola on my patio. To avoid the bright morning sun, I sat on a bench under the Desert Willow tree. A flower fell in my lap and I picked it up. My sister and I always called its pink orchid-like blooms "fairy skirts." A feeling of well-being rushed over me. Those memories used to make me cry, but now I treasure them.

I found myself picking another of our native flowers, the yellow Chocolate Flower. I took a whiff, loving that it actually smelled like its name.

More than once, I'd heard people say they had "never seen so many shades of brown" when visiting New Mexico for the first time. But I look beyond the sand, stucco buildings, and mountains to see a vibrant landscape. I was just about to count all the different colors visible from my vantage point, starting with the vast blue sky, when my favorite guest appeared.

I said, "Rudy! Are you hungry?"

Without waiting for his answer, I ran inside and got some raw hamburger meat from the refrigerator and put it on a plate. My prehistoric-looking friend twitched its long tail and blinked its yellow eyes as I cautiously set the food down on the stucco wall a few feet from him. He ran quickly over to the plate, just as a good roadrunner should, and started pecking at the food.

Rudy had been visiting me periodically for the past two years. I had no idea if the bird was male or female, but he was Rudy to me. I watched him stretch his crest up and down on his head as he ate. When he finished, he hopped down and disappeared into the brush of the empty lot next door without even a thank you.

I called, "You're welcome!" to my feathered friend.

Back to counting colors, I glimpsed my bottle tree a friend had welded for me years ago. It was practically hidden by my Apache Plume bush and I got a brilliant idea. I could put it next to my shop to perk it up. I nodded as I made the decision.

But hauling the bottle tree would have to wait because I had already planned to get a workout by riding my bike to the shop today. Riding the four miles to 16 Boxes with a backpack was doable. I figured I could easily be home before dark since the days are still long in August.

I didn't realize how tricky it would be to walk my bike through my narrow shop to store it in the back room – and that was without merchandise. In retrospect, I should have used two shorter containers side by side, since eight feet was not a practical width for a store. I frowned as I struggled to hoist the bike onto the overhead hooks.

After arranging teapot sewing kits on shelves, I jumped up and down on the floor to simulate the train's vibration. I was happy the practical pots didn't fall off. Hopefully, they would still be safe when the real train came by. The pincushion had fallen out of one of the teapot lids, so I glued it again, careful not to get poked by my sample pins.

I held the dainty red and blue teapot and thought of my grandmother, in Minnesota. She was quite a seamstress and always drank tea. The colors reminded me of the red and blue Norwegian flag that she proudly displayed in her living room. I put the teapot behind my counter to send to her.

I should also send something to my Abuela, Yvonne, in Mexico City. Since she didn't sew, I chose a ring made from a silver spoon. Abuela would love it. It went behind the counter too.

Standing on a stool, I hid two Bluetooth speakers behind the spines of some used books on a shelf. The rest of the day, I listened to music while organizing and pricing items. It was a tedious job but very rewarding, once the place filled with my treasures.

Jill's brothers arrived after they got off work and started their job out front. At around 7:30 p.m., I was sick of pricing items and remembered it was my turn to post a YouTube 'How To' video for an online repurposing club and got my supplies ready.

After setting up my laptop and lighting, I cleared my throat, smoothed my hair, put on a pleasant smile, and turned on the video camera.

"Hi, I'm Maria from Upcycled, my new shipping container store that will open this Saturday in Albuquerque. Wish me luck!"

I realized that was cheesy, so I got to the point. "Today, I'd like to show you how to make a safe from a book." I held up a book safe I had made last week. "It's a perfect place to hide keys or a small treasure."

"First of all, make sure to choose a book with an appealing spine and something that would be unobtrusive on your bookshelf. Today, I will use this copy of The Adventures of Huckleberry Finn, which I purchased for $3 at the antique store here in Albuquerque's newest shopping center called Out of the Box. "

I held the book and an X-ACTO knife up to the computer's camera and continued, "Open the front cover of the book. With your sharp utility knife, slice a large rectangle opening through the first few pages of the book."

I was just about to cut into the book, when a voice boomed, "Helloooo!" I hadn't even heard the door open and so was startled. I turned around to find Louise wearing a glittery purple cowboy hat and matching outfit. She paraded through the door and squealed, "This place is darling!"

I quickly pushed stop on my recording and waved to welcome my guest. "I'm so glad you came to see where I live, Louise."

The boisterous woman sashayed over to me, taking in the surroundings with wide eyes. "So, this is your treasure trove?" She reached up to twirl the globe above me, lost her balance, and almost fell on my computer. I jumped up and ushered her over to my jewelry display rack made from deer antlers. She picked up a silver necklace. "Maria, are these necklaces made from forks?"

There was no need for me to try and answer because she kept talking.

"Why the tines are bent to look like a heart, and here's a darling elephant. And this one looks like a hand with fingers crossed. They are all just beautiful and so clever!" She wrapped her arms around the whole antler rack as if coveting them. I cringed, hoping she wouldn't poke her eye out. She warned, "You better not sell them all. I need to get one for my daughter."

I jumped in before she could continue. "It's OK. If I do sell them, I can always find forks and make more. Oh, Louise, I made something for you." I reached into my backpack and handed her a small purse I made from a joke book. "You get the first one."

Her eyes opened wide and she read the title with a voice so loud it hurt my ears, "Speak Texan in 30 Minutes or Less!" She opened the clasp and looked inside. "This purse is as cute as a bug's ear! Thank you so much, I just LOVE it!"

I grinned as she turned it over to check out the hinges. Louise stayed a bit longer, choosing gifts for everyone she knew, then said, "Dearie, I will come back to buy out your store, but now, I must be on my way. I have a hair appointment. I don't come by this beauty naturally, you know." She touched her poufy hair and posed.

I wondered which hair salon in town did that style of hairdo?

Since I would have to start my tutorial over anyway, I grabbed my backpack and followed her to the door. Might as well deliver my new welcome gifts to the other shopkeepers now.

"I'm so glad you came by to see me."

She opened the door and said, "I'll treasure my new purse."

When we exited, Jack and John were finishing up by spreading mulch around the new plants by my steps. I said, "Wow! That looks so great!"

Louise stared at Jill's red-headed brothers and said, "I always wanted hair the color of yours. I tried to do it from a box once, but that was a terrible idea. I looked as though I was wearing an ugly red hat, which is what I had to do until I could pay a professional to dye my hair back to my normal color."

The guys smirked a little but kept working as Louise got in her Cadillac and drove away. I looked at the yucca with its bright red blooms and said, "How did you know I've always wanted a Brakelights Yucca?"

Jack, the older brother said, "Jill told us."

The fact that their parents had named the siblings 'Jack' and 'Jill' said a lot about them. The entire family was a hoot.

"Well, you did a bang-up job. I love it! When you're finished, just leave the invoice under the mat. And thank you so much!"

I took off to deliver my goodies to my new neighbors. As I looked back, I grinned at my new entryway.

As I knocked at the antique store, a jolt of excitement rushed through me. I love creating personalized gifts for friends and seeing their reactions.

When nobody answered, I moved on to the bakery where Mike greeted me. "I'm glad you caught us. We were just heading out. It's been a long day."

Pat stepped up behind him and agreed. "And we need to start going to sleep early with crazy early bakery hours in our future."

That was probably true. They would have to start baking super early to have their display case filled by opening time. Better them than me.

I handed them the clock made from a cookbook and said, "I made you a little bakery warming gift."

Pat held the clock and said, "Oh wow. You made this?"

"It's perfect for this place," Mike chimed in.

After a few more excited comments, they gave me hugs, a loaf of green chile cheese bread, and a cinnamon twist loaf as a thank you. Within seconds of smelling the bread, my stomach began to growl. When had I last eaten anyway?

I headed to the coffee shop to give a small handmade purse to Victoria but stopped in my tracks when I saw a couple standing on the porch. I was rather shocked when I realized 'The Barista' was in a tight hug with the ever-handsome Jett. I wasn't sure what to do, so I cleared my throat lightly.

Victoria saw me and curled her red lip up in a 'he's mine' sneer. Or maybe just an 'I'm so much better than you' taunt. Either way, I caught the unwelcome vibe.

Jett broke the embrace and caught sight of me. He squinted as though he'd never seen me before. His eyes seemed unfocused.

Before I could say a word, she took Jett's arm and led him into the coffee shop, crooning, "Babe, you must try my new Mocha Mint Frappuccino." As she turned to shut the door, she gave me an icy cold stare. My cheeks heated up and I did a quick 180, opting to move on to the brewery.

My face must have been flushed more than normal because when I stepped inside the door of the Rusty Railroad, Joey said, "Is it still hot outside? Your face is bright red."

Great. As if I wasn't flustered enough, I had to wear a big red sign.

I didn't respond to his question, but took off my backpack, set it on a table, and dug through to find the train clock I'd made from a coffee table book on railroads. I still couldn't believe Louise had this perfect book in her store.

Joey's eyes danced as he looked it over. "Maria, this is perfect! We were just discussing hanging a clock in here. I know just where to put it." He pulled me into a tight hug that lasted only a fraction of the time Jett and Victoria shared, but it was enough to make me wish for more.

Suddenly, Joey was gone. He darted through a side door and returned seconds later with a hammer. Standing on a chair, he pounded on a nail and hung up the clock. I couldn't help but chuckle aloud at his spontaneity.

"What?" His eyebrows raised at me.

"You sure don't waste time, do you?"

He shook his head and stepped off the chair. In a calmer demeanor, he said, "Nope. Hey, Maria, I have an idea. The staff is still learning the ropes. Can we practice on you?" Joey wore a tight-fitting, black Rusty Railroad t-shirt and when he pushed the chair back in its place, his bicep flexed. Very nice. He tilted his head, waiting for a reply.

I blinked and cleared my throat. "Sure. That would be great. I am pretty hungry." I'd forgotten to eat lunch and probably needed nourishment for the bike ride home.

Still holding the hammer, Joey pulled the chair out and motioned for me to sit, then he left to get a server. I ran my hand along the tabletop, amazed by the various types of inlaid wood. The next closest table had a different intricate pattern but was equally stunning. I should ask where they bought these. I'd love to replace my old dining table at home whenever I could afford it.

A blonde girl struggled to put a conductor's hat over her ponytail, then she bounced over to me. "Hi. Welcome to the Rusty Railroad. Can I get you something to drink while you look at the menu?" She handed me a black folder that felt like leather. Nice.

"Sure, I'll start with ice water. Thanks."

She scurried off to giggle with another teenage girl. Boy, did I feel old? Joey patted her on the shoulder, probably giving her some helpful advice. I turned my attention to the beautiful menu. The illustrations looked like they might be from a vintage book of trains. The food choices were equally surprising. They offered shepherd's pie, roasted chicken, elk sausage, and beef stroganoff. Not typical pub fare, although they did serve the New Mexico staple, green chile cheeseburgers.

I had just taken a sip of water when there was a bump on my chair. I turned around and found Carl holding a broom. I swallowed what water I hadn't lost in the bump. "Hi, Carl."

He didn't respond. His upper lip was lined with beads of sweat. Even though his long hair hung over his eyes, I could see that he was glowering at me. Earlier, I had thought he was shy or maybe even interested in me. Now, not so much. He moved back to the bar without a word.

I shook off the odd interaction when the server returned to take my order - shepherd's pie and a salad. I was a little uncomfortable being the lone customer until Joey sat down and slid a pint of beer to me.

When the beer spilled over the top of the glass, he shrugged. "Glad I'm not the bartender." He wiped up the spill with a napkin.

"This is our 'All Aboard Ale'. Oh, and dinner and drinks are on the house tonight."

His dimples were so deep I wanted to poke my finger in to see how far in they would go, but refrained.

Did he say free? I joked, "Really? Well then, I'm available any time you need a tester. By the way, this menu is beautiful."

"That's my brother, the graphic artist. He designed the menus, the signs, and t-shirts."

"Really?" I was impressed, especially since Jett's behavior a few minutes ago had not been impressive. "That's cool. I'm surprised at your wide variety of food with such reasonable prices." I took a sip of the beer, which was frosty and smooth. "This is yummy. I was afraid it would be too hoppy for me."

"Well, then don't try the Firebox IPA. Those hops will kick your butt. So, how's your place coming? Need any last-minute help?" He looked at me with those captivating warm blue eyes.

Afraid I might melt into the table, I looked down. "No. I'm good. But thanks."

He glanced over at the bar. "So, what was going on with Carl?"

I didn't want to jump to any conclusions and replied, "Oh, I don't know. He just kinda stares at me. Not a big deal."

Joey said, "We've already had some problems with him. He's not much for following directions and has a bit of a temper." He shook his head. "We needed a busboy and got his name from Larry."

My face must have shown my opinion of the landlord for he snorted then said, "I'll go check on your food."

Joey hopped up to talk to the servers. What a ball of energy. I couldn't help but watch his magnetic personality ooze as he spoke to his smiling staff. I'll bet everyone felt the same way I did around him.

Then, Joey walked to the bar and conversed with Carl. Even without hearing him, I could tell it wasn't a friendly talk by the way Joey stood with hands on his hips and head shaking.

When my dinner arrived, I thanked the server and took a bite of the salad. I was pretty sure the dressing and croutons were made in-house. Impressive. When I looked up, Joey had left the bar area, but the odd Carl still watched me. I turned away again and focused on my food. The blend of flavors in the shepherd's pie paired beautifully with the creamy ale. They must have one heck of a chef and brewmaster.

My attention was drawn again to the bar area when one of the young female servers hurried away from Carl. She rushed up to Joey and, with a big display using her hands, told him something and shook her head. From the way she glanced at Carl, it had something to do with him.

Joey stormed over to the bar where a red-faced Carl stood rigid. Then loud enough for all to hear, he said, "What were you thinking, Carl? You can't tell Misty that her shirt is too tight."

The statement may have especially been a problem since the girl was rather buxom. I watched as Joey took Carl's elbow and led him into the kitchen area. I heard indistinct shouting, then a clear, "Well, then you don't belong here. Grab your things and get out. We'll mail your check to you next Tuesday."

Wow, that went south fast. I watched wide-eyed as Carl burst back into the room, took off his apron, and tossed his rag on the bar, face redder than ever. He turned to leave, but the front door opened, and Jett entered, running smack into the irate man. Jett lost his balance and fell. He sat there blinking slowly until his brother helped him stand. Joey explained the situation while Carl paced around in an agitated state.

Jett limped over to Carl and tried to calm him down with an awkward pat on his shoulder.

Carl turned, pointed to me, and shouted, "It's all her f f f fault!" and then stormed out of the brewery.

Me? My fault? What was he talking about? What did I do? My face grew hot as everyone stared at me. All I could do was shrug.

Jett came over and sat beside me. He put his elbows on the table and his head on his hands. The dark-haired beauty was so close I could smell his aftershave or was it Victoria's perfume?

He spoke without eye contact, and his words were slurred, "Don't worry about Carl. He's gone now." He straightened the sugar packets, still not looking at me. "How was your...dinner?"

My heart was still pounding from Carl's odd declaration, but I took a breath and said, "Great. I am impressed with the food and beer. You have a real hit on your hands." I studied the man. He really should be pictured on the cover of a GQ magazine. I wondered briefly what kind of relationship he had with Victoria.

Jett continued to look away, this time toward the door. His elbow slipped off the table, but he caught himself. Wait. Was he drunk? I noticed a scrape on his hand as well as a red mark on his cheek, probably Victoria's lipstick.

I continued my part of the conversation. "Joey tells me the menus were your design. They are simply beautiful."

Jett didn't respond in any manner. It was as if he hadn't heard me.

Joey joined us and lifted the mood with his positive attitude. He pointed up. "Check out the clock Maria made for us."

Jett straightened and wobbled over to the clock. He turned and said with a smile, "Thanks. It's great."

Joey and I both watched him walk a little sideways through the kitchen door.

While Joey pondered his brother's odd behavior, I got my debit card out of my pocket and said, "Please let me pay for the meal."

After a beat, he turned to me with a genuine smile. "No way. We should pay you for being our guest guinea pig." There were those dimples again.

"Well, it was lovely." I fished around in my backpack past the bread loaves and found a five-dollar bill. "I can at least leave a tip for the service." I set the bill on the table.

"Fine." He pulled my chair out for me and walked me to the door.

I smiled. "Thanks again. Everything was delicious."

I stepped outside, surprised to find it already dark. I hadn't realized the days were getting so short. Dang it. Now I would have to ride my bike home in the dark. I hitched my backpack over my shoulders and headed back to my shop with difficulty, considering Larry hadn't yet installed lights. Where was that bright New Mexico moon? The sky was pitch black.

As I neared my container, there was a rustling sound. I moved forward quietly and thought I saw a dark form move underneath my window. I froze for a second, hoping the person didn't see me as I approached. As I walked, I fumbled for my phone to turn on its flashlight. Before I had reached it, I tripped over something and landed hard on my hands and knees. Ouch! Gravel was ruthless on bare skin. I sat up and checked my palms for blood, but it was too dark to see anything.

I was still a bit spooked and hoped the person skulking around hadn't heard me. I took off my backpack and laid it on the ground beside me. When I finally got my phone flashlight on, I shone it toward my building but didn't see anyone. I aimed the light at my hands and found messy scrapes, but my knees fared worse. Blood trickled down each leg. Wonderful.

What had cause me to trip? I pulled myself up to sit and turned around. With the light from the phone, I saw several books on the ground. OK. So, that was weird.

I stood carefully, brushed the loose gravel from my bloody knees and took a stiff step toward the books. I picked one up and shone the light on it. Just like the one I'd bought the day before, it was a copy of 'Huck Finn.' Had I dropped the books on my way out? Of course not. I knew that book was inside my shop beside my computer. It would be quite a coincidence to have two similar books so nearby. Surely, that sneaking figure hadn't stolen my $3 book. I cleared my head of the silly notion and squatted to look at the second book but fell backward in shock when I saw a hand attached to it.

CHAPTER 4

I slowly picked myself up again from the gravel. I hoped I had just imagined the hand. With a shaky grip on my phone, I illuminated the book and yes, the hand was truly there – age spots and all. I moved the light and saw an arm, then on to the pale face of the old man lying on the ground with wide-open eyes and bushy eyebrows. It was Mr. Harrison!

I squeaked, "Oh No!"

I took a moment to gain my composure and then spoke with a quivering voice, "Mr. Harrison, are you OK?" He lay motionless, so I quickly put my fingers on his neck. The skin was warm, but there was no pulse.

Trembling, I dialed 9-1-1 and said with urgency, "I need an ambulance at 555 Franco Street. I found a body! He doesn't seem to have a pulse. I'm in the new Out of the Box shopping center beside the turquoise container. Please hurry! Send the police too."

The dispatcher assured me someone would be right there and hung up. I wished I'd asked if I should give CPR to the man.

Unfortunately, I didn't have any other tenants' phone numbers yet. I hated to leave Mr. Harrison alone but knew I needed to get help. I loped back to the brewpub hoping someone there was skilled in emergencies. When I opened the door, I yelled with an unrecognizably frantic voice, "Help! I need help. Come quickly!"

Joey came out from the kitchen with a dishrag in his hand. "What's wrong?"

Jett sat at a table, head in hand, sipping a cup of coffee. He looked up slowly. A few of the staff members stopped what they were doing to listen.

I gulped, "It's Mr. Harrison. I think he's dead."

Joey's mouth dropped open and his eyes widened. "At his store?"

I shook my head. "No. Outside by my shop. Come quickly!" I turned and ran out the door, Joey on my heels. A silent Jett followed us as we made our way across the dark parking lot. I had trouble breathing and hoped I wasn't having a panic attack.

I managed to say, "I've already called 9-1-1."

When we got to the place where Mr. Harrison had been, he wasn't there. I looked around wondering if I had mistakenly been in another place, but my backpack was still in its spot. It was as if I was in an episode of the "Twilight Zone." Distraught, I said, "He was right here. I swear!"

Joey shone his light all around and said, "There he is."

The body lay about 10 feet away from where I knew it had been.

Jett said, "He probably crawled."

Although the comment irritated me since I knew he couldn't crawl without a pulse, I hoped his suggestion was true and that Mr. Harrison had miraculously moved that far. Joey ran to the body. He knelt, touched his neck and felt for life, and said, "I don't know how he got here, but he's sure not moving now."

When Jett and I approached the body, my phone flashlight lit up Mr. Harrison's pale face. He had a big red scratch down his cheek and the back of his white hair was stained with blood. I turned my head as a knot formed in my stomach.

As soon as Jett saw the gruesome scene, he moved a few feet away and threw up. He croaked, "I… can't. Gotta go lie down." He turned and hobbled back to the brewery.

I too felt sick but tried to hold the flashlight steady as Joey pumped the old man's chest like a pro. I turned my head and took a deep breath of fresh air to keep from fainting.

After Joey worked a while, he put his ear to the old man's chest, gave a big sigh, and shook his head at me. A tear slid down my face.

He stood and put a comforting hand on my shoulder. "Did you see anything else?"

I tried to breathe steadily and focus on Joey's question while wiping away a tear. "I thought I saw movement." I pointed to the back. "Maybe someone's still there?"

"I'll take a look." He started moving that way.

"Be careful."

Using his phone as a flashlight, he retreated behind my container. I wanted to go with him, but I wanted to stay put even more.

I sat on the gravel waiting in silence. It was so quiet I could hear my heartbeat – a fast, pounding in my ears. Adrenaline, I assumed. I'd never been so close to a dead body, and it made me shiver, despite the 80-degree evening.

Trying to get my mind off Mr. Harrison, I looked around for the books. They weren't beside him. I shone my light toward my backpack and where the old man had lain earlier. I vividly remembered the stack of books, but they were gone. Was I going crazy?

It would have been nice to have working security lights. Darn that lazy Larry. I limped over to my container, unlocked the door, and stuck my hand inside to turn on my porch light. Although it only lit my steps, the dim glow that spread over the side yard was better than nothing. What was taking Joey so long? And where was the ambulance?

I heard aggravated voices and crunching gravel, then two figures walked toward me. So, there *was* someone back there. When they came into the light, the two men were Joey and Carl! What was he doing behind my building? Was he the one I saw under my window? Did he have something to do with the death of Mr. Harrison?

Joey said with a semi-gruff voice as they walked, "And we're supposed to believe you were taking the trash out?"

Carl, still wearing a baggy Rusty Railroad shirt, stuttered, "It's t t t true. I had just dumped it in the b b b bin when I saw him. Then, when you c c c came, I hid."

Joey had Carl's arm in a vice grip. He asked, "Why did you hide?"

The sound of wailing sirens came out of nowhere, interrupting Carl's explanation, that is if he had one. I watched as the strange man grimaced and closed his eyes. Was the frown an indication he was guilty? Within seconds, an ambulance and two Albuquerque Police cars screeched in front of my building, throwing sand and gravel as their vehicles skidded to a halt.

With lights from the emergency vehicles illuminating the place, it became as bright as day. Two male EMT's worked on Mr. Harrison while a group of three uniformed police officers surveyed the scene. A man with gray hair wearing a baggy suit and loose tie glanced at the body and shouted to the EMTs, "Don't disturb any evidence!"

A young policewoman stepped over to us and said, "Can you tell me what happened here tonight?"

Joey nodded to me. The uniformed cop opened her notebook and I started to recount my story.

When I mentioned tripping over the books, Joey's eyes narrowed. Apparently, in the excitement, I hadn't mentioned that detail to him. The rumpled man joined in to listen and I continued the story up to the point when I'd brought the guys to help.

The plain-clothed man said with an eyebrow raised, "So, somebody dragged the body from there, to here?" He pointed out the two spots.

I nodded. A look of doubt spread across his face, but hearing the words out loud, it did sound crazy even to me.

Joey took over where I left off, "I applied CPR until it was evident that Mr. Harrison was deceased. Then, I scouted behind the building and found this guy, our former employee, Carl, crouched down in the shadows."

Carl stood silent with his head hanging low.

The seasoned officer turned to me with his lip curled. "And what happened to the books?"

I shrugged. "I have no idea. Maybe the person who moved Mr. Harrison took them? In case you are interested, one book was The Adventures of Huckleberry Finn. I remember that because I had just bought a copy myself yesterday."

He sighed and barked out orders to check out both areas I had pointed out. I watched as the officers snapped to business putting up crime tape and measuring areas. Someone took pictures of the scene, creating a macabre flash with each snap of her camera.

The cranky officer looked squarely into Carl's face. "You are under arrest in connection with the death of this man. You have the right to remain silent…" As he continued with the Miranda warning, I noticed Carl getting more and more agitated.

With his wild eyes, unkempt hair, and baggy Rusty Railroad T-shirt, Carl did look like a crazed killer, but he cried out in anguish, "I didn't hurt P P P Pops!"

Pops? Did he know Mr. Harrison? His eyes filled with tears as the younger officer slapped handcuffs on him. I started to feel sorry for the odd man.

The policewoman softened. "Was he your grandfather?"

Carl's tears stopped abruptly. "He's not my g g grandfather, Stupid!"

She made a face and led him to the squad car, protecting his head while putting him into the back seat. Simultaneously, Mr. Harrison was being loaded into the ambulance. I hadn't even noticed him being put on a stretcher. Everything happened so fast.

Just as the police car door began to close, Carl looked directly at me and shouted again, "It's all h h her fault."

Being the only non-police female in the area, all eyes turned to me. The older policeman growled, "Is there something you didn't mention?"

I shook my head vehemently. "No. I don't have any idea what he's talking about." So much for feeling sorry for Carl.

With a slow nod, the man whom I assumed was a detective, frowned, "You need to come down to the station to give formal statements. Both of you." He turned away and added gruffly, "Tonight."

I said, "Yes, Sir." Joey nodded.

The man growled, "Ask for Sergeant Barnes." He got in the squad car and turned the key.

It wasn't long before all the emergency vehicles drove away, leaving the two of us standing in a pitch-black parking lot.

After a few seconds of total silence, Joey gently put his hand on my arm. "Wanna ride with me to the station?"

I answered with relief, "Yes, please. I rode my bike today and don't particularly want to peddle downtown in the dark. Let me get my purse."

pedal

She already unlocked it to turn on the porch light

Still shaky, I hobbled up and <u>unlocked my door</u>. I stepped inside, closed the door behind me, and leaned against it. With my eyes closed, I took a deep breath, then counted to five. I exhaled slowly and then repeated the steps, just as my counselor had advised me to do in a stressful situation. And this constituted a stressful situation if anything did. I had started counseling just after my parents died and found it very helpful.

With my blood pressure almost back to normal, I flipped on the inside lights and walked to the back of my shop. I didn't notice anything at first, but as I passed the cash register, my pulse quickened. Something was wrong.

A flicker of light caught my eye; probably Joey's flashlight shining through the window. That was when I noticed a rip on my screen. A shiver ran down my neck as I stared at the large hole. I darted behind the counter, grabbed my purse, and hurried outside where I found Joey blessedly close sitting on the porch.

I said, "Umm. Maybe we should call the police back?"

He looked at me with wide eyes. "Why?"

"Someone's been in my shop. The window screen was cut."

He jumped up. "I'm not a detective, but mind if I look around?"

"Please do." I hardly recognized my wobbly voice. I led Joey inside and to the back of the shop, pointing to the screen and the large tear. He snapped pictures of the window.

After looking around, I cleared my throat and said, "I don't see anything else out of order."

He scanned the room as he walked. "I don't think your intruder was interested in money."

Puzzled, I approached my cash register to see what he meant. On the counter lay several bills that had not been there earlier - a ten and two ones. It was then that I noticed that the books I had bought at the antique store were gone. I did a double-take and realized the $12 was the same amount I'd paid for the books.

I stammered, "Um…I think the books I saw outside may have been mine because they were sitting by my computer earlier today, and now they aren't there. But why would someone take my books, and stranger yet, pay for them?"

Joey shrugged as he snapped a few pictures of the bills.

I asked, "Should we call Officer Barnes?"

He closed his eyes and sighed. "Let's just go down to the station and tell him the latest. If he wants to come back and check for fingerprints, he can."

That made sense to me, so we walked through the dark parking lot to Joey's jeep. My nerves jangled the whole time. When the engine started up, so did Herbie Hancock's "Take 5." On any other day, that song would make me happy, but on this horrific day, not even jazz could help.

Joey turned down the volume and asked, "Downtown station I assume? I mean the detective didn't actually mention which one."

I shrugged and said, "I assume so. It is the closest."

I closed my eyes as I rode downtown. Had I actually found a dead man beside my shop? This was all surreal and awful. Had Mr. Harrison broken into my shop to buy the books back? But, why? And how had he died?

I was on the verge of tears as I thought of his poor wife. "I hope the police were able to reach Mrs. Harrison. She must be devastated."

Joey said in surprise, "I didn't know he was married."

Not realizing my last thoughts had been spoken aloud, I looked up and cleared my thick throat, "Oh, I meant to tell you that I spoke to Mr. Harrison yesterday and he was much nicer than before. He said he was going to take his wife to Furrs Cafyteria for the early-bird special." With that simple thought, I couldn't contain my tears.

he didn't say where they were going

Joey frowned and said, "Oh. Wow, that's heartbreaking." He sighed and said, "Do you think Carl was involved?"

I wiped the tears from my cheeks and shrugged, holding out hope that the death was some sort of medical episode or accident. "Maybe he really was just taking out the trash."

Joey pulled into a parking space near the station, turned off the car, and said, "Well, it wasn't our trash. I took that out earlier. But, he sure acted upset. I wonder why he called him "Pops?""

I nodded. "Mr. Harrison told me Pops is his nickname."

Joey nodded. Before he opened his door he said, "But, how did Carl know him?"

I said, "No idea." We made our way toward the imposing building in silence, where I limped up the steps.

"Did you hurt yourself?" Joey asked, before running to grab my elbow and help me up the steps. Such a gentleman.

"Oh, yeah." I looked down. "I scraped my knees when I fell on the gravel. They're just a little stiff now."

He winced. "That sucks. Finding the body was bad enough."

I was touched by Joey's concern. He opened the door for me and I led him inside the lobby. The place was much nicer than the station where Kelly worked. I had gone to his police station several times with Jill when she dropped off his dinner and thought it was a real dive.

This waiting room seemed to be newly updated with Southwestern photographs on canvas displayed on brightly painted walls. The area was lined with windows, giving plenty of light to the live plants placed in the corners.

Even though this precinct was more welcoming, the connected molded chairs in the lobby gave it an institutional feel. Guess they didn't want anyone getting too comfortable in a police station lobby. I was surprised that there weren't any other people in the waiting room and chose a seat near the desk.

Joey asked the receptionist for Officer Barnes while I sat down, still feeling a little limp from my shock. I assumed there would be a wait. When he returned, he leaned down to look at my knees. His blonde hair fell in his eyes and he said, "Probably ought to clean those up before they get infected."

Before I could protest, he walked back to the counter. "Excuse me, do you have a nurse on duty? Or a first aid kit?"

I closed my eyes, embarrassed, and said in a stage whisper, "Joey, I can wait until I get home."

He came back with a white plastic first aid kit complete with a red cross on the lid. He gently dabbed at my right knee with a cotton pad soaked in something that stung – probably alcohol. I flinched, but relaxed when he applied some antibiotic cream. He covered it with a bandage and started on the left knee, this time kneeling in front of me.

I said, "How do you know how to do all this?"

"I've been certified in first aid since I was 12…I also…"

A loud, "Ahem" interrupted Joey's sentence. Sergeant Barnes stood at the door, looking even more rumpled than earlier if that was possible. I figured he was tired. I sure was. "Follow Me."

We did as he said and walked down a long hallway behind him. I was so glad to have Joey along since it would have been terrifying to do this alone. As we entered the stark meeting room, I wondered if we would be recorded as they do in 48 Hours or Dateline, but I didn't see any signs of a two-way mirror or camera. It was just a boring room with a table and four chairs.

In the bright fluorescent lighting, I got a better look at the detective. He wasn't as old as I had thought. Maybe only in his 50s, but his face was weathered with lines, probably due to our dry climate and extreme sun. He had since ditched his jacket and wore a wrinkled blue shirt and the loosened tie. With what seemed to be a permanent scowl, he took in a slow breath and pulled out a legal pad and Bic pen.

I jumped in and said, "Before you begin, I need to tell you something." I cleared my throat. "When I walked into my shop right after you left, I discovered that someone had been in there. My window screen had been cut." I chewed my bottom lip, waiting for his response.

"You called the police." It was a statement, not a question.

I swallowed. "No. You had just left and since we were on our way here anyway…We didn't touch anything, but we did take pictures."

The officer hung his head as if he was thinking, 'stupid people'.

Joey slid his phone across the table. Barnes studied the photos and looked at me, resting his head on his fist. "Anything missing?"

I pushed my hair behind my ears and said, "Well, I think I know whose books I tripped over. Several of mine were gone. Nothing else was disturbed and my purse was even sitting right by the computer." I regretted saying that immediately. "But the weirdest thing was that $12 in cash was left on the counter – the same amount I'd paid for the books yesterday at Mr. Harrison's antique store."

The officer leaned back in his chair, eyeing me with a look I couldn't decipher. His lined face, with graying beard stubble, was downturned in what I began to think was his usual look. The longer he took to react, the more I worried he suspected me of wrongdoing.

Unable to stand the silence any longer, I said, "Do you think maybe Mr. Harrison wanted the books back, broke into my shop, paid me back for them, then had a heart attack from the exertion of climbing through the window?"

He closed his eyes and finally spoke in slow response, "Let me do the detective work, Ms. Olson."

I nodded, feeling stupid for suggesting anything. I rarely made a fool of myself like that, but if I have ideas, shouldn't I help? I clasped my shaking hands together in my lap and vowed to stay quiet.

Sgt. Barnes put his chair back down on all four legs and studied the two of us. "Where were you during the evening?"

Joey looked at me and said with a shrug, "We were together at the brewery."

The detective scratched in his notebook and then asked, "Which one of you puked at the scene? The report says vomit was found five feet away from where the body was found."

Joey answered with a little smirk, "Oh that was my brother, Jett."

"Then why didn't we see him?"

I answered, carefully this time. "Well, when he saw the body, he got sick and went back to the brewery to lie down."

He rolled his eyes suggesting Jett was a wimp and then growled to me, "I'll stop by in the morning. You can both go." He ran his hand through his unkempt gray hair.

When I stood, my newly formed scabs started to sting. That and the restrictive bandages caused me to limp even more as we made our way down the brightly lit, endless hallway.

Joey walked beside me and said, "I can't decide whether to call you Gimpy or Detective Maria."

"Ha Ha. Very funny." I turned to him. "But don't you think that could have happened? He was pretty old. Couldn't he have had a heart attack?"

"Maybe. I just wonder why he bought the books back?"

"Right. There has to be more to the story." The image of the scratch on his face came back to me.

Joey pulled his phone from his pocket and made a call. "Is Jett there?... Oh, OK. I'll try his cell phone." He made another call but didn't get an answer.

We made our way back to his jeep. Joey beeped the doors open and said, "So, you live near Old Town?"

"Yes." I climbed into the jeep, buckled my belt, and shut my eyes, weary from the long day.

"Jett's not answering his phone. Do you mind if I stop by his house on the way there to make sure he made it home?"

"Of course not."

We rode in silence down Central Avenue, otherwise known as Route 66. Neon lights glowed from a few hotspots, advertising concerts and drink specials. A ride down this familiar busy street usually perked me up, but I felt a stab of sadness when passing an antique store.

A Railrunner train caught my eye as it pulled into the downtown Alvarado station; the big red roadrunner symbol on the side lifted my mood slightly.

We passed the Library Bar and Grill with its giant book and crazy titles: Tequila Mockingbird, Gone with the Gin, and Lord of the Onion Rings. Next to it, a few homeless people congregated in dark corners. Unfortunately, just like in most cities, we have a problem with poverty in Albuquerque.

My attention was drawn to the sky where a searchlight beam circled above the iconic Kimo Theater. The marquis also announced the big event – '48 Hour Film Project.' I couldn't help but glance at the beautiful art deco/southwest tilework in its entryway as we drove by.

I said, "I always love driving through downtown with all the good and bad it has to offer."

Joey nodded, then made a few turns, ending up in the Albuquerque Country Club neighborhood. We rode past the big houses I used to dream of living in as a kid. Many of the homes had manicured lawns with real grass, a luxury in this state. The jeep stopped in front of a large brick house with immaculate landscaping. I looked up at the massive structure. Wow. Jett must have some money.

He put the car in park and said, "I'll be right back." I watched him run along the walkway and up the well-lit steps, using a key to enter. He disappeared into the house.

While studying the grand 2-story home, I wondered if Jett lived there alone. What did I really know about him? For all I knew, he lived with that posh-looking Victoria.

Before I could analyze Jett's situation further, Joey bounded down the steps and back to the car. He nodded with a sigh. "He's OK. Just sleeping. Must have had a few too many, which is funny because I never even saw him take a drink today."

I nodded thinking he had sure seemed inebriated. I couldn't resist saying, "Now that's a big house," as we pulled away.

Joey pressed the accelerator smoothly and turned back onto Central Avenue. He spoke slowly, choosing his words carefully, "Jett was married briefly to an insanely rich girl, but they're going through a divorce. He's staying there until they settle everything."

I nodded at the new information, wondering what other interesting facts lurked in these brothers' past. But honestly, I was still too tired and unnerved about the death to worry about it now. After a mile of silence, we neared my neighborhood. I said, "You can turn right on San Pasquale. I live on Old Town Road."

Joey instantly started singing with a deep country accent, "I'm gonna ride my horse down Old Town Road. Gonna ride till I can't no more." He bumped up and down in his seat as if riding a horse.

When I stopped laughing, I guided him to my quaint house, which couldn't be more different than Jett's.

CHAPTER 5

Joey studied the exterior of my old home with a quizzical look. He was probably turned off by its small size or the wild native bushes that I'd neglected to trim. But he said, "It's really cool. And awesome that you live so close to Old Town. I want to see the inside someday." His face looked eager, like that of a child.

I lifted my eyebrows and shrugged. "How about now?" I wondered if I was being too forward, but I was still wired from the evening's events and knew I couldn't sleep right away. I explained, "I could stand the company for a few minutes."

He parked behind my truck in the narrow driveway and hopped out of the vehicle. We made our way up the brick path and through the quirky metal gate to the porch. The entry to my house was so old and worn compared to that of his brother that I was a little embarrassed. I noticed business cards stuck in the door jamb and pulled them out.

"What are those?" Joey asked, looking over my shoulder.

"Oh, cards from realtors. Seems there is a lot of interest in houses in this area, and they must love mine since I get a few every week."

"You would probably be able to sell it for a fortune. It's adobe, right? Not just stucco?"

I opened the door and scanned the living room hoping it wasn't too messy for a visitor. When all looked OK, I stepped inside and answered, "Yes. It's the original adobe structure from the early 1800s. My parents bought it from an old woman who had the house in her family for over a century."

Joey held his hands on both sides of the kitchen wall, "Check this out! The walls must be 18 inches thick." He rubbed his hand along the side of the tan wall and added, "I'll bet you don't even need heat or air in here with this built-in insulation."

I was touched that he was so excited about the old adobe home. Although most houses in New Mexico are the pueblo or adobe *style*, not that many were fully made of straw and clay. The ancient thick walls do keep the house cool in the dry heat of the desert and give it a quiet, soothing feel.

I answered, "Well, I do have a fireplace for the winter. And my parents broke down and put in central air in the 90s during an especially hot summer." I smiled. "But you're right, these puppies have the best insulation." I tapped the wall. "Not so great with cell phone reception though."

I plopped my backpack on the worn table and spoke my thoughts aloud, "I need to replace this old table with a cool one like those you have in your pub."

He looked at my scuffed table. "Oh. Glad you like them." I was going to ask where he got theirs, but he said in a rush, "Is that an original R.C. Gorman?" He walked behind the dining table to the large painting of a woman holding a baby, then moved to the painting next to it. "And a Dick Mason?"

Wow. Most people here know Gorman, but few I know are familiar with Mason's work. I looked at the iconic painting of a Dalmatian whose spots continue beyond the dog to meld into the background of New Mexico's spotted landscape. It has always been one of my favorite paintings.

I explained, "My parents weren't into many material things, as you can see by the furniture, but they loved local art. They almost sold these to pay for some…" I paused wondering how much to tell, "…medical expenses." I wasn't ready to tell him about my sister. "They ended up with a second mortgage on the house. So…if my shop doesn't make it, I'll lose the house or the artwork or probably everything."

He came in close, smelling slightly of aftershave. He looked down at me with warm blue eyes and said, "You'll make it."

A rush ran through my whole body. Why was this tall, rugged man toying with me?

He stepped back and gave me one of his infectious smiles. "As a matter of fact, I bet you'll have to beat the customers off with a stick, Maria."

I suddenly had a flash of Mr. Harrison being hit with a stick and turned to walk into the kitchen. "Can I get you something to drink? Water, tea, or beer?"

"Sure. I'll have water." He walked around looking at the other artwork, shaking his head as he examined each one.

I filled two glasses with cold water from the tap and couldn't help but smile at Joey's interest in the paintings. I walked to the living room and handed him a glass, then leaned against Mom's favorite but worn upholstered chair.

He said, "What's this?"

I looked up to see him scrutinizing the blonde doll, dressed in a Norwegian national costume. "I got her from Far Mor." I waited for his reaction.

He squinted and tilted his head as expected.

I explained, "In Norway, far means father, and mor means mother. Your father's mother is called Far Mor. A mother's mother is Mor Mor. It totally makes sense to keep track of which side a grandparent is from."

He nodded, "Brilliant. And a grandfather on a father's side is Far Far?"

"Yes! Anyway, the doll was my grandmother's when she was little and she gave it to my mom. Then Mom left it to me." I frowned. "Well, everything was left to me by default." I felt a pang of melancholy thinking of my parent's untimely death. That, coupled with the recent events, made me feel queasy and I took a drink of water.

As Joey quietly studied the doll, I leaned against the wall and remembered a time when Jill and I were nine or ten. We planned to go thing-finding like our heroine, Pippi Longstockings. But on that day, she spent the whole time talking to my dad about the doll. I gave up waiting for her and ended up playing with my little sister.

It made sense that she was so obsessed with the doll, coming from a family with all brothers. Even after all these years, she regularly stopped to check out the doll that fascinated her.

When Joey moved, I snapped out of my trip down memory lane and asked, "So, what do *you* think happened to Mr. Harrison?"

He shrugged. "Your idea could be right. He was old. A heart attack isn't out of the question, but the deep scratch on his face was curious."

My mouth dropped open. "You saw it too?" I didn't want to think about it, in case it indicated foul play. "And what about the missing books?" I felt silly bringing them up.

"I guess we'll have to wait to see what that *sweet* detective has to say." He laughed. "He was sure a Gloomy Gus, huh?"

That term made me smile. My dad used to call our neighbor that when he complained about everything. "Yeah, and I get to meet with him again tomorrow morning. Whoopee!"

"Do you want me to come by while he's there?"

"No. I'll be fine. Maybe he'll be in a better mood with a good night's sleep."

He shrugged a doubtful shrug. "Maybe. Look, I should go, but thanks for letting me see your awesome house." He carried his glass to the kitchen and put it in the sink.

"Well, thank you for the ride. I'll show you the rest and the courtyard another day. Oh, wait, speaking of the courtyard, would you help me put my bottle tree in my truck?"

He cocked his head. "Bottle tree?"

"Yes. It's just the thing to brighten up the exterior of my shop. I'll show you." I led him to the courtyard and flipped on the lights.

He nodded. "Oh. A tree with bottles!"

"Yep. Hold on." I ran to my storage shed and grabbed a large empty box and said, "Once we remove the bottles, it shouldn't be too heavy to carry."

We set to work taking the bottles off the metal stand and putting them in the box. We loaded the awkward stand and heavy box into the truck bed.

I touched his arm and said, "Thank you for that too. Now, I'm actually tired enough to sleep."

"I'm pretty tired." I walked toward the door.

"Good. Maybe you'll get a good night's rest."

"Hope so."

He looked down at me and said, "I can't believe you've been here all this time and I never met you. I'm like a botanist who just discovered a beautiful, one-of-a-kind, flower in my own backyard."

The line was unbelievably corny, and I started to laugh, but he looked so sincere that I didn't. Without thinking, I reached up and kissed him on the cheek. "Thank you."

He grinned and walked outside. A giddiness built up inside me as I heard his jeep's engine rev. He was probably the most unique guy I'd ever met. Maybe I should have told him that, but perhaps the kiss gave him the idea.

The next morning, I felt refreshed after a good night's sleep and shower. I stood by the kitchen window with coffee and a slice of Mike and Pat's delicious cinnamon twist bread and watched a pair of hummingbirds enjoy their own sweet breakfast from the red Penstemon flowers. The color reminded me of Victoria's lipstick, and I vowed never to buy that shade of red for my own lips.

I thought back on the night before and the tragedy of my neighbor dying. What had happened? If it wasn't an accident, who would have hurt poor Mr. Harrison? It could have been an outsider, but just in case, I started going through the names of people in the area. I could eliminate Joey since he was with me the entire evening. I doubted sweet Mike or Pat would have any ill will towards the man, besides, they had left long before dark. Louise's alibi was her appointment at the beauty shop.

Carl was an obvious suspect since he was found at the scene. It dawned on me that Jett was not with us until about the time Carl left. And he did have a scratch on his hand. Exactly what did I know about the brooding brother?

I drove to Out of the Box, still considering who would want to hurt the old man, but I hoped the police would determine the poor man had died a natural death.

Afraid to touch anything inside and not knowing when Sergeant Barnes would show up, I remained in my truck and admired the new landscaping. The pop of color from the blooming cactus complemented the spikey red yuccas and gave my place a happy curb appeal. The new additions made the turquoise container look even brighter. Nice job, boys! Maybe once the detective arrived, he could help me unload my new addition.

I glanced in the rearview mirror at the antique store, thinking of how sad it was that it wouldn't be opening this Saturday. Poor Mrs. Harrison.

The drab gray door slung open, and I did a double-take when Mr. Harrison stepped outside. What the? He was there standing on the porch big as day! But, that was impossible. He was dead!

Heart pounding, I ducked down and quickly accessed my phone's camera. I turned around, zoomed in and snapped a picture of the old man as evidence of what I saw. Then, I decided to video record him as he ambled toward his truck. I shook as I filmed him. After he retrieved papers, he hobbled back to his shop, alive as could be.

While I fiddled with my phone, preparing to call the police, there was a sharp knock on my window, causing me to drop my phone on the floor. I looked up to see Officer Barnes staring at me. I took a deep breath and blew the air out as I rolled down the window.

"You see a ghost?" he said in a monotone.

"I did! You won't believe it, but Mr. Harrison is alive! He just came out of his shop! Either that or I'm having a nervous breakdown." I glanced behind me, but the old man was out of sight.

The detective, again wearing wrinkled clothes, nodded slowly. "Yeah. That's Mr. Harrison," he said nonchalantly. "Ready to go inside?"

My mouth dropped open. "What are you talking about? Mr. Harrison was dead when they took him away in an ambulance. Right?"

He shrugged. "Yep. Let's go."

"But. How did I just see him?"

"Do I have to spell it out? One died. One didn't." He said this with an eye roll.

I froze as I considered this. Two Mr. Harrisons? Brothers? I asked, "How did you know there was a brother?"

"He came to the station last night to see your friend, Carl."

Carl? I wrinkled my nose. I was still reeling from the news of two Mr. Harrisons and then came up with an explanation for the differing personalities. I asked. "Are they twins? I mean, they looked so much alike, but acted so differently I was just sure he had a personality disorder, but it makes sense that there are two."

The rumpled detective pursed his lips like he was bored and apparently chose not to answer me. I studied his stern face, and thought he was about the age my father would have been now. I suddenly wanted my sweet, handsome father - wanted to hear him give me straight answers to my questions, unlike this jerk.

As I thought of the obvious differences in my dad and this detective, I wondered which Mr. Harrison had died? The grumpy one or the nice one? I couldn't pose the question that way, so I asked, "Can you tell me which one died?"

He sighed and answered, "Carl's uncle." He rubbed his hand across his neck.

I blinked, finally having a connection to Carl. He had said, Pops. So, the victim was the nice one I had spoken with." I felt sick.

Barnes blew out air in frustration. "Look, I have other cases to work on, can we go in now?"

"Oh, of course." I felt stupid to still be glued to my seat., so I stepped out of the truck and decided this was not the time or person to ask for help with my bottle tree. I unlocked my door, then took the Grass Man invoice from under the mat, stuffed it in my pocket, and led him into the shop. I was still dazed from the odd sighting, but pointed out the cash register with the mysterious $12 beside it. "This is where I'd left the books. My purse was sitting right there, but it wasn't even touched."

I walked him back to see the windows. With a small point and shoot camera, the detective took a few photos of the screen and countertop as he eyed the place over.

I followed him outside where he pointed to a big rock under the window. "Well, that's how he got in."

The old man must have brought the rock to stand on. I hadn't noticed it last night.

Back inside, Barnes growled, "Lucky nobody stole your teacup lights."

I was surprised by the surly man's use of the word teacup, and when he gave me a sideways glance in a playful gesture, I felt confident he had let his guard down and would finally give me inside information about the case. I relaxed against my display case and nodded, "So, what do you think?"

He ran his hand through his graying hair, preparing to tell me who broke in. But instead, he said, "I think you should shut your window, get a new screen, and for God's sake, hide your purse when you leave."

I shook my head, "No. About the case. When will we know the cause of Mr. Harrison's death?"

"Okay, you want to know what I really think?" He leaned in conspiratorially, "You just keep rescuing junk, and I'll do the investigating." The detective turned slightly and jotted something in a small notebook that had materialized out of nowhere

Ruffled by yet another snarky response, I narrowed my eyes, straightened my back, and said in a huff, "I repurpose interesting items – and people buy them…and they like them." I was infuriated that I had to defend my job to the man.

With a doubtful nod, the aggravating man said, "Preliminary autopsy report should be in tomorrow, but unless you're next of kin, you can read about it in the paper like everyone else."

Now I was getting hot and spoke louder, but it came out whiny, "But Sergeant Barnes, I found the body. He was right next to my building. Someone was in my shop. Don't I have a right to know something about his death, in case I'm in danger?"

He sighed and rolled his eyes, relenting, "I'll tell you if and when you should be worried."

Well, I guess that was a tiny win, so I calmed a bit. "OK, thanks. In the meantime, is there anything else I should do?"

As soon as the words came out, I shut my eyes. I'd just set myself up for another wisecrack. I wasn't wrong. He brightened and quipped, "Hang the bike a little higher. I almost hit my head."

He strode to the door without turning back or saying goodbye and lifted his hand in a slight wave before exiting.

What an exasperating man! I sure hoped he was better at solving crimes than soothing people.

I closed my window and locked the door before getting to work. I was still pretty spooked by the death and my teeth were clenched from my encounter with the detective, so I opened my mouth wide, then moved my jaw around and ended up yawning.

Back at the counter, I looked at the invoice for the landscape work, hoping the damage wouldn't be too bad. I read, 'No Charge – It's a shop-warming gift from your family at The Grass Man!'

My hand flew to my mouth. I was touched by the constant kindness of Jill's family. The lovely O'Briens had practically adopted me when my folks died. Someday, I will pay them back for all the good deeds they have bestowed on me.

While putting the "invoice" down, I bumped my laptop, waking it up. There on the screen was a frozen picture of my door - obviously, the end of the video I had started yesterday. I sat on my tractor seat and started the recording over so I could see how my tutorial looked. There I was, talking. The lighting was good. I nodded in approval. The volume was OK. Even my hair looked nice for a change. Too bad, since I'd have to start all over. I also realized I'd have to choose a new book since Huckleberry Finn was missing.

As the video continued to play, I heard Louise enter in her big, boisterous way. I watched myself turn around towards the door and welcome her. Then, I saw myself press a button on the computer. Wait, why didn't the video stop? Good grief, I hadn't stopped the recording at all. Suddenly, there was Louise's ample purple rear end taking up my whole screen. I looked at the time of the entire video – it had recorded for two hours and three minutes. I didn't even know the computer would record that long. Good to know, in case I ever want to make a full-length movie.

I was about to delete the recording when it dawned on me that the laptop camera may have caught the break-in! With a burst of excitement, I fast-forwarded through the video. It was fun to watch Louise zip around the shop in triple time. Then we left the shop and there was a lot of nothing. I kept scrolling but all I could see was the front door. Pretty boring…until at the 1 hour and 50-minute mark, when a shadow crossed over the screen. I paused the playback, afraid of what I might see, then bit my lip and pressed 'play'.

My eyes grew wide as the shadow grew larger. My heart rate doubled, just as it had when I found Mr. Harrison's body. When I heard a low grumble, like someone stubbing a toe, I turned up the volume to maximum. Staring at the screen, I tried not to blink for fear of missing something.

Slowly, an arm came into the frame, the same arm I'd found holding a book the night before. It reached past the computer to the stacked books. The close shot of the hand revealed age spots and craggy fingernails. Although I knew it had to be Mr. Harrison, my heart gave a little flip when I heard his familiar low voice say, "Now Flick has no reason to kill me. I got the darned books back."

I didn't know what that meant, but I continued to watch and listen. He spoke more softly. "Here you go, my dear. I'm sorry I couldn't let you keep these. Perhaps you'll find some other books to use for your projects." The weathered hands carefully unfolded a ten and two one-dollar bills and placed them on the counter.

I could hardly breathe as the old man hobbled to the front door and opened it. When he turned around, there was a clear view of Pops, the man I'd recently befriended and found dead last night. Now, I knew which twin had died. My throat constricted as the sweet man locked my door behind him and left, books in hand.

I stopped the video, sick that I'd caught the last moments of his life on a recording. My eyes welled with tears.

After I wiped my eyes, I watched the video again, still wondering how he had died. And who in the world was Flick?

I knew I should call Detective Barnes, but I was still so aggravated with him, that I opted to wait. Maybe I could figure the whole thing out on my own. Far Mor always says, If you've asked for help to no avail, do your own research. After all, I needed to know if I was in danger.

CHAPTER 6

I was so engrossed in thought I nearly fell off my stool when someone knocked at my door. It was the second time in a day that I was startled by a knock. But in my defense, finding a dead body could make a person jumpy. I tiptoed across the floor and looked through the peephole. All I could see was a mess of red hair.

I unlocked and opened the door in relief. Jill said, "Looks like the boys did their job."

I smiled. "I love it, but your family shouldn't have done this for free!"

She shrugged. "You are family."

I shook my head and said, "Jill, you are a sight for sore eyes. I have so much to tell you. Why aren't you at work?"

Jill waddled in, lugging a purse the size of a shopping bag, and said, "Dad's having the office painted and didn't want me around the fumes. I came by to check out the new bakery. I'm starving." Jill scanned me from my face to my bandaged knees and frowned. "What in the world?"

I shook my head. "You won't believe it when I tell you."

Jill's blue eyes grew big. "Well, get started then."

I opened my mouth to speak, but suddenly Jill's face made a familiar pout. "But I'm famished. Can it wait a minute?"

Although I was shaken by my new findings and anxious to tell her the whole story, I knew better than to get between her and food. I nodded.

As we walked across to the bakery, she said casually, "In case you're wondering, I'm carrying bricks in my bag."

I raised my eyebrows and hands in question.

She explained, "I'm trying to build up arm strength to carry Sophia in her carrier." Without taking a breath, she continued at high speed, "I'd kill for a cup of coffee. The doctor says I can have a cup a day, but I'm being super cautious. You'll let me have a sip of yours, right?" The crazy girl sounded like she'd already had a double shot of espresso.

Jill waddled up to the bakery entrance, flung the door open, and with a comical face sang, "I smell something wonderful!"

When we entered the brightly painted store, my eyes were drawn to the clock I'd made for Mike and Pat. It looked adorable hanging above the door against a light blue wall. I was glad I'd chosen the larger hands for it was easy to read.

Mike poked his head around the opening to the kitchen. When he saw me, he lifted his flour-coated hands. "Back again?"

"Yep. I'm already hooked on your bread. This is my friend, Jill. Jill, this is Mike, co-owner of Baking Bad."

She said cheerfully, "Hi Mike," then looked with a frown at the empty bakery case. "So, don't you have anything yummy to try?"

"Oh, we sure do. Been working all morning perfecting our eclairs, but we also have muffins, bagels, cream puffs, and some pastries too. Come on back."

We followed him and his trail of flour through the door where trays of goodies were stacked on tables. Pat carefully iced cinnamon rolls. He looked up. "Hey girls. Come to satisfy your sweet tooth?"

"I already had your amazing cinnamon twist this morning, but my friend Jill has to get a preview." I turned to Jill. "This is Pat. He's the other half of this operation."

Pat, a good foot shorter than Mike, stood by him and said, "Actually, I'm a third and he's two-thirds."

Mike smiled down at his partner and patted the top of his head with a smile.

"Ooh, can I get a picture of you guys all covered in flour?" They posed, showing off their hands and coated aprons. I snapped a pic with my phone and asked, "Are we your first customers?"

Pat beamed, "No. Our families have been by, and Louise stocked up for winter, I think."

I looked at the goodies and made my decision immediately. "I want a buñuelo! I can't believe you have a Mexican pastry! Now if you just had some lefse for the other half of my heritage, I'd be in heaven."

Mike wrapped the crispy pastry and handed it to me. "We've been working on a Norwegian almond cake. You might like that."

I squealed, "Sweet! My grandmothers would be thrilled. All I need now is coffee to go with this."

Mike said, "Are you going to 'The Barista' or do you want some plain old coffee here?"

"I think I can handle your plain old stuff." I gave a wink and nibbled on my crunchy cinnamon fritter, savoring the flavor and memories it brought as I waited for Jill. She took forever ordering a whole bag full of baked goods to take to her family. "I just can't stop," she said. She licked her lips.

I poured my own coffee, paid, and turned to leave with our orders in hand when Mike asked, "Is it true you found Mr. Harrison last night?"

I turned back and said with a sad nod, "Yes, sir. Not a fun evening." I shook my head.

Jill stared at me. "Is this what you wanted to tell me?"

I nodded and sat down at one of their small tables. Jill joined me and pulled a raspberry-filled bismark from her bag and said nonchalantly, "Who's Mr. Harrison?" She took a bite and moaned.

I answered, "He's the owner of the antique store next door." I grimaced and said, "I found him dead just beside my shop."

Jill's eyes widened, and she nearly choked. "He was dead?"

Mike wrinkled his nose. "That must have been horrible."

At a loss for words, Jill furrowed her brow.

I told them the details and then summed it up with, "It was an awful evening. Then afterward, we...Joey and I had to go to the police station and tell the detective what we knew."

Pat shook his head. "Wait. Why did Carl blame you?"

"No idea." I perked up as I grabbed my phone, "but you won't believe this. Look at who I saw this morning!" I pulled up the video of the living Mr. Harrison coming out of the shop and held up my screen for all to see.

The guys' eyes widened in unison.

Jill cocked her head at the phone and asked, "Who's that?"

Mike and Pat said, "Mr. Harrison!"

Jill's look was skeptical. "What? But you said he died last night."

I shrugged, "I did. He did. Apparently, there are two of them. Brothers. Twins I guess."

Pat slapped his hand over his mouth.

Mike slowly nodded, "Well, that sure explains a lot. One day he'd wave to us and the next day he'd sneer. I thought he had a screw loose."

I nodded and took a sip of hot coffee.

Pat's gaze swiveled to Mike, "Maybe that's who was shouting over there yesterday – the two brothers."

I swallowed, ready to ask what they'd heard but the door jingled, and Victoria strode in wearing a brightly flowered sundress and dark glasses. Her nose was in the air, and she didn't even look our way.

Pat switched into customer service mode and said politely, "Hello, neighbor. Victoria, right? Can I get you something?"

She cleared her throat and said in a snotty tone, "Do you have anything gluten-free?"

He motioned for her to follow him, saying, "At this time, we have only one offering. The oat bran…" His voice trailed off as they walked into the kitchen area.

Mike said, "duty calls" and followed after them.

"Who is that?" whispered Jill with a mouth full. "And why would you go to a bakery for something gluten-free?"

I shook my head. "That's Victoria, owner of 'The Barista' coffee shop. So far, she hasn't been very friendly. Maybe she's just shy."

"Shy? That's not the vibe I got."

Jill was probably right. Unable to wait, I unwrapped my crisp and took another heavenly bite. I lifted my coffee cup for a drink, but it was empty. "Jill, did you drink all of my coffee?"

She shrugged. "I couldn't help it."

A shrill laugh came from the backroom as Victoria said in a sharp tone, "Oh yes. Of course, Jett and I are spending all our free time together. Why we had a blast yesterday. You know, he's just a doll and would do absolutely anything for me!"

Jill and I looked at each other, suppressing giggles at her blatant arrogance. I whispered, "I saw them hugging yesterday and wondered. Now I know they are an item."

Jill voice wasn't much of a whisper. "I'm pretty sure everybody, including the dead antique store owner, heard that she's dating Jett. Sounds like she's sunk her claws into him pretty deep."

I replied, "I can't believe she's his type, but there is a lot I don't know about Jett."

One of the bakers said something I couldn't hear, and Victoria replied in a loud sing-song voice, "That's the reason we got our shops here, so we could be close to each other. Duh!"

Jill clamped her mouth shut comically then said, "Still think she's shy? I think she's a b…" Before she could finish the word, Victoria re-entered the lobby with a straight face, carrying a small sack. The boys trailed behind her.

I said, "Hi Victoria."

The uppity woman lifted her sunglasses to see who spoke, pursed her lips, and nodded ever so slightly at me. Upon seeing Jill, she scrunched her face, put her glasses back on, and swaggered out the door.

Jill waggled her head and said, "Well, isn't she just a peach?"

I wondered why Victoria was so rude to my friend. Was it because of Jill's wild red hair, or that she was so obviously pregnant? Then I caught sight of the red jelly running down Jill's chin. So, maybe that was it. I leaned over with a napkin and wiped the raspberry filling off her face. How in the world could this silly girl raise a child, when she was such a mess?

Mike entered and said, "Don't worry about Victoria. She's just a prima donna."

Jill snorted and then placed her hands flat on the table. "OK, back to the earlier conversation. So, the antique twins looked so much alike that none of you knew there were two of them?"

The three of us gave sheepish shrugs.

She continued, "So, which one died?"

I sighed. "The one that was nice to me, nicknamed Pops. I don't know how he died, why his body was moved, or where the books are now." When I clasped my hands, I felt the bruised scrapes on my palms and frowned. I felt ashamed babying my superficial wounds when people had lost a family member.

I said, "I should stop by to give my condolences to the other Mr. Harrison. Anyone want to come?"

The bakers shook their heads slowly, with wide eyes.

Jill, in her peppy voice, said, "I'll go." She grabbed her bag of goodies and stood up to leave. "Thanks, fellas!"

I stood, threw away my empty cup, and told Mike and Pat, "I'll keep you informed if I hear anything."

As we headed to the antique store, Jill said, "Those two kinda remind me of Mitch and Cam."

I thought of the gay couple from Modern Family and laughed. "They aren't nearly as goofy, but I can see what you mean."

When we reached the entrance of the antique store, I knocked. The silver car was parked to the side, so I assumed he was there. When there was no answer, I knocked again. We shrugged at each other and turned back toward my shop.

Jill announced, "That was some night you had. But at least you got to hang out with one of the hunky brewery brothers. Since Jett's off the market, how's the other one?"

My face flushed at the thought of Joey. She noticed and said in a rush, "You like him!" Jill did a little hop of excitement, which couldn't have been easy with her heavy purse, big belly, and bag of pastries.

When we entered my shop, I saw my computer and burst out, "Oh, I forgot to tell the others about this! Come here, Jill!" I led her over and cued up the recording. "It turns out I accidentally caught Mr. Harrison on video just before he died."

I pushed play and watched as she studied the video.

Jill's eyes and mouth were open enough that I could see food on her tongue. How was she still eating?

"What?" She commented as the video played, "Flick? Who's Flick?"

"Maybe his brother? Who else would want the books back? And that could be why they argued."

Jill took in a sharp breath, turned to me, and exclaimed in a loud whisper, "Maybe he killed him?" then she added even more dramatically, "Good thing the brother didn't answer the door just now or we could have been next!"

"Ha! Right." I laughed but when I saw my friend's knitted eyebrows, I realized she was serious. I waved it off. "I'm pretty sure we're safe." But Jill had planted the new idea in my brain. Did Mr. Harrison have something to do with the death of his brother?

I was just about to push stop, but I heard a new sound on the recording. "Listen!" We both held our breath and heard muffled voices, then the sound of a train approaching. I pushed pause. "Did you hear that? Someone's talking."

Jill yelled, "Rewind it!", so loud I covered my ear in pain and kept my hand there in case she made another seismic outburst.

I ran the video back a bit and turned up the volume to max. This time, we strained to listen. There were definitely two voices; one probably Pops, but the sounds were so muffled we couldn't identify any voice or words. As the Railrunner passed, we heard what sounded like a scuffle and crunching gravel, but weren't sure due to the noisy train.

"Could you understand anything?" she asked, staring at me with blue eyes as round as saucers.

Frustrated, I shook my head. "Nothing."

Biting her fingernail, Jill said, "What are you going to do with this? Turn it in to the police? Maybe we could go to a lab where they can enhance the audio like they do on CSI?"

I considered both of her suggestions and shook my head. "I don't think we could afford the testing ourselves, and I can't stand

Sergeant Barnes. He'd just make fun of me if I gave him any information, but maybe I should?"

Jill pouted as she pondered for a moment, then squealed, "I know! Let's do a ProCon! It'll be just like old times. Is the notebook here?"

I smirked and said, "Yes, it is. I always keep it nearby." I grabbed my worn pink spiral notebook from behind the counter and sat on the car seat bench.

She rushed over to sit beside me and opened her bag of goodies again.

After flipping through to the first blank page, I wrote, 'Should I tell the police about the video of Mr. Harrison?' Then, I drew columns and the word pros at the top of one column and cons above the other.

Jill and I had been making our ProCon lists in this very book since fifth grade. A few former topics included, 'Should we get our ears pierced?' 'Should Jill let Stevie Mack kiss her at Molly's party?', 'Should we go stag to the spring dance?' and 'Should we go to an in-state college?' In each of those instances, we went with the pro even though the kiss with Stevie Mack turned disastrous when Molly's mom caught them kissing and made everyone go home early.

All of our important questions, with our scientifically formulated answers, were forever documented in this hot pink notebook covered with Lisa Frank dolphin stickers.

Under pro (to tell the police), I spoke the words as I wrote, "Because it's the right thing to do."

"And why shouldn't you tell them about it?" she probed, taking a bite of yet another donut.

"Because Sergeant Barnes is aggravating." I made that entry under con.

Jill licked icing from her lips and said, "OK, so under con you can also put, 'We can figure it out ourselves.'"

I added that then shrugged. "But, it would take time and my shop opens in three days, and investigating a murder could be dangerous." I wrote both on my pro lists then added another. 'We have no experience solving crimes.'

Looking at the list, I said, "Two against telling the police and four in favor." I realized it had been my own ego preventing me from doing it immediately. I just didn't want to be chided by Barnes. I sighed. "Guess I'll call him."

Jill looked at me. "Yeah, you probably should. Besides, you don't have to prove to this policeman that you are smart. We know you are."

I tipped my head and gave an exaggerated pout. "Aw. That's so sweet." I pointed at my friend. "But I'm going to remember you said that. I'll call him in a bit."

She put on a flirty grin, "So, tell me about last night? Did something exciting happen with you and the brother? What's his name again?"

"Joey. And nothing happened. He did bandage my knees like an expert though." I walked over to her and bent to show her his medical prowess.

Just as she leaned over to look at my bandages, Larry's whiny but gravelly voice boomed. "Well now. It looks like I've walked in on some sort of kinky girl party here."

Argh! I had to put an alarm on that door. I was already tired of him walking in and startling me. I stood and straightened my shirt and stammered, "Um, I was just showing my friend how... well, I got some scrapes on my knees..." I rolled my eyes. Larry wasn't worth taking the time to explain. Besides, his one-sided smile gave me the creeps. "Oh, never mind."

When the disgusting landlord ogled at my bare but bandaged knees, I wished I hadn't drawn attention to any of my body parts.

"Want me to take a look?" He started to squat.

Disgusted, I crossed my legs, and said, "No. I'm fine."

"So, I heard you had some excitement last night." The annoying man sauntered over, sat on my tractor seat and pulled a toothpick from his pocket, and started picking his teeth. Even more annoying was the unpleasant odor emanating from him.

I said in a snarky tone, "Yes, and it would have been easier to manage if there had been outdoor security lights."

"Oopsy." He shrugged and continued, "I'll get around to that soon. So, did you really trip over his body?" His eyes danced.

Repelled by his morbid interest, I said, "No, I fell over some books."

Larry shrugged, stood up, and turned to Jill. "So, who's this beautiful ginger?" His tongue played with the toothpick in his mouth as he looked her over.

As expected, Jill's face screwed up in disgust. She usually didn't mind the term ginger, but coming from Larry, it sounded lewd. And who flirts with someone who is obviously pregnant? I didn't have to wait long for her comeback.

She sat taller and said with a head waggle, "I'm Maria's best friend. And I have a huge policeman husband who will be stopping by regularly to visit her." Jill's eyebrow was lifted high as she glared at him. Gotta love my protective bestie.

I was so ready for him to leave, but asked, "Did you need something, Larry?"

He leaned against my counter, gave a smirk, and asked, "You gals know Alex Chandler?"

Everyone in the state knew the name of the distinguished entrepreneur and real estate tycoon. We both nodded skeptically.

Larry puffed up his chest and said with a confident shrug, "Well, I've worked with him for years." He crossed two fingers together. "We're like this. Yep. I'm a pretty big deal."

I had trouble believing that, but waited to hear the point of his story.

In his squeaky voice, he continued. "As a matter of fact, I was at his place last night helping him get ready for his hoity-toity benefit this Thursday." He paused as if he expected us to ask for his autograph or something.

"That's nice?" I said, still wondering the point of his story.

"You know, I can probably score a couple of free tickets for you girlies if you want."

Jill jumped at the chance to see him squirm out of the offer he couldn't possibly honor. She folded her arms and said, "Sure. We'll take the tickets. Thanks."

Larry didn't even flinch - just nodded and made a click with his mouth then nodded. "Alrighty then." He turned to me, "You ready to open on Saturday?"

"Yes. I'm good to go."

"Okie dokie. I'll bet news of a death here will be good for business."

Shocked at his statement, I blinked. "What?"

"Yep, I can see it now on the news..." He held up his fingers like they were scrolling across the screen. "It'll probably read, 'Antique store owner dies just before his shop opens.'"

My face scrunched up in horror. "Well, that would be awful."

Jill shut her mouth enough to say, "How would that be good for business?"

Larry shrugged. "Eh, you know what they say; any publicity is good publicity." He sucked in a deep breath and said, "Well, I'll just mosey on down to get some work done."

He scuffed his boots all the way to the door, turned back, and pointed at me. "Don't want you running around in the dark anymore, missy. And you know, you could just call me to be your escort at night." He raised his eyebrows suggestively and exited.

Jill looked horrified. "Eew. You said he was creepy, but seriously? And that scraggly blond beard and greasy hair doesn't help. How does a lowlife like him own such a cool place?"

I shook my head. "He's just the manager. The owner is out of state. Texas, I think."

"Too bad *he's* not in Texas. Gross."

"Dang that Larry. Now he got me worried. I'm afraid I'll be cursed if people find out someone died right there." I pointed in the direction of where the body was found. I hadn't even considered how publicity might affect our businesses.

Jill waved a hand in front of her nose and said, "I doubt anyone will even pay attention to an old man dying anyway." She gagged and waved some more, "Do you think he wore enough aftershave? And what was that other rank smell?"

"I think it's a mix of chewing tobacco and B.O." I wrinkled my nose.

Facing an empty corner of the room, I said, "I want to run to the junkyard over on Silver Avenue. I need to get my mind off all this for a while. Wanna come?"

"Sure. Maybe this place will air out while we're gone." She pinched her nose.

When we went outside to my truck, I sighed. "Shoot. I have to get this out of here before I can bring more stuff back."

"What?" She leaned her head over the truck and turned to me. "Your bottle tree from home?"

I pulled the tailgate down and nodded. "Won't it look cute beside my shop?"

"Absolutely. Let me help." She moved toward me.

"Nope. Not in your condition. I think I can get it by myself."

I pulled the metal stand along the bed making a scraping sound so horrible Jill held her ears. Luckily, the stand wasn't as heavy as I anticipated, and was able to slide it off to the ground. Then after dragging it across the gravel, I positioned it in just the right spot beside my steps.

Jill appeared, holding two empty wine bottles. She stuck them upside down onto two long spikes. It wasn't five minutes before the tree was in full bloom with colorful bottles reflecting the bright New Mexico sun.

We stepped back and said in unison, "Perfect."

When Jill and I pulled into the junkyard parking lot, we were enveloped in a cloud of dust. The area, surrounded by a fence topped with barbed wire, was sealed with a heavy gate. I parked by a rusted red truck with a beat-up sign reading, 'Smitty's Salvage'. I said to Jill, "Why does a place full of junk, need such protection?" I pushed the buzzer on the gate and waited.

"Oooh, Maria, Look! There's an old broken birdbath. You could use that, couldn't you?"

I looked through the chain-link fence at the cobalt blue ceramic stand. Even though the bowl was cracked, I knew it would look great with succulents planted in it. "Good eye, Jill."

A stout man in grimy overalls came out of the building wiping sweat from his forehead with a bandana. "Can I help ya?"

"Hi. I've shopped here before. Aren't you Smitty?"

He squinted, trying to see me in the bright sun, and said, "Oh yeah, need some more bike parts?"

"Actually yes. How much do you want for the blue birdbath?"

"Eight bucks. But it don't hold water."

"That's OK. I'll take it. Mind if we walk around a bit?"

He spit on the ground. "Go ahead. I'll put 'er over by your truck. Ring the bell if ya need sumpin." He opened the gate and lifted the heavy blue stand as if it was made of foam rubber and placed it by my truck.

Jill tiptoed through the field of broken debris with her mouth agape. "It looks like a tornado came through here."

"I know. Isn't it great?" I watched my step as I moved excitedly towards a pile of old bicycle parts. "Hey, grab any wheels that have good spokes and put them in a stack. Rust is OK and don't worry about the tires. I'll take them off anyway. Take the chains too."

"What are you making this time?"

"Oh, on Pinterest, I saw this cool way to set colored glass between the spokes and make yard spinners or wall artwork. I also want to make a table. I have a whole corner waiting for my bicycle creations!" I handed her a pair of gloves.

She shook her head as she put them on. "Should you really be shopping today, when your store opens so soon?"

Ha, what an ironic statement. Jill is just as impulsive as me. Once we get an idea, we get crackin' on it. As if I'd said that aloud, I added, "Besides, I've got to have projects to work on during my slow days in the shop. I refuse to twiddle my thumbs."

She nodded as if that made perfect sense. We started grabbing the straightest wheels and putting them in a stack. I'd brought tools so I could take bikes apart if needed. I spotted a cute pink bicycle basket and put it in the growing pile.

Jill started laughing." Oh my gosh! Check that out."

I followed her gaze straight above us to a huge billboard looming over the junkyard. It featured an enormous, handsome Alex Chandler standing with the Sandia mountains in the background and the slogan 'Luxury at its best, right here in ABQ.'

It wasn't that the billboard was funny since we'd seen the handsome older man's face plastered all over town touting his properties. What made me chuckle, however, was that the rich man with the iconic salt and pepper hair pointed directly down into the junkyard. And just under his finger, were the words, 'Location, location, location!'

I chuckled and said, "How much do you want to bet he didn't plan on this actual location for his billboard?" I-25 was directly behind us. Surely from that viewpoint, the sign looked like he was pointing to the foothills of the mountains rather than into a junkyard. He could only hope that was the case.

Jill said, "It was probably Larry's job, to choose the spot for the sign."

I chuckled at that and picked up a set of handlebars. "Sounds about right."

"Do you believe anything that creep said?"

I scoffed. "No. He probably just did an odd job at one of Chandler's properties and thinks they are best friends now."

CHAPTER 7

As I disassembled some handlebars, I heard a squeak. I figured it was just Jill twirling a tire again, but the sound came from the other side of me. There was the squeak again. "Did you hear that?"

She stood up straight. "Yeah. It sounds like it's coming from that bathtub."

I put down the handlebars and we crept over to the filthy tub and peered in. There was a disgusting-looking animal inside. I jumped back and said, "What is it?"

Jill peered over the edge, her head cocked, "It's too big to be a rat but too small to be a dog."

I inched closer to get a good look at the creature. Matted from head to toe, it had long black and gray matted hair sticking out everywhere, like a coat of bad dreadlocks. I took my phone out of my pocket and snapped a picture of the strange animal. Its little beady eyes lit up when it saw us and scrabbled along the side of the tub trying to get to us. If it was a wild animal, wouldn't it have tried to get away from us?

Conjuring up my nerve, I carefully put my hand down inside the tub. The thing ran toward my hand, tongue out, trying to lick me. "I think it's a dog, just a tiny gross one." Its toenails clicked as it tried to climb up the porcelain to me. "Look, it can't get out by itself."

Leaning over the side, I picked it up and caught a whiff of a nauseating odor. I held it at arm's length. "Oooh, you stink." The critter wriggled in my hands as we inspected it. I said, "Look. The poor thing has burrs embedded in its skin."

Jill came closer and pulled her head back and to the side, "Phew. That thing smells worse than Larry. But look at those cute bright eyes. What's it doing here?"

I shook my head. "And how long has it been here?" I carried the little thing back to the gate, holding it in front of me to avoid the smell, and rang the bell. When Smitty came out, I held it up to him and said, "This is the worst junkyard dog I've ever seen. Not very ferocious."

He squinted again, but not because of the sun this time. "What is it?"

"We think it's a dog. It was in a bathtub and couldn't get out."

"Well, it ain't mine. Folks dump dogs near here all the time. Prolly just fell in while it was scoutin' round for food. You can have it. That one wouldn't do me no good anyhow, not like my Pit, Brutus. But, he runned off." The big sweaty man started telling a story about how in his day, Brutus caught someone who had broken into his place and nearly took off his arm.

While he rambled on, the stinky pup curled up in my arms and got comfortable. I looked at Jill and said, "Guess we could take it to the shelter."

"Or you could clean it up and keep it?" She said, her brilliant blue eyes dancing.

I gave a sideways glance at my friend for that remark. "No."

As Smitty droned on about his amazing dog, Brutus, I whispered, "Let's stop by the vet's office and see what they say about it." I peeked into the small face hidden beneath wild hair and tried to imagine its story.

Jill held the stinker while Smitty went inside and brought back a warped plastic butter tub with some water. The poor tiny creature drank and drank while he loaded everything in my truck.

"Thanks, Smitty. You know I'll be back." I paid Smitty for the rusted goods with cash. He wiped his sweaty head with one of the bills, reminding me to always wash my hands after handling money.

With a guffaw, he said, "Let me know what you do with that there rat you got."

We drove with windows down to diminish the dog's rank odor. Jill cooed at the dog then held it up and said, "It's so matted that I can't even tell if it's a boy or girl."

We stopped by a vet's office. After the staff and patrons gathered around to stare at the unsightly animal, the vet confirmed it was indeed a dog, and probably a teacup poodle. He checked the animal's eyes and teeth and determined it was about four years old. They gave it more water and carefully trimmed away the worst mats and burrs. Only then, did they announce it was a female.

"It's a girl!" Jill squealed. "I just knew it."

She weighed in at a whopping 3½ pounds and had no tags, microchip, or tattoo. The vet suggested getting it groomed, then waiting a few days before getting shots. I had no intention of keeping the dog, but knew she had to have a bath.

We drove to Pet Palace, a local pet store with signs posted for grooming, and showed the dog to a woman wearing a pink paw-print smock. She set down her clippers and took the pup. "Oh, poor little baby! She must have been in agony with all the mats. I have no other choice but to shave her down completely."

"Shouldn't take me but an hour or so. But don't worry, the hair will grow back soon and she'll be just adorable." So, we left the dog there to be washed and shaved.

Driving to my shop, I asked, "Who would leave a tiny dog like that to fend for itself?", disgusted at the thought. "She could have been eaten by a coyote. That happens you know."

Jill said, "Idiots. Well, she's safe now. What are you going to name her?"

I whipped my head over to Jill. "Name her? If I do that, I'll have to keep her and I don't want a dog. We'll take her to a no kill shelter once she is fixed up." Jill pouted.

I faced the road again and rolled my eyes. I had to be firm with her. As if I was explaining to a nine-year-old why we couldn't get a dog, I stated, "I'm starting a new business in three days and I've already wasted half a day when I should have been working on my pricing. You keep her!"

"Seriously? We already have Rosco, Snowball, Pitter, and Patter. Plus, a baby is on the way. Remember?"

I understood her house was pretty full with a dog, a cat, two birds, and an incoming child, but that sure didn't mean *I* needed a dog.

She brightened, "I think you should name her Stinky. No, Tubby because you found her in a tub, but she's too skinny for that." I could hear her wheels turning as she thought of other names. "If it was a boy, you could name him Matt because of all its mats. Ooh, how about Pipsqueak?" She laughed at her own plays on words.

I rolled my eyes as I parked by my shop. I wasn't about to let Jill persuade me to keep her, but I had to smile at her ideas for names. Stinky and Tubby were out, but Pipsqueak kind of fit.

As I got out of the truck, I remembered my little sister's stuffed bear, named Zia. I had always thought if I ever got a pet, I'd name it Zia, but I had no intentions of telling Jill that.

I gave my keys to Jill so she could go inside to get out of the heat. Then I unloaded the bike parts and lugged the birdbath and extra rims behind my container. I didn't want my new shop to look like a junkyard. Not yet anyway. I felt uneasy walking past the area where I had found Mr. Harrison. I kept my head up to avoid seeing any blood but my stomach turned just the same.

Inside my store, the cool air rejuvenated me. I slumped onto my stool and said, "I guess I should price stuff today. Wanna run some errands for me so I can get to it?"

"Sure!" She grabbed her keys before I could tell her what to do. She winced and held her stomach.

I tensed up, ready to race to the hospital. "Is it the baby?"

She laughed as if I was hilarious. "No. I'm just hungry."

"Whew! Well, I have some snacks here."

"It's ok. I'll just pick up lunch for us while I'm out."

"Great. Can you stop by the dollar store and get more price tags like this?" I showed her a package of the kind I used. "Then, if you're still out, go back to Pet Palace and get that pup?" I shook my head at the thought of a dog, but said, "I really do want to know what she looks…and smells like now."

I dug into my purse and cringed as I held out three precious twenties. "I hope this covers the grooming." I hadn't had a pet since I was six and that was only a goldfish, so I had no idea what it would cost to groom a dog.

"I'll split the cost with ya, girl," she said as she took only one of the bills from my hand and bounced out the door.

I was overwhelmed looking around at all the products that still needed to be priced. It wasn't easy to determine the appropriate value of my creations. The cost of materials was generally low, but I had to be compensated for labor and still keep prices affordable. I turned on some music to motivate me, took a deep breath, and started with jewelry.

I had gotten more than half of my items marked and wondered what was taking Jill so long to run three errands. Within seconds, I figured it out. The redhead stormed in, loaded down with an array of bags: one from the dollar store, several from Pet Palace, and another from McDonald's.

I smirked, "Did you remember the dog?"

"Yep. She's right here." She set the bags on the counter and a skinny, black head poked out from under her chin.

I couldn't believe how tiny the dog's head looked without hair. I pulled myself up off the floor where I sat amid baskets of items. I looked at a cloth sling holding the dog.

"You bought that?"

Without blinking, she said, "No. I purchased some fabric and whipped it up while I was gone." She lifted her eyebrow and pursed her lips and said, "Of course, I bought it. It's so handy! It keeps your hands free and look at how cozy she is."

She lifted the dog out for me. I took the tiny smooth body from her and held it in front of me, amazed by the lack of hair. What a transformation! With bare ears and nose, she looked nothing like a poodle, but more like a cartoon rat with huge eyes. A tiny pink bandana was tied around the shaved neck, and I had to smile at the odd sight – "A rodent with accessories!"

Jill squealed, "You should see what else I got!"

I groaned. "Jill. Why did you buy anything? I'm not keeping her." Just as I said this, the dog slipped into a natural position in my arms. I was surprised at the warmth of her little body.

Jill said, "You can't resist that face, now can you?"

I looked down at the dog and dang it if a cute little tongue didn't lick my chin. I whispered, "Are you in cahoots with Jill?"

"You should see her extra-extra-small sweater. We need to keep her warm as long as she's furless." Jill pulled out a tiny pink sweater and slipped it over the dog's head and put her minuscule paws through the armholes. "I also got food, a collar, and a leash."

"You are crazy! Why did you buy so much?" But then I remembered how she had been in a baby store. Her cart was filled in no time. Jill was the shopping-est girl I knew.

The little dog snuggled in close to my chest and looked into my eyes with what I took as adoration. I lifted her head up to my nose to see if she smelled better. Much better. Then she licked my nose and I melted. "Why do you have to be so darned sweet?"

In a babyish voice I swear I never used in my life, I said, "You are a little cutie, aren't you?" I held her in one arm and started pulling stuff from the bag. "How much did this set us back?"

"Actually, I got the bowls, collar, leash, and poop bags at the dollar store. The groomer only charged twenty bucks because the dog was so pathetic, but she hopes you'll bring her back for future grooming." Jill gave a wink. "Plus, she gave me a 20% off coupon for Pet Palace, so I went shopping there for the rest. So, not much at all!" Jill finally took a breath. "And we have fish sandwiches, fries, and tea. We should eat before the food gets cold."

"Well, I hope you kept the receipts, because…" I said shaking my head at Jill realizing there was no point arguing with her. I poured a little food and water into the tiny red bowls and put them on the floor, then set the dog down and opened my sandwich wrapper. "I am famished" I admitted.

"Oh, I left the best thing in the car. I just had to buy it. And it's my treat." She waddled out to her car and returned with a bright yellow dog bed. When she handed it to me, I saw it had a red Zia symbol in the center. Oh no. Now that was a definite sign.

The simple circular Zia sun design originated in Kelly's reservation, Zia Pueblo. It was adopted by the state and is the only symbol on the New Mexico state flag. The bed was perfect for a tiny New Mexican pet. I couldn't help but say, "It's so cute!" I put the colorful bed back in its bag to keep me from looking at it.

As we ate, we watched the pup sniff around the shop. She eventually made it to her food bowl and ate a few kibbles, then lapped up the water with her delicate tongue.

Jill's mouth dropped open. "Jeeze! She's so dainty. Rosco is so loud and sloppy, the whole room is soaked when he gets a drink."

The little dog pranced with a high step over to me and stood on her back legs, patting lightly on my shin, signaling me to pick her up. I said softly but firmly, "No. You stay down while I eat." Surprisingly, she seemed to understand and lay down at my feet as we ate. She looked so mournful, that I relented and took the yellow bed from its bag and placed it on the floor. Without expecting a result, I said, "Get in the bed." I turned back to my food.

Jill said, "Well, would you look at that. She just toddled over and jumped in. Amazing."

Wow. She really did. With a few turns, the little thing lay with her head resting on the side and looking up at us with those sweet dark eyes.

Jill bit into a fry and said with her mouth full, "She's such a smartie! I wonder who taught her those commands?"

My stomach clenched at the thought. "What if she wasn't dumped at Smitty's but she got loose and her family is looking for her? Should we try to find her owner?"

"Maria, you're overthinking it. She didn't have a collar, a microchip, or any information and wasn't even spayed. If someone wanted to keep her, they would have taken much better care of her. By the looks of her, she had obviously been on her own for a long time. And remember, you saved her life."

I let out a big sigh. She was right. I looked at the little sleeping darling and before thinking, I said aloud, "If I was to keep her, I would name her Zia."

Jill clapped her hands and said, "Woohoo! Now you have to keep her! It's a perfect name!" She sang, "Maria has a dog and I am a Godmother!"

I laughed, then closed my eyes, wondering what in the world I had gotten myself into. Snapping back to my practical self, I said to my friend, "OK. Enough dog talk. I can't even think of that now. I should re-record my 'How To' video."

She said, "You'll have to choose a new book since Huck Finn is missing."

I started back towards my storeroom and joked, "He's probably back on the island with Jim."

She groaned at the quip then gathered up all the fast-food trash. "I do love me some Twain."

I picked up an old cookbook I'd gotten from Louise, figuring it would work, and went back to my stool. As soon as I sat down, I realized I had forgotten to call Sergeant Barnes about the video. That's OK. I'd just e-mail it to him. I smiled, realizing in this manner, I could avoid seeing him in person and his sarcasm.

I clicked through my video files to e-mail the clip to him, but couldn't find it. Hmm. Where was that file? I checked in documents to see if I'd saved it there.

Panicked, I said, "Uh, Jill? I can't find the video. It's gone!"

Jill said, "What's gone?"

"The footage of Old Mr. Harrison in my shop." I started feeling sick. Had I accidentally deleted the evidence?

She leaned over me, slurping her last dregs of iced tea from a straw. "We just watched it this morning. How could it be gone?

Rubbing my temples, I said, "I should have called Sergeant Barnes as soon as I saw it."

"Let me look." She took my place at the computer and tapped on the keyboard while I paced nervously, then said, "Maybe it's in your deleted files."

She shook her head after searching. "Nope. Can't find it."

I started sweating. "I don't know what to do now. If I tell the detective I had it and lost it, he'll think I'm a total idiot. I mean it could have been important." I was especially sad that it was the last recording of Mr. Harrison.

"Stupid computers!" she exclaimed. "Sometimes mine will just go blank in the middle of a file and I have to start over. I'll ask Kelly about it tonight."

She looked at me and said softly, "Don't beat yourself up, Maria. You were going to call him - it was decided by the ProCon list. Just don't tell him about it. It didn't show that much."

I raised my eyebrows in disagreement, "It proved who broke into my shop."

She cringed. "Well, there is that. Look, I've got to go. I stayed way longer than planned. Mom wants me to go over the receipts from last week." She gave me a little hug and said over my shoulder, "It's going to be fine."

"Please tell your parents I love the landscaping!" I gave her a tight squeeze and said, "Thanks for everything."

I was lucky to have such a good friend.

As Jill carried her 20 lb. purse to the door, she turned back and gave a bright smile, "Have fun with Zia tonight!"

I'd already forgotten about the dog and when the door shut, I looked down at the pup curled up in her bed and dressed in a tiny pink sweater. Despite my frustration over everything, the little dog dressed in a tiny pink sweater made me smile.

Left almost alone, I was consumed with worry about the missing video. What had happened to it? I decided to wait until I got home to film my tutorial.

While debating on how much to price a book clock, I tried to remember everything I could about the missing video. A train had passed by, but what time was that? The video would have had a timestamp. Too bad it wasn't available.

I jumped up and dug through my backpack to get the latest Railrunner timetable and found the weekday schedule. A northbound train went by at 7, but that was before I even left my shop. The next Railrunner, a southbound, should have gone by after its 8:45 departure, which would have been just when the scuffle occurred. I had encountered the still-warm body at around 9:15, so maybe this information gave me the time of the death. I jotted that into my phone notes so I wouldn't forget, or lose it.

CHAPTER 8

By late afternoon, I had finished pricing everything. I felt a little better and decided to attempt to deliver the purse to Victoria again. I woke up the exhausted dog and hooked the little leash onto her mini collar so we could take a little walk. I stood beside my building, delighted to find that she knew how to walk on a leash and even better, how to do her business. After I cleaned up after her, we walked to the dumpster to throw away the little bag.

As we walked back to the parking lot, she stopped and sniffed around on the ground, and picked something up.

"Zia, what is in your mouth?" It was my first time using the name and I smiled.

She looked up at me while holding something silver in her mouth. I bent over, gently pried her teeth open, and pulled out a small silver charm, shaped like a spoon. "That's odd. But, it's kind of pretty." The charm was so tiny, that I knew I would lose it in my pocket, so I carefully stuck it in my cellphone case for safekeeping and continued across the parking lot with my small thing finder friend beside me.

Upon reaching Victoria's shop, I picked up Zia, took a breath, and climbed the steps. I tapped on the door and waited. There was no response so I poked my head inside. Zia peeked in from her own vantage point, clamped under my left arm.

I didn't see anyone, but I winced as a loud screech pierced my ears, "You can't bring a dog into my establishment. Are you crazy?"

Taken aback by this strong reaction, my face flushed. I jumped away from the door. Why did this woman make me so upset? I hadn't even planned to take Zia inside.

Victoria's perfectly made-up face appeared at the door, her eyes burning into mine. As I thought about her sharp statement, my embarrassment turned to anger. What if I had been a customer with a service animal? Would she treat them like that?

I'd had enough of the "Barista's" rudeness and without thinking, I lifted my head and lied, "She's my emotional support dog." Although I dislike people who cheat the system, I justified my statement as my own kind of quality control for our shopping center. I added with confidence, "You know, a service dog?"

Victoria opened the door wide and narrowed her eyes, "I don't believe you. What's your disorder? You look fine to me. Where are your papers?" Her face had turned purple and her lips tightened as if she was protecting her shop from a bomber instead of a poodle.

She held the door open with her polished hand directly in front of my face. I couldn't help but notice the silver charm bracelet with a variety of cups, coffee pots, and spoons! The charm Zia found must belong to her, but in my emotional state, I didn't want to tell her I found it. Not now anyway.

I replied calmly, "Victoria, you know you aren't allowed to ask those questions. It's an invasion of privacy according to the American Disabilities Act."

She squinted as I spoke, then lifted an eyebrow. "Well, we'll just see about that." I could picture her googling the ADA as soon as I was gone. Disgusted, I turned to leave.

I felt a little guilty deceiving her and turned back around to fess up that Zia wasn't really a service dog. But, just as I started to speak, she said, "Well, I don't know how that dog could be a comfort to anyone. It looks like a rat."

Her comment changed my mind yet again. As much as I wanted to get away from her, I took a breath and went with the sugary approach. I handed her the purse I'd made from a book about coffee, titled 'Celebrating the Bean'. With a sincere smile, I said, "I made this for you – to wish you good luck starting your business."

Her eyes widened and then narrowed as she took the little brown purse from me. She examined it with a wrinkled nose. A bit flustered, she said, "It's way too small for me to use as a purse, but I suppose I can find a place for it."

Not quite a thank you, but at least she didn't throw it back at me. I said, "Well, OK. I guess we'll keep moving. Goodbye."

The door closed behind me and I shook my head wondering how anyone could get along with that woman. And why in the world did Jett like her?

I walked to the brewery next and stood on the porch while the hostess went to get Joey. I had to laugh when the big, rough Joey emerged and immediately said in a baby voice, "So who is this?" He stepped outside, picked Zia right out of my arms, and held her over his head in his palm. Zia wagged her tail and took in the high view of the world.

"It's my new dog, Zia. I found her at the junkyard. This is what she looked like this morning." I took my phone from my back pocket and found the unbelievable 'before' image of her in the rusted tub. He stared at the picture in astonishment.

"No! That can't be the same dog."

"It is."

"Well, it's sure the funniest junkyard dog I've ever seen."

I said, "That's exactly what I said to the owner."

Joey laughed and took the dog inside the brewery, yelling, "Jett, come see this!"

Now that was the perfect response to my new crazy-looking dog. I smiled and followed him inside.

Jett joined us, looking nothing like he had the night before. He seemed refreshed and had a sparkle about him. His captivating dark eyes toggled from photo to dog and back. As he petted Zia, I was happy to see his gaping smile when she licked his hand. He said, "I think she's got personality."

I nodded. "Indeed."

Joey turned to me. "So Maria, how are your knees today?" Both brothers glanced down at my bandages.

For some reason, when these guys looked at my legs I didn't feel creeped out at all. "Oh, they are much better. A skilled doctor bandage them last night."

Jett smirked. "So, Dr. Joe worked his magic?"

"Yes, he did."

Joey perked up. "Hey, did our friendly neighborhood detective show up this morning?"

I rolled my eyes. "Mm-hm. He was no help to me but got the info he needed. Hey, did you guys know there were two antique store owners?"

Both guys looked surprised, apparently not aware of that fact.

I added the most important part. "Identical twins!"

I figured they would be shocked about this, but Jett's face crumpled. He cleared his throat as if he might say something important, but Joey spoke first. "Twins? That's crazy. Which one died?"

I was still focused on Jett's odd reaction, but said, "It was Carl's uncle, Pops…" I frowned and said, "the one that was so sweet to me the other day."

Jett shook his head, almost as if he was angry, but still didn't say anything. He turned around and walked off.

Joey watched his brother head toward the kitchen. He handed Zia back to me but was clearly deep in thought. I wasn't sure what to do or say at the awkward moment, but tried a light approach. "Well, I guess I'd better take my ferocious dog home with me." I turned and said, "See you later."

I felt uncomfortable with the silence that followed, but just as I reached the door, Joey's warm voice said, "Oh, yes you will."

Without turning back, I smiled, opened the door, and walked into the heat of the day.

I buried my grin in the little shampoo-scented dog and walked back to Upcycled. What an interesting day. How strange that Jett changed gears and left as soon as he heard which man had died. Moody people baffle me.

Once in the shop, I realized how tired I was and decided to call it a day. I packed up most of the dog gear and my laptop so I could re-film my video from home tonight.

Since I wasn't in the mood to cook, I drove through Blake's Lotaburger and got a green chile cheeseburger and fries. After parking in my driveway, I carried my belongings in from my truck, shaking my head at all the dog paraphernalia Jill had gotten.

There were more business cards stuck in the screen door. I knew I could make a pretty penny if I sold the house, but I was determined to make a go of my new business and keep the home if possible. After all, apart from spending two weeks at Hummingbird Music Camp, I'd never lived anywhere else.

I looked at Zia, and joked, "You better not eat too much and become a financial liability, or out you go!" Her sweet black eyes looked so innocent that I couldn't see her being a liability. I took her out of the sling so she could investigate her new home.

I set up my demonstration materials on my old dining table as I munched on my burger. Then, with the new old book in hand, I scooted my food away and started filming myself again. At one point, while the camera recorded, Zia jumped up on the table and laid her head on her paws, and watched me. I hoped she was out of the camera shot but was so engrossed in making my tutorial that I didn't really care. So, what if she photobombed my video a bit?

I posted the video, relieved to check one more thing off my list. At least if this video vanished from my computer, it would still be somewhere in the cloud.

I collapsed in front of the TV, finished eating, and finally started to unwind. I must have fallen asleep because when I woke, the music from the 10 o'clock news blared. The leading story was about fires burning in the Jemez Mountains due to the extreme drought. I frowned, hoping the flames would be contained soon. I loved to take the short drive up to hike among the tall Ponderosa pines; besides, that's where Hummingbird Music Camp is located.

Breaking news scrolled along the bottom of the screen, taking me out of my mountain reverie. "Investigations are ongoing in the 'Out of the Box Murder'. One person of interest, the victim's nephew, Carl Harrison, was released from custody this morning."

I sat up so fast that I knocked my plate on the floor. Murder? Darn. I was still holding out hope that Mr. Harrison died from natural causes. An unsettling feeling crept into my stomach but I was fairly sure it was the grim news rather than the hot green chile.

I had hoped the public wouldn't find out about the incident but now it was all over the news. I remembered Larry's theory that any publicity was good publicity. Did he have something to do with the announcement? I shook my head in disgust.

Not only that, why did the media always have to give kitschy names to tragedies? It was disrespectful to the family to give Mr.

Harrison's death a grim title. The "Out of the Box Murder", seriously? How awful. What about his poor wife?

And now, not only did all of the shop owners lose a peer, our new center would be known for the murder before we even opened. I didn't see how it could be good for business. I flung myself back on the couch, feeling tears well up in my eyes.

Zia rushed over, climbed on my chest, and licked my face. How did she know I was upset? I blinked away the tears, focused on her bright eyes, and said in a croaky voice, "You know what? Maybe it will be nice to have a little friend live with me."

I pulled the little pup closer and cuddled her into my neck. She licked my chin until I said with a giggle, "That's enough, pipsqueak."

As much as Zia turned out to be a great, yet unofficial, emotional support animal, I was wired from the news and needed fresh air. I would take my new dog for a stroll through Old Town.

I clipped on her tiny leash and we walked past other old adobe homes, admiring my neighbor's moonflower. Its giant white flowers were so vivid in the moonlight, they practically glowed.

We walked a few blocks until we reached the iconic square, surrounded by stores famous for art galleries, souvenir shops, and restaurants. The evening was completely still tonight. There were no Mariachi bands in the gazebo nor Native Americans selling their wares on the sidewalk by my favorite restaurant. Every time my family went, I had to sit by the tree growing inside. It was quiet and dark with everything closed for the night. The only sound was faint music coming from a jazz bar on a side street.

Glancing across the square, I was awestruck by the full moon as it illuminated the San Felipe de Neri church in a gorgeous glow. This church built in 1790, held not only my baptism and Quinceanera, but was the site of my sister's funeral, and later, that of my parents. The moonlight glinted off the beautiful towers, bringing tears to my eyes.

When we finished a slow lap around the square, I noticed little Zia panting so I carried her the rest of the way. I forgot just how short her legs were.

Once in bed with the little warm body snuggled next to me, my phone rang.

It was Jill calling to check on me. "Hey girl, are you okay?"

"Yeah. I'm alright. I just can't believe they named it the 'Out of the Box Murder.'"

"Um. Did you watch channel 7?"

"No. I saw 13."

"Well, they just mentioned you on the news."

"What? No, they didn't." Surely Jill was kidding. Why would I be of interest?

She continued, "They said you found Mr. Harrison's body." She paused then said slowly, "And they said the police will question you more later."

I couldn't hold back my frustration and said, "What? It's not bad enough that I had to find the body of a new friend, but now they announce on TV that I could be a suspect? Jeeze. Probably that darned Barnes. Now I'm never going to get to sleep."

"Actually, the announcer said you *and* some other shop owners would be questioned further." She spoke softly. "Sorry. I guess I shouldn't have called."

I felt bad ranting at her and said, "It's OK, Jill. It wasn't your fault."

She asked. "Do you think Larry called the station? I'll bet he wanted the marketing ploy."

"Who knows what he would do? Jill, thanks for the head's up. I don't know what else Barnes needs to ask of me, but at least I've been warned that he may call."

After hanging up, my head whirred. I got up and took a Melatonin with a glass of milk to help me relax. Back in bed, I thought about the timeline of the murder, the video, and who could possibly want to hurt Pops. Carl was upfront in my thoughts but I didn't know why. And how could we market our businesses in a more positive light? Besides a small article in the paper last week, our only big publicity was a murder and I doubted that was going to be a real customer magnet, even if Larry thought it was.

The supplement must have worked, because the next thing I knew, my alarm went off. I opened my eyes and jumped back to find an animal in my bed. Then when I saw those eyes all cute and snuggly, I remembered I now had a dog! Zia must have been exhausted too for I never felt her move all night.

I packed up my pup and drove to the shop where Louise stood on my steps waiting for me. Her pantsuit could have belonged to a large elf, it was so green.

"Joey told me about your new fluffy friend. I just had to come to see it."

I handed Zia to her through the truck window and then got out. "She's not exactly fluffy yet."

"Well, I'll be hornswoggled! This is the teensiest dog I've ever seen! Is it still a puppy?"

"Nope. She's full grown. Probably 4 years old. I sure hope her hair grows out by winter."

"Oh, it will. I used to have a poodle named Trixie and believe me, her hair grew fast. She had to be groomed every six weeks.

They're smart too – although I'd barely call this one a dog, she's so puny." She put her down on the ground.

I sucked in my breath. "Wait! She doesn't have her leash." I scrambled to get it from my purse.

"Have you tried letting her off lead to see if she runs away?"

"No. Should I? I mean…" I felt uneasy allowing her to walk untethered, since there was a major roadway nearby, not to mention a train track and coyotes in the area.

She waved her hand down. "Heck yeah. There's no traffic here yet. Besides, we've gotta be faster than those tiny legs. Let's just see what she does."

We watched as the dog explored the ground, tinkled, and hopped up the steps to my shop. She turned and waited for me.

"Looks like you may not need a leash. Around here anyway." Her bright green earrings bobbed as she said this. I noticed however that her hair didn't budge.

"Hmm. Maybe?" I was still apprehensive about letting Zia off-leash completely.

Louise helped carry my stuff inside, looked around the shop then abruptly said, "Well, I've gotta get going. Let me know if you need anything." She barged through the door in a comical way. I knew she was eccentric, but that behavior was strange even for Louise.

I looked around for Zia to make sure she didn't follow the woman outside. When I didn't see her, I stepped outside, and there stood Louise, with my pup stuffed in her shirt, possibly in her ample bra. The silly woman looked at me with a sheepish expression, just waiting to be caught.

"Ha Ha. Very funny, Louise. Give me my dog back," I kidded.

She lifted Zia out from her shirt and handed her to me. "Be careful. Someone could steal that little one as easily as shoplifting a necklace."

I laughed as she left, but thought about her last words and said, "Zia, you'd better bark if someone ever tries to steal you for real."

I wondered if Louise had heard about the death of Mr. Harrison since she didn't bring it up. When Zia was back on the floor, she climbed right into her yellow bed. She looked cozy sprawled out across her namesake, the big Zia sun. Her eyes were glued on me as I attached a chain-link gate to the wall. I was surprised that she didn't flinch at the noise of the drill.

I talked to her while hanging necklaces, earrings, and bracelets on the links. "I'm glad I have a good stock of products, so I don't have to work overly hard my first week. Maybe the murder will be solved soon so we can have a nice opening day. Right, Zia?"

Before the dog could answer my rhetorical questions, my phone rang. When I picked up, a man's voice barked, "Olson. Come in this afternoon for more questions."

Olson? Not Miss Olson or Maria. Seriously this detective sure had nerve. I remained silent, then figured I could fight fire with fire and said, "Barnes, I would love nothing more than to see your friendly face again." I smirked at my own grit.

Unfortunately, he didn't seem to notice my bravado and added, "Bring both of your boyfriends this time." Click. He was gone.

First of all: Grrrr. Second of all: they weren't my boyfriends.

The only good thing about going in for another visit with the detective was hopefully I could get more information. I'd like to know if I was safe. Maybe Barnes would even tell us who did it.

Zia stayed at the shop while I walked to the brewery. Joey stood out front, sanding a large round piece of wood, his tight t-shirt accentuating his biceps. Oh wow. How did I miss those before? I was going to sneak up and surprise him when Victoria, dressed more for a party than for work, intercepted from the left carrying two cups of coffee.

"I see you didn't need the assistance of your mouse today."

Her voice was so smarmy I wanted to slap her, but I looked her directly in the eyes. "She's back at my place, holding down the fort as my guard dog. She's a very capable poodle."

"Mmm." She pursed her lips and looked at me as if I had a bad case of B.O. I almost lifted my arm to take a whiff, but I knew she was just trying to intimidate me. After all, I had just taken a shower.

Joey turned and gave me a youthful smile, "Well, look who came to visit – Maria!"

All the intimidation Victoria had thrown at me dissipated with Joey's infectious tone. Victoria rolled her eyes and walked up the steps to the brewery. I watched in amazement as she somehow opened the door without spilling any liquid from the cups. I could never be that graceful.

I smiled at Joey and walked closer. "Whatcha doing?"

"We needed another table, so I'm finishing this one." He ran his sandpaper in a long stroke down the length of the wood.

I took a closer look at what he was working on. It was an inlaid masterpiece, similar to the one I had studied at dinner. "Wait a minute. *You* made the tables inside?"

This was unbelievable. I ran my hand along with the various colors of wood, looked up at him, and then back down.

"Sure did. Don't look too closely at the one in the corner of the pub. I had a problem with the finish. I'm hoping nobody will notice it there, since it's so dark in that corner."

I was flabbergasted by his talent. "They are amazing, Joey! I admired those tables and meant to ask where you bought them." So, these guys were both artists. One the woodworker and the other a graphic designer. "I just can't believe you made them."

He shrugged. "Thanks. I love working with wood. And sanding is a great stress reliever. So, how are you? Haven't run into any more stacks of books outside, have you?"

I shook my head. "No. But, we've been ordered by our favorite detective to come in for more questioning – today. And we have to bring Jett."

I felt bad I got them involved in the whole thing, but then again, I was glad I wasn't in it alone.

He threw his head back in exasperation. "What else does he need to ask? I told him all I remember."

I shrugged. "All I do know is that my name was mentioned on the news last night. I wasn't too thrilled about that."

"Well, that's not right." He looked confused as he lay down his sandpaper and leaned against the sawhorse crossing his arms.

Despite the distraction of his bulging muscles, I said, "Oh, and I don't know if you heard, but the media has dubbed Mr. Harrison's death, 'The Out of the Box Murder.'"

He groaned and held his hand to his forehead, apparently sharing my misgivings. "No way."

"Way."

He let out a breath. "That's disrespectful for his family and it sure won't help our businesses either."

I nodded. "That's what I thought. So, I just stopped by to give you the fun news about seeing Barnes again. Guess I'll meet you guys down at the station. How about 1:00?" I smiled a fake smile.

"I'll tell my brother. I'm sure he'll be thrilled." He rolled his eyes. "But we'll see you there."

I found it hard to turn away from this handsome guy and his cool tables, but couldn't find a reason to stand there gawking either. So, I made my way back to the shop where I spent a few hours repurposing bicycle parts. I didn't have the equipment or materials to start on the colored glass-in-the-spokes project but managed to make some adorable coasters and bookends from sprockets.

Afterward, I tackled a bigger project that took hours. I sat on my front step and used pliers, a hacksaw, wire, and a lot of elbow grease, but finally, put together a small table with three bicycle rims and a piece of glass. It would be a nice big-ticket item.

After scrubbing the grease and dirt from my hands, I ate the chicken salad I'd made that morning and drank some water while looking over my shop. It was filling up quickly. For a second, I was giddy with anticipation of opening day and then I remembered a murder needed to be solved.

Zia pranced back and forth by the door. I smiled at how cute she was until I realized she was telling me something.

"Oooh, I'm sorry. Do you need to go potty?"

She gave a little bark, the first one I had heard out of her. It finally dawned on me that it was her answer and I jumped up. I smiled as I opened the door, pleased that she would tell me when she needed to go out. She hopped down the steps and found a place to do her business by the side of my building.

I said, "Good girl, Zia. Will you be okay staying here all alone while I go to the police station?" I could swear she pouted at me.

She stood right where she'd picked up the charm and I remembered it was still in my phone case. Since it had been so near where the body was first seen, I considered telling Barnes about it, but wasn't sure if that was a good idea.

As we walked back inside, I said, "I wish I could take you with me to the station, but I really shouldn't."

CHAPTER 9

When I met the brewery boys in the police station lobby, Joey gave me a warm smile. On the contrary, Jett stared at his watch as if he had a pressing engagement. The place was much busier than last time. A young woman sat by the window wiping her eyes while a couple nearby was involved in a heated argument. I tried not to focus on them as I sat down in an orange plastic seat.

I was getting as comfortable as I could in a molded seat, when Sergeant Barnes entered. He didn't say a word – just jerked his head toward the hallway.

We followed him down the corridor like lambs being led to slaughter. The only difference this time was Joey's imitation of the sergeant's gruff walk. I suppressed a giggle.

Back in the same bleak interrogation room, Sergeant Barnes sat in front of us again. This time he faced Jett. "So, you are the brother who couldn't hold down his dinner?"

Jett furrowed his brow, undoubtedly surprised by the crassness of the detective. He cleared his throat and replied, "I was a bit…under the weather."

Barnes folded his weathered hands on the table and growled at our trio, "Just what aren't you telling me?"

When his penetrating gaze turned to me, I started to squirm and looked down at my hands, noticing I'd left some grease under my fingernails. I finally looked up and shrugged blankly wondering which of my withholdings he meant.

I decided I should tell all, but before I could speak, there was a shift in my chest, causing all eyes to narrow at me. I bit my bottom lip and looked down at the odd lump. My face reddened as I explained, "Oh, um, I just got her yesterday and didn't want to leave her alone." A tiny head popped out of my vest as if she knew I was talking about her.

Joey brightened, leaned forward, and said softly, "Well, hello Zia!"

She wiggled a little in favor of the attention and squirmed as her tongue tried to reach him.

"You…are…kidding…me." Barnes closed his eyes in dismay.

I could feel my face heat up. "She'll be quiet. I promise." Since he was already mad at me, I came clean. "So…there is something else that none of you know."

I told them the whole story of the video recording that had continued after I left my shop. "It showed Mr. Harrison on film, leaving the money on the counter. Then when he left my shop, there was a definite confrontation outside, but I couldn't hear who else was talking."

Barnes' chair lowered to the floor. His eyebrows lifted as if he was finally interested in something I'd said. His voice was even a smidge upbeat, "Great. Hand it over." He held out his hand.

Oh crap. Guess I should have told the rest. "Uh…it's gone." I winced, then continued with my 2nd confession du jour. "My friend and I left the shop to go to the junkyard and when we got back, it wasn't on my computer anymore. I don't know how it disappeared." I shrugged. "If I erased the recording it sure wasn't on purpose."

Barnes stared at me in uncanny silence. I wasn't sure he was even breathing. I shifted uncomfortably in my chair wondering if or when he would speak. After a full minute of this, he finally took a deep breath and said with his eyes shut, "Un..be..lieveable. And you didn't think to show me the recording when you saw it?"

"Well, I did plan to..." I couldn't tell him about our ProCon list for fear of total embarrassment, "but, it had disappeared by the time I was ready to send it. You see, we found this dog and..."

I trailed off realizing my excuse was lame. I sighed, readying myself for him to throw something at me or send me to bed without dinner. But the officer just said quietly with clenched teeth, "So, did your friend also witness the video before it vanished into thin air?"

"Yes! My friend, Jill, did. Here is her name and number." I held out a Grass Man card. He didn't take the card, so I inched it toward him on the table and sat back, determined not to say anything else that might upset him.

With a grumpy shake of his head, Barnes went on to another topic. "And all three of you were together the entire evening of the murder until the sickly one left?"

My heart started pounding. Jett hadn't been with us until after I'd eaten. I waited for him to say something, but when neither guy spoke, I said, "Well, there were a few minutes when I didn't see Jett, but I think he was at Victoria's place?" I nodded to Jett so he could give his alibi. He just sat stone-faced. Great. Now I ratted out one of my new friends.

The officer turned his head slightly to Jett. "Victoria?" He cocked his head and pursed his lips. "Please elaborate, Mr. Roth."

Hearing their last name for the first time made me realize how little I knew of these brothers. Why, they could truly be a pair of madmen for all I knew, but I shook that thought off with an internal laugh.

I focused on Jett as he slowly nodded. He took a deep breath and said, "That's right. Victoria Yates owns the coffee shop across from us. I helped her at her store on Monday evening. When I came back to the brewery, Maria was finishing her dinner." He looked directly at the detective and said, "I promise I had no reason to harm that man. I never even met him."

I took in a breath. That was a lie. I remembered they had issues with the brewery permits and parking areas. I also vividly recalled Jett being so mad he said he could kill him. No. Wait a minute. That was probably his grumpy brother. Maybe Jett had never met Pops.

I realized I looked like I was scrutinizing Jett by squinting and cocking my head, so I yawned and cleared my throat to seem more casual.

Barnes nodded suspiciously at Jett, then turned to Joey. "How about you. Anything to add?"

I glanced nonchalantly as Joey spoke. "No sir. My brother and Ms. Olson told everything as I remember it."

I knew there was no way Joey was involved since he'd been with me all evening. That was a comforting thought. I rubbed Zia's head, waiting to hear Barnes' response.

The detective stood and picked up his notes. "Go on. You can leave." I assumed the rude dismissal was directed at all of us. I was flabbergasted. Weren't we allowed to ask anything?

In frustration, I leaned forward and placed my hands on the table abruptly, and spat out all my questions. "But the news report indicated it was truly a murder. Is that true? Did Carl have something to do with it? What should we do? Am I in danger?"

With no expression, he replied, "Yes. Doubt it. Nothing. Maybe." He turned and left the room.

The door slammed shut, leaving me speechless. Did he just answer all my questions in one fell swoop? I had asked so many I couldn't even remember the order, so his answers didn't help me at all. I sat open-mouthed and looked at the guys.

Joey said, "I get the feeling he doesn't want to talk to you about it."

We walked down the steps of the police station in silence. I let Zia down on the gravel and she pitter-patted around the rocks then squatted and peed. At least the three of us had something to watch as we stood uncomfortably on the sidewalk.

I finally broke the silence. "Jett, I'm sorry. I have a problem being too forthright. I had to mention that you were gone." I shook my head, "I know you didn't have anything to do with Mr. Harrison's death." I pleaded for forgiveness with my eyes.

"No big deal," Jett said this without looking at me, but his voice was terse. He turned and got inside his Mercedes.

I winced and picked up Zia, looking at Joey. "Guess I should learn to keep my mouth shut."

"He'll be alright. Some girls find his dark, brooding personality irresistible."

I didn't find his behavior alluring at all, but I smiled a little anyway. I hoped it was just Jett's nature to be aloof and that he wasn't too angry with me. "Well, I'd better get this little one back to the shop."

Joey smirked and said, "I wasn't going to say anything, but while we were in the waiting room today, I thought you looked a little lumpy." He nodded at my chest.

I laughed. "I didn't mean to smuggle her in, but she was so comfy in my vest I forgot to mention it. She's like my little Roo."

His face turned uncharacteristically solemn. "Hey, um, would you do something for me?"

"Sure?" I said, expecting him to ask if he could borrow my truck, or have me make a clock for his girlfriend.

"Um." He looked down at his shoes. There he was hem-hawing around again.

"Just spit it out, Joey. I'll probably say yes unless you need a kidney or want me to have your baby. Those I'd have to think about for at least a day." Did I really just say that?

It did get a chuckle out of him. "You mean, you wouldn't just automatically have my baby if I asked?"

I was mortified, but he laughed and then came to the point. "OK, I wondered if you would go with me to the junkyard to help find train paraphernalia for brewery decorations."

"Well, why didn't you just say so? Of course. I never mind a trip to Smitty's. When do you want to go?"

"I was thinking tomorrow? Say 11:00? I'll drive."

"Perfect. I'll see you then." I turned toward my car, still a bit embarrassed about the baby comment.

He unlocked his jeep with a beep and then said, "Later, smuggle girl."

I smiled as I unlocked my own door.

After making a run to the bank, I felt a jolt of excitement as I put bills and change in my antique cash register. Of course, filling it with customers' money would be way better. I lifted Zia onto the counter and she sniffed the machine.

If only my mom could have seen the beautiful cash register and my new mini-dog. I imagined her, hugging Zia in one arm while running her other hand along the ornate brass designs. She'd push her long black hair behind her ear and say something like, "Maria, everything is muy bueno. But, mi Hija, fill this cash drawer con rapidez. Perrito must be spoiled."

Although Mom had been a seventh-grade English teacher, she was famous for mixing her Spanish and English at home, to keep us sharp, or maybe confused.

Sighing, I put Zia back down on the floor. I should give my condolences to the surviving antique store owner. It was the right thing to do. Before I left, there was a polite knock at my door. I pulled it open to find Kelly, hulking there with a stoic expression. Behind him, Jill stood wearing a goofy smile and a red polka dot maternity dress that made her look huge.

I brightened. "Well, look at you two. Come on in."

Jill, a good foot and a half shorter than her husband, pushed past him and handed me a gift bag without saying anything. She stared at me with wide eyes and lips shut tight, trying not to talk.

"What's this?" I asked, in bewilderment. "My birthday is months away."

She was practically bouncing. "Open it."

I lay the bag on the counter and pulled out a box. I read aloud, "Motion-activated security camera?" The picture and description on the box indicated it was an especially high-tech version and probably expensive. "Wow! This is so cool. Thanks so much!"

Kelly said in a flat voice, "You can watch your shop from an app on your iPhone."

Jill piped up, "And it will alert you if there's any movement!" Her grin was contagious.

"It's amazing!" I held the box to my chest, feeling tears well up. "This is perfect, but I'm sure it was far too expensive. You shouldn't have."

Jill pulled her long hair up in a ponytail with one hand and fanned her neck with the other. She said, "We have some extra money now. This guy just got a new job!" She let go of her hair and patted her tall husband on the shoulder.

"Congratulations, Kelly!" I wiped my eyes as I looked up at the guy who I'd grown to love as a brother. There was no mistaking his Native American ethnicity with his wide face, high cheekbones, and thick black hair. He was striking, I'd always believed he could be an actor or model, but I doubted that was his new job, or that this modest man would ever be interested in calling attention to himself in that way.

Just as I opened my mouth to ask about his job news, the curtain to my storage room moved.

Jill said, "Oh, Kel, you haven't met Zia!" The dog toddled out to us. Jill picked her up and handed her to Kelly. Zia looked extra tiny in his extra-large hands. His face instantly softened. The sight gave me a preview of how he would look holding their baby when she arrived in a few weeks.

Watching the couple admire the dog, I was sure they would be loving parents, despite Jill's wild demeanor. At least little Sophia would have parental balance with calm Kelly as a dad.

There was a loud knock at the door. When I answered it, a balding man in blue coveralls holding a toolbox and a roll of screen, read from a paper, "Maria Olson?"

I narrowed my eyes. "Yes?"

"I'm here to fix your window screen."

I glared at Jill, wondering if she was responsible. I was surprised since I'd forgotten to schedule a repairman. I glared at Jill. They had already done way too much for me. But she shrugged. Maybe Larry had stepped up to the plate. I led the man to the window in the back. He started to work right away replacing the screen.

Jill let Zia down and said, "We should go, Maria. Kel only has today off before starting his new job, so we're going on one of our last dates before our lives change forever." She looked up at Kelly with adoring eyes and then gave me a hug. I thanked them again and the two left me alone with the repairman.

While the guy worked, I downloaded the app for the camera on my phone and read about the features of the new toy.

The man, whose embroidered name read Marvin, moved outside. I could hear the whir of a drill as I tried to decide where to put my small camera. Not long after, the door opened and Marvin said, "OK. All done."

He showed me the new screen. I thanked the guy and said, "How much do I owe you?"

He said, "Someone already took care of it."

I couldn't imagine Larry paying for the repairs and asked, "Who?"

The man shrugged. "Dunno. Boss just sent me out and said it was covered." He got in his truck and left.

Puzzled, I locked the door behind him and wondered if Jill and Kelly had arranged it, after all, but it is impossible for Jill to keep any kind of secret. Hmm.

I stood on a stool to put my new camera on a top shelf, hiding it inside the opening of a candle holder. In the disguise, it looked like a wide black vase. Nobody would ever know it was there.

I clicked on the app's icon and voila! I could clearly see most of the shop including myself standing by my counter looking at my phone. I sighed and was relieved that I had new security measures in place. I refused to rely on stupid Larry anymore.

Thinking of the landlord and the way he kept just walking into the shop unannounced, I decided to make a door chime. I needed to know when a customer arrived anyway, in case I was in the back section or just to know when people were leaving if I was distracted by other shoppers. I'd read about loss prevention tactics and knew this was an easy measure to take.

I searched door chime ideas on Pinterest, my favorite site for Do-It-Yourself ideas. I've posted quite a few pictures and How-tos of my own creations there.

I debated whether to make the chime from bottle caps or silverware. I had used a lot of silverware for my jewelry and realized

I didn't have enough, so chose bottle caps. I had a plethora of them – I do love that word.

In my tub of odds and ends, I grabbed the gallon baggie containing hundreds of bottle caps. While leaning over the tub, I spied a broken toy xylophone and had an epiphany. I quickly dropped the baggie of bottle caps and grabbed the toy along with some fishing line, a piece of wood, pliers, nails, and a hammer. I sat on my front porch, ready to work. My curious dog sat in the shade watching me.

I worked on the project for about 30 minutes, taking apart the little instrument, and making sure the bars that would hit each other sounded nice together. Even with limited musical instrument experience, I was aware that some tones would clash being next to one another. It was fun to play around with the different sounds.

Once finished, I screwed in an extended hook on the inside of the door, high enough that nobody would walk into it. I then hung the new chime up. It looked so cute with the colorful rectangles hanging just so. I opened and shut the door a few times to hear the musical tones. Adorably perfect! Nobody could sneak up on me now.

While the door was still open, I looked at the depressing-looking antique store. I'd forgotten to go there with all the interruptions. I picked up the dog and carried her across the hot gravel parking lot and up the steps.

I knocked and whispered to Zia, "This could be a mistake. Be ready to run." After a few beats, the door creaked open slowly. Wait a minute. The building was brand new. How did it already creak? White hair came into view, but instead of the grumpy man I had expected, there stood an old woman with a slightly hunched back.

She looked up at me with cloudy blue eyes and said in a tired but friendly voice, "Can I help you?"

Not knowing who the woman was, but figuring she was a relative, I spoke up, "Hello. I'm Maria, I own the turquoise Upcycled shop over there." I pointed behind me. "I just wanted to stop by and give my condolences on the loss of Mr. Harrison. He was very kind to me the one time we met."

The little woman nodded. "Well thank you, my dear. He was the sweetest man I knew." She cleared her throat and said, "I'm Milly. Pops and I were married for 64 years. I just don't know what I'll do without him." Her eyes filled with tears as she spoke. She brushed them away and gave a faint smile.

"Oh, I'm so sorry. It must be just terrible to lose your husband. I shouldn't have bothered you." I stammered, "It's way too soon to have visitors. I'll leave now, but please let me know if I can help in any way." I realized I'd talked way too much and turned to go.

"Wait, won't you come in? I'm here alone now and could use the company…Maria, was it?"

"Yes. If you're sure." I turned back and followed her into the dim store, still feeling bad for bothering the grieving widow.

She said, "I just stopped by to pick up a few favorite antiques before they are sold." She stopped beside an old Victrola and cautiously eased herself down onto a wooden armchair then motioned for me to sit on a piano stool. "Here, let's visit."

I sat down on the beautiful oak stool and couldn't help but swivel a little. I did refrain from twirling all the way around due to the somber nature of the visit. I shifted Zia in my arms. "I hope you don't mind, but I have a little dog with me." I was glad I remembered to announce her presence this time.

She looked more closely at my black bundle and said in surprise, "So you do. I hadn't noticed. Why that's a tiny thing."

"Indeed." I smiled. "So, Milly, are you planning to help run the shop now?"

She shook her head. "At my age, I don't have any interest in working in a store." She clasped her weathered hands and lay them in her lap. "I'll leave it to Flick to run. They were partners, you know - Pops and Flick. Those boys did everything as one." She looked as if she would cry again.

I asked, "Flick and Pops? Those are sure interesting names."

She brightened a bit. "They are, aren't they? I'll tell you the story if you like."

Nodding, I said, "Please. I love stories." I do and there was nothing pressing I needed to do. Plus, she must have needed to talk to someone and any information could help with my investigation.

She looked down at her knobby, arthritis-riddled hands as if the memories were written there. "Back in the late 40s going to the movies was all the rage. Why, you could see a show for only a quarter." She looked up and giggled in the cutest way, endearing her to me instantly.

Milly continued, animated. "The boys...they're twins you know... had the most coveted jobs in our small town - working at the local movie house. And they were only in high school! Jonathan worked at the concession stand and Joseph ran the projector."

Hearing of their jobs I could now understand their nicknames.

Smiling as she reminisced, she said, "That's where I met my dear Jonathan. I would go to every movie possible with my friend, Margaret, just to see him." Her eyes stared into space as if she were reliving the scene. "He smiled so sweetly each time he handed me my popcorn."

She looked back at me. "He was such a friendly boy. Well, it wasn't long before the other kids started calling him 'Pops'."

I smiled at the cute nickname for someone who sold popcorn.

She continued with a wave of her hand, "Then, Joseph, never to be outdone, came up with his own nickname, 'Flick', since he ran the projector."

She stood briefly and took a framed picture from the wall and handed it to me. The sepia-toned photo showed two identical-looking men with dark hair, standing in front of the Guild movie theater. As I studied the photo, I thought of how simple life must have been then.

"Why they were the most handsome boys around, and out of all the girls in town, Jonathan chose me!" Milly beamed.

I wasn't sure if it was because of the excited manner in which she spoke, the antiques surrounding me, or the photo, but I was transported into her memories. For a moment, I could see past her wrinkles and hunched shoulders to envision a tall young girl with bright eyes and dark hair.

A lump formed in my throat as I looked back at the old photo. Blinking away tears, I said, "That's so sweet. So, you got married?"

"Yes, and my girlfriend, Margaret, married Flick." She watched to see my response.

"Really? How cool that two best friends married twins. That sounds like the plot of a movie."

She smiled. "For almost 60 years, the four of us did everything together, that is until Margaret passed away a few years back." Milly's facial features drooped again.

I changed the subject and asked brightly, "Do you have any children?"

She shook her head. "No. Pops and I weren't blessed with children, but Flick and Margaret had six. The Harrison name is now being carried on with great-grandchildren."

I took in all the information. She sighed and said, "The funeral will be Friday morning at ten. I don't expect you to come, Dear, since you didn't know him well." She smoothed her hair into place. "Flick, I mean Joseph, will need some time, so the store probably won't open until Tuesday or Wednesday."

"Oh, of course. He must be terribly upset." I knew firsthand that losing a sister was traumatic, but losing an identical twin must be like losing a limb.

She nodded slowly. "Yes, he is distraught, especially over the manner of his brother's death." Milly looked up at me and cocked her head. "Oh my, you aren't the dear girl who found Pops, are you?"

I was sad to admit it but did. "Yes, Ma'am. The experience was terrible, but nothing like what you have been through." Why had I even compared my situation with hers?

"You poor thing. Well, I must wait for that nice Detective Barnes to investigate to see what happened." She shook her head. "I'm fairly sure it wasn't a heart attack. My Jonathan was in good physical health. His doctor said he had the heart of a 70-year-old."

I nodded at the news he was in good shape. Wait a minute! Did she call Barnes nice? Maybe he has a twin too!

CHAPTER 10

I shook off the ridiculous notion that Sergeant Barnes had a nice twin and asked Milly, "You don't know of anyone who might have wanted to harm your husband, do you?" I was thinking specifically of Carl.

She scoffed. "Heaven's no. Everyone loved Pops. Now Flick, on the other hand, has had his share of enemies in his life. He's a little harder to get along with. Have you met him?"

Not quite knowing how to answer truthfully, I said, "I tried, but he wasn't very…receptive." That put it mildly.

Thinking of the difference in the men's personalities, I wondered if someone had tried to kill Flick, but accidentally got Pops? That would seem more plausible than anyone hurting Pops.

The words, "I just want to kill him," popped back into my head. I considered Jett's odd behavior that night and after. Could Jett have targeted the grumpy brother and got Pops by mistake? I shook my head at the thought. Surely not Jett.

Milly broke the silence by continuing, "But, Flick is mostly bark and no bite."

I thought about another quote I'd heard this week. 'Now Flick won't have to kill me,' and asked, "Did the brothers get along?"

"Oh, you know…there was sibling rivalry. Flick was ornery and even a little jealous of his brother. You see, Pops had a knack for making friends and I might add, making money, so there was always some tension there. It especially got bad when deciding to open this antique store." She looked around the shop wistfully. "Flick didn't want to share the business, but he would need a loan, so Pops offered to take on the financial responsibility if he could be a partner and work at the shop."

I let that sink in. Flick didn't want to share the business. Would that be reason enough to kill his brother?

A man wearing a ball cap came in the back door of the antique store and yelled, "Hey, Aunt Milly, when is Carl coming to help?"

I stiffened. Carl? He was coming over? I didn't want to see him here. I couldn't get a good look at her other apparent nephew, since he was way back past the desk.

She answered, "He should be here in a bit. Be patient, Arnie. He's having a hard time, you know." The guy grunted and walked back through the door with the same gruff demeanor as his father.

I realized my knee had been bouncing since the mention of Carl. What if he blamed me again in front of this sweet lady?

I ventured nervously, "So, Carl is one of your nephews?"

"Yes. He's Flick's youngest son by many years. Pops worries…" She closed her eyes and corrected her mistake, "*worried* so much about Carl's temper. He tried to get him to see a counselor, but that didn't go over well at all."

My leg stopped moving at the possible motive and I said cautiously, "How did Carl react to that?"

When Milly didn't answer right away, I worried she might think I was prying, but she took a deep breath and said, "Well, he held his hands over his ears and started rocking. That's what Carl does when he doesn't want to hear something. The doctors say he has something called Asperger's."

Ahh, that would explain Carl's social awkwardness, but maybe not the temper. "Hmmm." I nodded, unsure of what else to say. I switched gears, hoping to wrap up the visit. "Is there anything I can do for either you or Mr. Harrison?"

"No, but thank you, Maria. If I think of anything, I know where to reach you."

I stood to leave. "It was so nice to meet you, Milly. Again, I'm sorry for your loss. I hope you'll come to visit my shop sometime."

She stood and walked me toward the door. When it opened, the sun shone brightly on Milly's dress, which was a beautiful, vivid pink that I hadn't noticed in the poorly lit shop. I opened my mouth to comment on the color when she faced the parking lot and said, "Oh, Hi! You're just in time."

I turned reluctantly, expecting to see Carl, but instead, saw Mr. Harrison ambling toward us.

"Flick, meet your neighbor, Maria."

Even from a distance, his scowl was well pronounced. Oh boy, this wasn't going to be fun.

As he slowly pulled himself up the steps with the use of the handrail, I studied the face of this possible murderer. The brothers' features were so similar it was uncanny, but the expressions couldn't be more different. Instead of the relaxed weathered smile of Pops, this face was craggy with furrowed brows and downturned lines throughout.

As he reached the landing, I held my hand out to him, saying, "Nice to meet you, Flick."

He pursed his lips and frowned. Maybe I should have called him Mr. Harrison. After an awkward moment, he gave a skeptical nod. I put my hand down, realizing he wasn't going to shake it. "I'm so sorry for your loss, Mr. Harrison. I'm sure you miss your brother terribly."

"Indeed." He stared at the floor.

It was a bit of a relief to hear him speak sincerely and I felt a pang of sympathy.

But then he continued with a gruff voice, "The old goat was supposed to work the store on Friday. Now we have to go to his damned funeral instead."

My mouth dropped open. Surely I hadn't heard him right. But I guess I had, since Milly slapped him on the shoulder playfully and said, "Joseph, be nice."

He growled, "It's hard to be nice when your brother's dead and your son was arrested for something he didn't do." He eyed me as if I was suspicious.

Too hastily, I said, "So, you don't think Carl had anything to do with Pops' death?"

His face suddenly turned crimson and I saw an eerie resemblance to the son in question. Flick shouted, "Hell no!"

Horrified that I had upset the man, I quickly said, "I'm sorry. I shouldn't have asked that." I felt awful to upset either of them. For heaven's sake, he was mourning.

The old man looked as though he might have a heart attack right in front of me. My own heart raced as I scrambled for something to say. Milly piped up, putting her hand on his shoulder, "Now go inside, Flick, and take your pills. The doctor said you shouldn't get upset. You're already under too much stress."

He turned with a huff and stormed inside letting the door slam behind him. Milly stood beside me on the low porch, shaking her head. Attempting to explain, she said, "Flick is much nicer when he takes his medicine."

My face must have shown my guilt for she put a gentle hand on my hand. "It's not your fault. A lot of people, including the police and even his own brothers, wondered if Carl was involved. I'd better go check on Flick. Have a good opening day, Maria." She leaned across and tapped Zia on the head, then gave an exhausted sigh and turned to go in.

Poor, poor lady. I felt so bad for her, but as much as I wanted to feel sorry for Flick, I wasn't so sure he or his son weren't involved in Pops' murder. Now, I had a new reason to investigate - to solve the murder for sweet Milly.

I faced my shop and bent to set Zia down, but the gravel was so hot I feared it would scorch her little black feet, so I carried her to the shady side of my container. Still baffled by the old man's outbursts, I said to her, "At least he didn't blame me as Carl had. What was that about?" Zia just looked at me without answering.

Arriving at my building, I saw that my new plants were looking thirsty in this heat. There was no outdoor spigot, so I opened the door, put Zia down in her little Zia bed, and went to my sink. I filled a plastic cup with water and made three trips from the backroom to the plants. The dog watched me walk back and forth from the comfort of her yellow pillow. I needed to get a bigger container, or I'd get the bulk of my 10,000 daily steps just watering plants.

On my third trip, I noticed my box of empty wine bottles in the storeroom. I remembered a Pinterest post with wine bottles as self-watering systems for flower pots. Why not use them for outdoor plants? It was worth a try, so I grabbed a couple of bottles from the box. After filling them, I pushed a cork into each, then tapped a long nail all the way through each cork. By removing the nail, I left a small hole to drain water. With a spade, I dug little holes in the gravel surrounding the plants and turning the bottles upside down, poked them in the ground.

Studying the practical bottles, I felt nothing. They needed major perking up. I pulled the bottles out of the ground, dusted them off, and emptied them. The labels had already been removed, leaving a blank glass canvas, and so I went to work painting flowers with acrylic paints. Once dried, they looked so cute and bright, sticking out of the ground like flowers themselves.

Were there now too many bottles at my front door? No way. You can't have too much colored glass.

With a new idea in mind, I looked up a phone number and dialed it. A female voice answered politely, "Rusty Railroad."

"Hi, could I speak to Joey, please?"

After a few moments of silence, I heard a cheerful, "Joey here," that made me smile.

I disguised my voice in a low growl and said, "Roth, I'll need you to come in for more questioning. Gotta squeeze out any information from you that I can. I'll make sure to be as aggravating as possible too, so hurry on down."

"You can't trick me, Maria. Barnes would never speak in so many words. What's up, girl? You're not breaking our date for tomorrow, are you?"

Did he say date? I was glad he couldn't see me because I felt my face flush. In my regular voice, I said, "No, we're still on for the junkyard, if you can call that a date. I wanted to ask you to save any wine bottles you happen to come across – especially blue ones. I have a new project and think they would look great in blue."

"Sure. We sell wine here too so I should be able to grab a lot. I'll keep a box just for you."

"Great. Thanks. So… see you tomorrow at 11?"

"Yep."

The rest of the evening was spent making more watering bottles to sell. After packing up to go I said, "Zia, want to go home?"

She jumped out of her bed and ran to the door wagging her tiny tail. What the heck was up with this dog? How did she understand English so well? Of course, maybe she just wanted to go outside.

I packed up my truck and leaned down to pick up Zia, but she wasn't underfoot. I looked for her, but couldn't see her around the truck. I looked further and saw her running across the gravel parking lot, making a beeline for the antique store. I called her, but she kept going. What in the world? I chased after the dog, wondering what she was doing. She stopped, turned to look at me, then kept going as if she was daring me to follow.

I didn't want to cause a disturbance at the Antique store by yelling, so I used a loud whisper. "Zia! Come."

She went toward the back door and sat down. I followed and ducked down under the window. I picked Zia up to reprimand her, but just then a low gravelly voice came from the only window located at the back of the store.

"Of course, I looked at them! Yes. Just as you suspected, First Editions, but they're gone now!"

There was a little pause, but I couldn't hear the other voice. I started biting my lip when I realized he must be talking about the books I had bought.

"Well, he was supposed to retrieve them but as you know he can't now, since he's dead!"

I shook my head at his blunt statement and in the silence that followed, I strained to hear another person but couldn't. When Flick's voice started up again loud and clear with an answer, it became evident I was listening to one side of a phone conversation. "Yeah. A pretty penny. At least $10,000 for all four, but don't blame me about them being gone! I don't even know who he sold them to."

My eyes widened. They were worth how much? I looked at Zia to see if she was as surprised as I was, but her eyes looked just as beady as usual.

After another moment of silence, his voice came back even louder, "More books? Hell no! Find someone else!"

There was the unmistakable sound of a landline phone being slammed down, not that I'd heard one in years. Whoever spoke to Flick sure didn't get what they wanted. He just got riled up.

I held Zia, gently clamping her back legs under my left arm, glad to leave Flick alone to stomp around his store. A cool breeze passed by and a shiver of dread ran through me as I considered the books' worth and possible connection with Pops' death.

With adrenaline pumping, I ran across the parking lot and jumped in my truck. I looked around, relieved to see an empty parking lot. After releasing Zia onto the passenger seat, I drove away as if I'd just committed a crime. Apparently, detective work can make a person paranoid.

Once inside my house, I locked the door behind me and relaxed a bit. I tried to process what I'd heard. There was no way to know who Flick was talking to, but it sure sounded like the books I had bought were first editions.

I turned on my laptop to look up the two titles I remembered of the books in question. I discovered the first edition value for those two, even if they were in so-so condition, was up to $8,000. And I only spent $12 for all four of them!

Just the thought that Pops could have been killed because of the books unnerved me. In addition, I felt sick thinking how close I came to slicing into a first edition copy of Huckleberry Finn.

As I rolled my shoulders, trying to loosen my uneasy feelings, I considered the grumpy Flick. What motive would he have to harm his brother? If he truly didn't know I was the one who bought the books, then he wasn't the one to see Pops carry them out of my shop that night. But…maybe he *did* know and lied to the person on the phone.

I jolted when I pictured Carl with his head bent to look at the books in my hand when I saw him that morning. Is that what he meant by, "it's all your fault?"

I typed what I knew so far into my phone, knowing I do best by keeping notes.

1. Pops sold four books to me for $3 each and then got in trouble with his brother for selling them.

2. Carl saw me with the books just after I bought them.

3. Pops broke into my shop, bought the books back, and had a confrontation with somebody outside of my shop, resulting in his death.

4. Somebody wanted the books. Who? And why?

5. Flick was jealous of Pops and didn't want to share the shop with him.

6. Somebody, probably Victoria, lost a charm near my shop.

7. Jett, who had a beef with Flick, was not at the bar the entire evening and seemed to be drunk.

8. Carl has a temper and was upset that Pops wanted him to see a counselor.

9. Someone could have killed Pops by mistake, meaning to target Flick.

10. The killer could have been someone completely unrelated to Out of the Box.

It was a grim list. Was I crazy to get involved in a murder investigation? Smiling to myself, I added an eleventh item: My dog might have investigative skills.

To clear my mind, I made a traditional Norwegian dinner complete with boiled potatoes, and a can of fish balls. I sat on the couch to eat.

Zia surprised me by jumping up on the couch with no problem. That was some distance to jump with her 4-inch legs. It would be like me jumping on top of my bookcase, or even onto the roof.

Her eyes followed my fork as I dipped bites of the mild cod and potatoes in the creamy horseradish sauce and chewed the savory bites.

"Sorry, little one. This is not dog food."

When I finished eating, I called my grandmother in South Dakota.

Her lilty voice answered, "Helloooo?"

"Hi, Far Mor. It's Maria."

"Oh my, sweet, sweet dear. I've missed you so. It's so good to hear your voice."

"I'm calling to tell you that I just made Fiskeboller from your recipe. This time the horseradish sauce was perfect. It was delicious and I thought of you."

"I'm so glad somebody is still cooking Norwegian food. I doubt your cousin Erik will ever even try, not that I would expect a big city lawyer to worry about that."

Being the only granddaughter, I felt a special bond with my Far Mor and wanted to make her happy; not out of guilt, but because I loved her deeply.

I said, "I wish I could tackle lefse, but think I'll wait until you come to see me for help with that. Oh, and I'm mailing a package to you, so be on the lookout for it in a few days."

"Aren't you just the sweetest thing? Are you about ready to open your new shop? I sure wish I could see it." Her thick northern accent was so cute.

"Yes, it's Saturday morning. I'll send you a picture as a text message, so be looking for it on your new smartphone."

"If I can't figure it out, I'll have my little neighbor, Braden, help me. Your Far Far won't be any help. Is everything OK? You sound a little sad. Are you worried about your new business?"

I could never hide my feelings from this grandmother and so spilled everything about the murder. "I wish you were here to help me investigate. With your sixth sense, you would have it figured out in no time."

Years ago Far Mor solved a mystery in her small town. She was so good at it the police still call her for advice on other cases when stumped. She has even been featured in the paper for her expert sleuthing.

In her usual bright and happy voice she said, "Maria, just remember to look for the small details that nobody else thinks matter. But, most importantly be careful."

"I will. Oh, speaking of small things, I got a new dog!"

She was delighted to hear about Zia. I also told her Jill was close to delivering, then asked her opinion on a special baby gift I was considering for her. I felt better after talking to Far Mor.

My grandmother in Mexico is equally sweet and loving, but on the opposite end of the spectrum, being distracted by so many family members nearby. I must have thirty cousins, most of which I've never met. And the majority of the large family live within minutes of my grandmother's house, if not inside it. Abuela always seems to be busy babysitting, hosting birthday parties or cooking large quantities of enchiladas and tamales. Whenever I do get the chance to talk to her, the call is usually interrupted by some drama. Someday, I plan to bring her here so we can spend quality time together.

I snapped a picture of Zia sitting on the couch and texted it to Far Mor. The nearly black dog was surprisingly photogenic as long as I used good lighting. If I took more photos of her, I could make my first dog scrapbook. I looked from my phone to Zia and said, "So, why were you sneaking over to the antique store anyway? Did you hear someone talking and wanted to check it out?"

She jumped off the couch and toddled to her food bowl, apparently giving up on the hopes that I'd give her any fish balls.

Hours later, after doing laundry and showering, I sank into bed with a still full belly and a tiny dog snuggled next to me. I finished reading a mystery about a cat in the Capitol building. It was cute, though I doubted any cat could solve a mystery. But then again, Zia was pretty smart. Maybe she would help me solve my mystery.

CHAPTER 11

I woke to a tiny tongue licking my face with great fervor. I opened my eyes and found beady black eyes staring at me. I let Zia out in my courtyard, happy to think there was a safe place for her to do her thing without me hovering over her.

After dressing in my favorite Hamilton t-shirt, I drove to the shop, with my dog sitting in the passenger seat. As I pulled up, I was surprised to find Jill sitting in her car beside my door. Her window was rolled down and she watched me approach. I got out and said, "What are you doing here? And why so early in the morning?"

She frowned. "It wasn't my choice. Your favorite policeman ordered me to meet him here at 9:00."

"What? Why?"

Jill raised her eyebrows. "Seems like someone told him I was witness to a video and now he needs my statement." She pursed her lips.

I nodded, feeling a bit guilty for giving Barnes her name. "Oh yeah, but why didn't he have you go to the station?"

She shrugged.

I shook my head. "Well, now you'll get to see how weird he is. Come on in."

We entered the shop and I pointed out my new camera.

As soon as she looked up, her demeanor changed to a grin. "Good camouflage, Maria." She made a silly pose and flung her hair around provocatively at the hidden camera.

I instantly heard a ping on my phone, indicating movement in my shop. That was cool, but I needed to figure out how to stop it from alerting me when I'm the one moving or it would ping all day. I showed her the app. and after she showed me how to switch it to stay mode, she posed with even more outrageous moves and laughed at her images on my phone.

I set my laptop on the counter, ready to show Jill my tutorial video. I wanted to see if Zia had truly photobombed the shot. The door opened, making the new chimes tinkle. We turned, expecting to see Sergeant Barnes, but it was Larry. Oh, brother! If I was super lucky, I'd get to see both of my favorite guys at the same time.

"Hi, Larry," I said in a monotone.

"Hey, hey sweet things. So, I hear you had some work done around here – got your screen fixed?" He slithered towards us and gave a wink to Jill.

Ick. I felt sick just being near him. And there came a waft of his strong odor. I said, "Yep. It's important to feel safe." This was said with a hint of sarcasm since he still hadn't fixed my lights, but Larry didn't catch it. I figured if he was the one who had paid for the screen he'd start bragging about it soon.

"Can't be too careful." He leaned his elbows on the counter and started pushing keys on my cash register just like a little kid might. Jill and I shared raised eyebrows wondering what he would do next.

This guy was annoying as heck, but I realized he may know something I could use. It was time to pick his brain. "So, how well do you know Carl? I heard you suggested he work at the brewery."

"Carl?" He shrugged as he walked around the store fingering one item after another. "His dad said he needed a job and was too clumsy to work at the antique store. I knew the J boys needed some help cleaning, and told them to check him out. He's an odd duck, but I figured even *he* could handle a mop."

I nodded, trying to think of something else to ask him. I said, "Hey, Larry, did you hear the news report last night? They mentioned Out of the Box."

He nodded, acting almost happy. "Yeah. It's in the paper too. I had to talk to several reporters to get the story straight."

So, he *was* connected with the report. I ventured further, "So, now that we know it was a murder, any ideas who might have been involved?"

He shrugged. "I dunno? The gates were open that night. Could have been anyone." He said this without any emotion, then looked up and lifted his hand to my globe lamp, twisting it until the world spun around. I started to object for fear it would come off the hook, but he let go and pulled his hand down, and said, "Welp, you probably want to know why I stopped by, huh?" He pulled something out of his pocket and sucked in air between his front teeth. "I told you I was kind of a big deal? Here are your tickets to the fundraiser tonight." He gave a sideways smile.

Jill and I looked at each other in surprise. Were those really tickets for the posh event?

"See, I can make the world turn just for you ladies." He glanced up at the twirling globe and smiled at his cleverness.

I rolled my eyes at his lame attempt at humor. Could this guy be trusted? I leaned forward and took the tickets as if snatching them from the mouth of a lion, then stepped back to stand by Jill. We looked at the invitations, which were embossed on linen cards. Fancy.

I managed to control my excitement as I handed one to her. I said more casually than I felt, "Thank you, Larry. I think we can still go, right, Jill?"

I watched her silently salivate. She nodded with wide eyes.

Puffed up with his inflated ego, Larry said, "I gave tickets to that sweet barista, so she'll be there," Under his breath he added with a disapproving scowl, "probably with that brewery brother."

He reverted to his old smarmy self and pointed to his chin, "But you won't see this fine face there 'cause I have to oversee another property tonight." His squeaky voice sounded so funny bragging.

I nodded, trying to hide my relief that we wouldn't run into Larry at the gala, or worse yet, have to sit with him. That was an awful thought. But, I may still have to deal with the snobby Victoria.

He sighed, "But, for now, I have to stop by Baking Bad to check on their A/C unit." He leaned in conspiratorially, "But, it could be a ruse so those boys can check *me* out?" He howled at his own remark.

Eew. Larry was even worse than I imagined if that was even possible. He turned to the door and handed Jill something as he scuffed by. His strong odor lingered in the air again after he left.

"What did he give you, besides the creeps?" I asked.

She looked down at her hands. "His card. He gave me his card with his phone number underlined." She looked up and said, "Seriously?" She tossed the card in the trash and jumped up and down. "A real live Gala! I can't believe it." She twirled around, then looked down at her enlarged body and frowned. "What in the world can I wear?"

I looked at my pregnant friend and said with a shrug, "I don't know?" Then added, "Shoot, I don't even know what *I* should wear. It's been ages since I've worn anything fancier than a sundress and sandals. Don't worry, we'll come up with something." I started to read the invitation when there was a loud knock.

I opened the door. Sir Grumpiness stared at me with his craggy eyes, uncombed hair, and signature wrinkled suit. Behind him, another officer leaned into the backseat of the police car. I said with no more excitement than my greeting to Larry, "Come in Detective Barnes."

He entered, looked at Jill, and said with a scowl, "This the witness to the video?"

"Yes. This is Jill. Jill, this is the always effervescent Sergeant Barnes."

Jill looked a little nervous and held out her hand. Instead of taking it, he said, "Sit." She made a funny face at that and sat in her usual spot on the car seat bench. We followed his gaze to the door, where a tall dark officer entered, carrying a bag. When the man looked up, we saw that the policeman was Jill's husband, Kelly!

Startled, I wanted to ask my friend what he was doing there. But, just as I opened my mouth, the detective growled. "Standing Wolf, if you can't find that video on the laptop, just tag it and we'll take it back with us."

Why did Barnes call him Standing Wolf when his last name was Standing Bear, or for that matter how did he know Kelly at all?

Jill's eyes were huge when she saw her husband. Her mouth opened, but Kelly looked at us with a 'don't say anything' look. I followed his lead and casually looked away, that is until I went into panic mode as the rest of Barnes' statement sunk in. I turned to the detective, "Wait. Why would you take my computer?"

He closed his eyes as if I was too stupid for words. "The video is evidence."

"But, you can't take it from me this week!" My mind whirred, "Saturday is opening day. I have to have it to run my business."

"Better hope this guy finds it, then." He nodded at Kelly.

I wanted to slap the smug look off Barnes' face as he towered over Jill in a menacing stance. He said, "So, you saw this supposed video of Mr. Harrison taking the books and leaving the money?"

Supposed? If he didn't believe there was a video, why was he taking my computer? I could only hope Kelly would find the missing file today. Oh boy, if Kelly's new job is being the IT man for Barnes, I sure felt sorry for him.

Jill's attention wasn't on the detective because her head was cocked and staring at her husband in disbelief. Kelly acted as if he had never even seen the two of us before.

Barnes cleared his throat waiting for her response.

Since Kelly's back was to Jill as he sat on my tractor seat clicking around on the laptop, she finally turned to Barnes and said, "Yes, I saw it."

"Tell me about it," Barnes ordered, notebook open, ready to record her statement.

She told the same story I had but with fewer details - not surprising since I had seen it more times and she was clearly distracted.

The gravelly voice asked with annoyance, "And what about the voices you heard from outside?"

She focused her attention fully and scrunched up her face as though she was still listening to the voices on the recording. "Well, it sounded like arguing. Two voices. Maybe one a little higher than the other. We wanted to try to enhance the sound before contacting you." She sat up straighter and threw her shoulders back.

"But you didn't contact me." He said with a drone.

Oh no. I recognize this posture. Jill is feeling comfortable enough to ramble or is trying to get her husband's attention. Either way, she would drive Barnes crazy.

Jill became more dramatic as she spoke, "At first, Maria wasn't sure if she should tell you about the video, but we did our pro and con list to decide whether to tell you or not and the pros won, so she truly was going to call because we always follow through with the winner, but as you know, the video was gone when we came back from the junkyard, so by then it was a moot point and now I guess you'll just have to take our word for it."

He stared at her with eyebrows touching. Instead of reacting to the content of her statement, his response was, "Remarkable. Do you ever breathe?"

Sometimes even I am amazed at the length of Jill's run-on sentences. I glanced at Kelly, who couldn't contain a smirk, but Jill just shrugged, her face turning pinker than usual.

The detective said, "You might want to read Olson's shirt." He nodded at me.

I looked down at my <u>Hamilton the Musical</u> t-shirt and read the upside-down quote, 'Talk Less. Smile More.' I wanted to tell Barnes, 'No. *You* should read it.' After all, I'd never seen him smile.

Arms crossed, Barnes said, "Explain this pro and con list?"

Jill looked at me. Unfortunately, my frown didn't dissuade her from telling all to the man.

She shrugged. "It's in Maria's pink notebook?"

I jumped in with, "It's just a little game we've played for years." My head was now sweating. I didn't want to get in trouble for hiding evidence.

When Barnes stuck his open hand out at me, I had little choice but to fetch the notebook. I leaned behind the counter and retrieved my pink spiral notebook we had used for decision-making forever. I opened it to the correct page and handed it to him.

Much to my chagrin, he flipped back to the beginning of the notebook and read-aloud, "Should I let Jimmy Sanders hold my hand at the movie?" He turned a few pages and read, "Should we buy thong underwear?" He rolled his eyes at that.

My face burned with embarrassment and I willed him to jump to the last page, but he went forward only a few pages. "Should we room together at UNM?"

I interrupted before he could read any more, "See it's just all silly stuff."

Finally, he shook his head and flipped to the last written page. Again, he read aloud, "Should we tell the police about the video? Pro #1: Telling the police is the right thing to do. Pro #2: We don't have time to investigate. Pro #3: It could be dangerous. Pro #4: We have no experience investigating murders."

I took hold of the book, trying to take it from him before he could read the cons, but his hold was like a vice grip. He glared at me until I let go and faced the floor. I sure didn't want to make eye contact with the detective.

Barnes nodded slowly then continued. "Con #1: We can do it ourselves. Con #2: Barnes is a big jerk who doesn't listen to me anyway."

I scooted to look over Kelly's shoulder and said a little too loud and quickly, "Sooo, how's it going, Officer Standing Wolf? Have you come across the video? I sure hope you can find it before you leave." I nudged him.

Kelly concentrated hard on his work He was too engrossed in searching the laptop's documents to answer.

Barnes said, "Leave it, Olson."

His remark sounded like a command you would make to a dog. I was going to say something in protest, but Barnes was already asking Jill more questions. The thought of a dog reminded me that I should let Zia out. I gladly left the infuriating man to find my sweet pup sound asleep in the back room. I don't know how she slept through all the people stopping by. Maybe she just didn't care. "Hey little one, wanna go outside?"

I leaned over and picked up the warm bundle, who stretched her tiny black paws out and yawned. She was so cute I could hardly believe she was mine. I carried her through the shop, ignoring Barnes, and stood on the front porch while she did her thing. Looking across the way, I thought of the phone conversation I'd overheard the night before but refused to share the information with Barnes as long as he wasn't sharing anything with me.

I followed Zia back into the shop and noticed Jill leaning over her husband, whispering in his ear. The poor guy's face had turned maroon, which is difficult to do with such a tan complexion.

The detective stood, writing in his own notebook, and didn't seem to notice the extreme flirting going on across the room.

I walked up to him and asked only one question to avoid confusion like last time. "Sergeant Barnes, is Carl Harrison still your main suspect?"

He didn't answer but looked down at Zia. His expression was one of disgust. "Your rat…is wearing…a sweater."

I looked at the skinny, practically hairless dog in her darling pink sweater and got defensive. It was the second time someone had called my sweetie a rat. I refused to dignify his statement with a response. I repeated, "Is Carl Harrison still your main suspect, and am I safe now?"

"Nope," he said, still staring at the dog. I had done it again; asked two questions at once. Did he mean, No, Carl Harrison isn't the main suspect or No, I'm not safe? Or both? He stood and said, "We're done here. Tag the computer and bring it along."

Kelly gave a slight wince, probably expecting me to explode, but, of course, I couldn't be mad at my buddy. He shut down my laptop, unplugged it, and followed Barnes to the door.

Barnes' parting remark was, "Good thing you got your window screen fixed…and nobody will ever notice that camera." His eyes flicked up to my hidden security camera before he scoffed and walked out the door. Kelly gave me an apologetic glance as he closed the door behind him.

"Argh! See what I mean? Detective Barnes is the most annoying man in the world!" I took Kelly's place on the stool.

Jill shook her head. "I thought you were exaggerating, but he truly is a jerk. However...I sure do like his new IT guy."

"Did you know Kelly was working for *him*?"

"No. He just told me the guy he was helping this week was a real hardass. The officer who had the job before him warned him not to make any waves. Must be why he didn't tell Barnes that he would be interviewing his wife."

That did explain Kelly's odd behavior. "Poor guy. Barnes could have at least learned his last name. I'm surprised you didn't get him in trouble with your flirting."

"Kel's pretty good at ignoring me. Besides, that detective was distracted by Zia. I'm sure he didn't notice."

"I don't know. He sure spotted my hidden camera." We both looked up at what we thought was well-hidden. I put my hands to my head. "How will I get by without my computer?" I leaned my head back in mock agony and in real frustration. Lowering my head, I looked at my phone and saw it was already 10:00. "Hey, did I tell you I'm going to Smitty's with Joey at 11?"

She raised her eyebrows and said. "Ooh, la la! Nothing says romance like a date at the junkyard."

I laughed, "It's not a date. I'm just going to help him pick out some train stuff."

"Well, you better be back in time for OUR date tonight. What time does it start?"

I grabbed the elegant ticket from my purse and read, "7 p.m. Oh my, it's black-tie! We do have to dress up."

"Well, I hope I can find a dress to fit over this monster baby bump. How about we meet at Savers when I get off work? That way I can get a dress without dipping into Sophia's college fund?"

"Good idea. We might as well buy gowns at the thrift store since these tickets could be some Larry printed just to impress us. I'll meet you there at 5:15."

"Guess I'd better get back to The Grass Man. Thanks so much for forcing me to meet Sir pain-in-the-booty Barnes." She gave an eye roll.

"You bet! I'll call you next time he comes around and you can join me."

"Only if his tall, dark, handsome sidekick is with him." She turned towards the door.

How sweet that she was so crazy about Kelly, even after three years of marriage. I hoped to be so lucky someday.

She turned and said as an afterthought, "But, please don't call me when Loser Larry shows up. What's up with him? He must really like girls with watermelon-shaped bellies."

I grimaced at the thought of him being into pregnant ladies. I said, "He's gross, but I think he's harmless."

As she walked out the door she said, "You know… Larry has a key to your shop. He could have walked in and erased your video while we were gone."

CHAPTER 12

The thought of Larry using his key to come into my shop whenever he wanted, gave me the creeps, but I highly doubted he would care about the recording. At least I had my trusty camera now – as long as I remembered to turn it on every time I left.

I had a lot to do before going to the junkyard with Joey in 45 minutes. I smiled just thinking of being alone with him, then told myself to focus.

Since I didn't know how long I would be without a laptop, I needed to set up a manual sales recording system. Using a ruler, I drew columns in my black, shop notebook to keep track of sales.

My phone rang, scaring me so much that I drew a squiggly line down the page. "Hello?"

"Is this little Maria?"

The only person who called me that was Far Mor, but this was definitely not her voice. The thick drawl gave her identity away. "Louise?"

"Honey, I just want to tell you that Saturday morning, all the shop owners are meeting in the parking lot at 8:15 for a little pep rally to get us going. Make sure you are there, Darlin'."

"I'll be there, Louise. Thanks for calling." What a funny lady.

I planned to take Zia with me to the junkyard since I had promised Smitty he could see her all cleaned up. She'd be fine in my sling while we tromped through the clutter. When I arrived at the brewery, one of the waitresses walked out the door. I said, "Hey, would you mind telling Joey that Maria is on the front porch?"

She said, "Sure," turned around, and went back inside. The girl came right out and said cheerfully, "He'll be right here," then bounced down the steps, unchained a bicycle from a rack, and took off. That reminded me that my bike still hung in my storage room. I should start riding again soon.

Joey appeared at the door and said, "Come on in."

I shook my head, "Oh, no. I've got Zia. We'll just wait for you out here."

"Well, I'm ready now." He stepped outside into the heat and took his keys from his pocket. "Let's go, girls!" He tapped Zia gently on the nose.

We rode in his jeep to the junkyard, talking about opening day the whole time. Being with him was so comfortable, it was as if we'd known each other for ages. I said, "So, what kind of railroad stuff are you looking for? There's no guarantee Smitty will have any at all."

"Anything, really. I just need to decorate our upper level. We probably won't need the extra space for a while, unless it starts getting crowded, but I want to be ready." He crossed his fingers. "There are so many microbreweries in the Albuquerque area. Too much competition."

I had thought about that when I first heard about the new Rusty Railroad. Little brewpubs were popping up all over town. But now that I'd seen theirs, I thought it would be a big hit. "Your layout, menu, theme, and beer are all winners. If you can just get people in the door, it won't be long before you'll open the upstairs."

"Unless the murder killed our business." This usually upbeat guy looked uncharacteristically worried.

So I wasn't the only one nervous about Saturday and sighed in agreement. "Oh, Sgt. Barnes came by today. I can't seem to get one day without seeing him."

"Oh, joy. Was he any more helpful than before?"

"No. As a matter of fact, he took my computer to try to find that missing recording. And now I have to keep track of my sales on paper."

He looked at me with concern. "Do you want to borrow a laptop from me?"

That was sweet, but I didn't want to impose. "No. But, thank you. Hopefully, it will just be for a few days."

We pulled into the dusty parking lot and I introduced Joey to Smitty. "He's looking for anything train-related." Then, I showed him the new and improved Zia.

Smitty took off his stained hat and scratched his head. "Well, look! That thing cleaned up perty good. It sure is itty bitty."

I had to smile at that term coming from him and waited for his whole spiel about Brutus, but instead, he pointed to a bin of railroad spikes and sent us on our way. As we scoured the area, my wheels turned at the thought of cool products I could make from the spikes. If only I knew how to weld. Might have to add that new skill someday.

Joey stopped so quickly in front of me, that I ran into his back, nearly squashing Zia.

He said, "Sorry, but look at that."

"What is it? Another dog that needs rescuing?" I joked as I looked around his shoulder.

His eyes were round and he was breathless. "It's a…it's a…"

For a second, I thought he might be having a medical episode but I followed his fixed gaze to a rusted round piece of metal.

"I think it's a drumhead," he said as he walked toward a sign leaning against a shed.

"A what?"

He picked up the large round piece of metal and looked it over. His eyes sparkled as he said, "See how it's almost as big as a bass drum? This one is for…" He balanced the object against his stomach and rubbed some of the rust off with his t-shirt. That was an act I'd probably never do, at least not with this prized t-shirt. He read with excitement, "…the Northern Pacific Railway."

"Cool?" I said, not knowing what else to say.

He must have realized I didn't have a clue what the thing was, and explained, "These used to be attached to the last car to advertise that specific company. I've never seen one except in a railroad museum. And to think this is just sitting out here rusting."

His excitement over the piece of metal was almost contagious. I said, "Don't tell Smitty it's special or he'll raise the price."

"I don't even care. I'm thrilled and can't wait to show Jett."

Joey was too excited to look around anymore, so he happily paid Smitty $40 for his treasure and a box of railroad spikes. As we started the trek back to Out of the Box, he turned to me from the driver's seat and said with huge eyes, "I can't believe that! You must be a good luck charm. Can I just keep you with me all the time?"

I laughed. "As tempting as that sounds, I'm not so sure I was the reason you found your dumbhead."

He smirked. "Drumhead, silly."

His use of the word good luck charm reminded me of the charm I'd found. I turned my phone over and saw the spoon safely encased under the clear plastic.

Joey sighed, "Well, this should sure perk Jett up."

Aha. Finally, a chance to ask about his brother's moodiness. I said, "So, has Jett been down because of his divorce?"

"Yeah. His moods have been all over the place. He's been spending a ton of money, dating questionable people, and has acquired a short fuse."

I figured he meant Victoria and was relieved to know Joey wasn't impressed with her either. I held Zia up by my face and cuddled the girl. Just thinking of Victoria's anger toward the pup made me feel protective.

At a stoplight, he said, "Although I kid Jett that he's finally grown into his broody dark looks, I've been pretty worried lately. He was so low last week, I worried he would hurt himself."

I frowned, sorry to hear that. "That's too bad." I thought Jett's being under the influence recently couldn't help the situation. The phrase, "short fuse" stuck with me.

The light changed as well as Joey's spirits. He smiled. "I hope his work with the brewery will provide some stability and distract him from his problems."

"I hope so too." After a beat, I asked, "So, is he normally outgoing and talkative like you?"

He laughed. "Um. No. For years, my parents called us Penn and Teller, usually to get me to stop talking or him to join in the conversation."

I laughed at the comparison between the two magicians, one gregarious and the other silent.

Joey eyed the Twisters restaurant up ahead and he asked, "Are you hungry?"

"If you're talkin' a carne adovada burrito, then yes I am."

He pulled into the drive-thru. We ordered food which we devoured on the way back to the brewery. Twisters had the perfect amount of spice. My lips tingled a little with the heat of the sauce, but the tortilla, potatoes, and cheese mellowed it out perfectly. Yum. I drank my water and let Zia lap from my cup afterward realizing that even though she hadn't gotten any spicy food, she was probably thirsty from being a black dog in the sun.

Once we unloaded his purchases, I looked at the time on my phone. "I'd better go, Joey. Thanks for the burrito. It was fun, even though I didn't buy one thing at Smitty's. That's got to be a first for me."

"Next time." He winked. "See you tomorrow."

"Okie dokie." I saluted him and started walking backward on the gravel, wondering what had possessed me to say okie dokie, or to salute for that matter. He didn't seem to mind though as he hopped up his steps, carrying his big prize.

As I turned around, I heard voices coming from a black Mercedes parked by the coffee shop. I saw Jett through the open window, sitting in the passenger seat. I slipped behind a recently planted yucca outside the brewery, glad to have such a large barrier so I could listen and not be seen.

Victoria, sitting in the driver's seat, said in a quieter voice than normal, "I'm so glad you took out that antique the other day." Then, she must have moved, because her voice became muffled.

I peeked around to try to read her lips but felt a sharp pain on my cheek. I jerked back and rubbed my face, realizing how close I'd come to being poked in the eye with a yucca spike. It brought back a memory of a time, when as kids, Jill and I witnessed a big grasshopper leap up and impale itself on a sword-shaped leaf of a yucca beside our house. Those plants could be deadly.

Being more careful not to get blinded, I focused my attention on the car again and heard Victoria say, with her typical shrillness, "...practically ancient and just in my way." What old antique was she talking about?

As though put out, Jett said, "You could have just talked to Flick, instead of making me do that." Jett rubbed his forehead.

I pictured Mr. Harrison as 'the old antique.' A spoiled elitist like Victoria probably *would* think Pops was ancient. What if Victoria had Jett kill him? Was he looking uncomfortable out of remorse?

She responded, "Well, I hated Flick as much as you did." Then she cooed, "Besides, I wanted *you* to take care of it. I owe you big time, now." I could see her rubbing Jett's shoulders.

He pulled away and said, "Well, you didn't tell me there were two of them."

How likely was it that they were talking about the death of Pops? It could really be that he'd killed Pops by accident, meaning to go after Flick. My mouth went dry. I shook my head. No. Jett would never do anything to harm either of them…or would he? The sullen brother had acted pretty strangely the last few days.

Jett pulled away from her and said, "Look, I've got to go. I have a lot of work to do." He paused then said, "Shouldn't you be working on your coffee shop today?"

I watched the prissy barista bat her eyes and whine, "I already worked there this morning for like an hour."

Although trying to make sense of the conversation, I was baffled that she'd worked only an hour in her shop. Then I realized with all my visitors and excursions today, I hadn't worked much more than that myself. Most other days it was more like 10 hours there.

He said, "I'll pick you up at 6:30 for the gala. And Victoria, please be ready this time."

When Jett got out of the car, he rolled his eyes, apparently frustrated with his new girlfriend. As he walked towards me, I moved so quickly that I caught my sleeve on the yucca and my shirt ripped.

I stood still, hoping he hadn't heard the tearing sound or worse yet, seen me. The yucca trunk wasn't wide enough to cover both of my legs.

When the crunch of gravel stopped, I held my breath, realizing Jett was standing still. Crap. Not only was I probably in view, but so was my shadow since a dark squatty version of myself lay on the pink crushed rock.

I assumed I was safe when his footsteps resumed, and he climbed the wooden steps to enter the brewery. I took in a gulp of air and watched Victoria's car drive out of the complex.

I was a bit unsettled by the conversation and walked back to my shop, wondering what antique had been taken out. The gala would be a perfect chance to spy on the beautiful, but suspicious couple.

I took Zia from her sling and let her walk beside me,. She was probably glad to stretch her legs after being held for hours. I assessed the damage to my favorite t-shirt, frowning. I could have polished the drumhead with it after all since another Hamilton was shot. I snorted aloud at my own Hamilton joke.

Once home, I showered and felt energized. Zia and I sat on the couch for a minute. I turned to look at her barely fuzzy face. "You've met Jett. Do you think he could hurt someone?"

She looked at me as if she pondered the question. I waited. "Well, I can't wait all day for you to answer. I've got to go. Aunt Jill and I have a big night and I don't want to be late."

I started to get excited about the evening and gathered up what I would need to take to Jill's. I gave Zia a treat and left.

Although Savers had the typical used-clothing smell, it was a great place to find treasures. Since I was a few minutes early, I perused the housewares section. I found a few cups and saucers, vases, and a new globe, all of which went into my cart to repurpose.

Within moments, I heard Jill calling me from the formal wear section. "Maria! Get over here! I need your help."

I looked across the store and spotted her red hair with no problem. She was already looking through the gowns. I pushed my cart over to her, surprised to see a great selection of dresses. "Wow, a lot of people must just wear something once, then donate them. Hmmm. Good for us."

"Right. So many prom dresses. But, what size should I try? I don't see a maternity section." She looked puzzled as she pulled out hangers and cocked her head reading the labels.

"I don't know. Just grab anything that might fit."

She started holding up gowns to her body, most of which would not work, but after going up from size 8 to 18, she found several to try on. I found a few gowns in sizes 4 and 6 that I hoped would work for me. One cream-colored dress was gorgeous and only $12.99.

Once we were settled in side-by-side fitting rooms, I heard panting coming from Jill's cubicle. Then the sound turned to groans, then giggles followed by laughter.

"Do you need help?" I ventured.

"What I need is a miracle to get out of this one," she said with a snort.

When I opened her door, there she stood, boobs practically popping out of the top of a tight stretchy hot pink dress. The fabric color was 3 shades lighter in her belly area since it was stretched so tight. She turned her back to me and there was a good 8-inch gap where the zipper should have closed. The sight was truly hilarious. As much as I dislike disturbing other shoppers, I couldn't control my laughter. Even at a thrift store, there was a good chance we'd be evicted if we didn't calm down.

I started to tug on the dress, pulling it down, when that didn't work, I tugged it up. I hoped the fabric wouldn't tear. No matter how much I tried, the dress didn't budge. With a gulp of air, between fits of laughter I said, "How in the world did you get this on?"

Her voice was muffled with her mouth covered in fabric. "I don't know! It was stretchy and I kept pulling on it. And here I am." At this point, I'd moved it up, causing her arm to be stuck up in an awkward waving position. She said with a snort., "Take a picture of me."

"Seriously?" Only Jill would ask that. Most people would die before having a picture taken at a moment like this.

She huffed, "Dang right. I want to show Sophia what I went through for her if she even thinks about having a baby too young."

I took a few pictures of the scene, giggling the whole time, then worked on the dress until it was deemed useless. I said, "Wait here."

Her eyes gave me a 'duh' look and I scooted to a cashier with blue hair and tattooed sleeves. "Excuse me, do you have a pair of scissors? I need to cut my friend out of a dress."

The look on the girl's face was priceless. She flared her nostrils so much I thought her nose ring might pop out.

I quickly added, "Don't worry, we'll pay for the dress."

She gave me a sideways glance and slowly handed me a pair of scissors.

I carried the sheers to the room and held them up to my friend. "It's either this or a crowbar."

I started cutting the pink fabric and finally freed Jill, saying "Guess you're not going to be pretty in pink tonight. Let me help you with the rest." I moved my garments into her fitting room and we took turns trying on more dresses in the small space, making sure this time, none were death traps.

After ten more minutes of awkward dressing in the tiny room, we found the perfect outfits and walked to the cashier. Our giggles erupted again when the same girl saw the shreds of polyester on the counter and remarked, "Wish I could have seen you in that."

Jill responded immediately by holding up her phone and showing her the photo. We got the reaction we expected as she laughed in surprise.

We dressed for the gala at Jill's house. Less than an hour before it started, we rushed around bumping into each other. At a quarter 'til seven, we were about as fancy as we were going to get. I looked in the mirror at my used, cream-colored beaded gown and thought I looked pretty good.

Jill sighed and said, "You look awesome, Maria. I'm so jealous of your body right now. You have a waist!"

She nudged me aside to get a full view of herself in her green gown. "And here I am, looking like Kermit the frog after a buffet of all the flies."

"Are you kidding? Jill, you're beautiful. Like a princess." It was true, the emerald color complemented her gorgeous red hair and green eyes.

"A pregnant princess?"

"OK, so a beautiful enchantress."

The front door opened, and Kelly entered. He froze when he saw us. I'd say he was speechless, but then again, he usually was.

He walked up to Jill and said, "Wow!"

Jill's face changed into a smile as she flirted, "You like?" Her eyebrows were lifted in anticipation of a favorable answer.

He eyed her from head to toe. "Maybe you shouldn't go out looking so ravishing."

She fluttered her eyelashes at him. "I promise I won't even glance at anyone else." She tapped him on the chest. "Just be here when I get home, big boy."

I shook my head and said, "Enough, love bugs. We should go. Good-bye, Mr. Standing Wolf." I smirked at him.

His shoulders lowered and he said, "That man..."

As I shut the door behind me, I felt bad reminding Kelly of his new boss. But it occurred to me I now had a spy in the police department. Maybe Kelly could tell me what was going on. This new thought excited me as we got in Jill's Prius.

"Jill, I have new suspects besides old Flick and weird Carl."

"Who?"

"Jett and Victoria."

With her hands on the wheel, she turned to me with narrowed eyes. "Isn't that one of the brewery brothers?"

I nodded and told her about the conversation I'd overheard.

Jill said, "Well, it does sound odd, but why would the old man be in Victoria's way?"

I shrugged. "I don't have everything worked out, but something wasn't right about that conversation and I mean to dig further."

CHAPTER 13

Jill acted giddy pulling into the valet station of Alex Chandler's newest hotel. I climbed out of the car as gracefully as I could. The driver helped extract Jill from her driver's seat, then drove off in the green car with the Grass Man logo on the side. It didn't exactly fit in with the Lincolns and Jaguars we saw, but it was better than my truck.

Jill grabbed my hand as she toddled in her high heels, working hard not to lose her balance. She complained, "I think my shoes have shrunk. They seem so tight."

I looked at her feet and saw that they were swollen. "I don't think it's the shoes that have changed size."

As we approached the entrance, two men dressed in tuxedos simultaneously opened the tall front doors. Before us stood an elaborate, never-ending marble staircase leading up to heaven I could only assume. It was like a scene straight out of a glamorous movie. We watched, mouths open, as elegant men and women, dressed in their finest, ascended the steps gracefully.

Jill looked at me in horror. I think she imagined us clambering to the top only to trip on the hems of our evening gowns and fall down the entire length of stairs. At least that's what I pictured. After all, neither of us had worn heels for a while, and no long gowns since Senior prom.

I turned and whispered to a tuxedo-clad man, who I hoped was working and not a guest, "Is there an elevator nearby?"

"Certainly, Ma'am. Right this way."

Jill nudged me. "He called you Ma'am."

I said, "It's just because I look so sophisticated tonight." I held my head high and winked at her.

The man led us around the stairway to an elevator with beautiful copper doors. He pushed the up button and waited with us. I looked at our reflections in the shiny door and was glad I had pulled my hair up. We looked every bit as elegant as the other guests here. I suppressed a giggle thinking that ours were probably the only dresses bought at a thrift store.

When the doors opened, the man leaned in and pushed the only option, Level 2, on the board, then bowed and left us to ride up.

The doors closed and Jill said, "Did he think we didn't know how to run an elevator just because we couldn't operate stairs?"

I smirked just as the doors opened to a gorgeous foyer. It was truly like a fairy tale. We walked forward, mouths agape as if we had just stepped off the hay truck. The ceiling, made completely from glass triangles, was maybe 30 feet high. I could imagine Daniel Craig or some other James Bond, crashing through the glass in order to save the world.

My soaring imagination halted when a man wearing white gloves asked for our invitations. I fumbled as I opened my cream-colored clutch, the one my mother had carried when attending nice affairs years ago. I retrieved our tickets and handed them to the man, praying they were official. He inspected them as I held my breath.

Instead of being tossed out as imposters, the man said with absolutely no inflection, "You are sitting at table number 13. Enjoy your evening." He graciously waved us to the ballroom.

I leaned over to Jill and said, "I've never seen a man wear white gloves before. Maybe you should get some for Kelly."

When Jill started giggling, I said, "OK, let's pretend we're rich and famous just for tonight." I added, "In order to do that, we'll have to act calm and dignified."

She looked at me and smirked. "Wouldn't it be awful if my water broke and ruined this brand-new carpet?"

I looked at her in shock then down at the expensive-looking carpet. "It couldn't, could it? You're not ready to pop, right?"

"No. I'm just kidding. The doctor said I've got another two weeks."

Rather than the confident air I hoped to give off, my nose scrunched with worry. I took a deep breath and tried to relax my face.

As we walked, I smiled pleasantly at the fellow guests, trying to guess their professions. I leaned over to my friend and whispered, "At least if you do go into labor here, I'll bet there are plenty of doctors to help you deliver."

We walked through the doorway into an ornate room full of crystal chandeliers. Each table was topped with a cream-colored tablecloth, elegant place settings, and a vase holding beautiful lilies.

"Oh my." Jill said, "So, this is how the upper 2% live."

A combo played light jazz in the far corner near a dance floor. A cocktail waitress carrying a linen-covered tray offered us drinks. I took a glass of red wine, immediately regretting the decision since I wore a cream-colored dress. I sipped the drink carefully. When I looked at Jill, she surprised me by holding a glass of wine too.

"So, you can't do coffee, but you can have wine?"

Without looking at me and with a comical look of superiority, she said, "I'm not going to drink it. I just want to hold something." She lifted her nose and looked around with a haughty expression.

I grabbed her hand. "There is a bar over there. Let's go get something you can actually drink." I led Jill to the well-stocked bar and asked if they had anything non-alcoholic. Jill chose a sprite and traded in her glass for the pop. I looked at the tables. "I wonder which one is 13."

Jill made a face. "Unlucky 13."

"Stop being negative. It's going to be an awesome evening." I pointed at a small stylish frame on a nearby table displaying a calligraphed number 4 and said, "Let's find our table and put our bags down so we can mingle."

We casually walked from table to table, finally finding ours on the other side of the huge room. After placing our purses at two empty places, we carried our drinks and walked among the beautiful people.

I whispered, "Do you recognize anyone?"

"Not yet." She looked around. "Wait, I think that couple over there had us install turf a few months ago. Jack said their house in the Northeast Heights was amazing."

I scoured the room but didn't recognize anyone. I heard a familiar voice and turned to see Jett talking with an older woman. I grabbed Jill's arm. "Look. It's Jett."

"Oh My! He is even more gorgeous in a tux!"

He was indeed striking with those chiseled features and dark hair. I watched him, wondering if he could possibly have murdered the old man. I started over to say hello; after all, even if he was a killer, he wouldn't be dangerous in a public place.

As I neared him, I heard Victoria's obnoxious laugh and did a 180, and walked right back to Jill's side. I held my glass in front of my face, so the barista wouldn't see me. We watched as she sidled up to Jett and slid her arm through his. Her dress was a beautiful red number that accentuated her knockout figure and red lips. She truly looked outstanding.

I continued to stare across the room at her when a deep voice came from behind me. "I don't believe I've had the opportunity to meet you two lovely ladies."

I turned and found myself looking straight into the grey eyes of multi-millionaire, Alex Chandler, himself.

I stammered, "Uh. Hi." Oh no. This was it. We were going to get tossed out on our ears because he didn't know us. I felt my face redden.

"So, what brings you lovely ladies to this event?" He asked with a suave, yet sincere expression.

I took a deep breath. "Hello, Mr. Chandler. My name is Maria Olson. This is my friend, Jill Standing Bear. You're right. We have never met you but have seen your face all over town." Now, that was the stupidest thing to say to a famous entrepreneur. I closed my eyes in embarrassment.

Thankfully, Jill spoke up, "We were given the invitations by Maria's landlord who says he knows you? His name is Larry."

I chimed in to explain, "Larry B?" I studied the handsome white-haired gentleman to see his response.

He nodded, "Oh, of course. Larry!" He tipped his head back and laughed. "Sure. He said he knew some fine ladies who needed a night out. And I believe he was right." He turned to Jill and nodded at her protruding stomach. "You look like you are embarking on a life change soon."

She patted her tummy and said, "Yup. In a few weeks."

Chandler smiled and said, "I'm so glad you gals could join us. I look forward to seeing old Larry tomorrow at our weekly coffee. He's something else, isn't he?"

Weekly coffee? I could barely control my surprise. I nodded warily and said, "He's something else, all right. Thank you so much for letting us join you, Mr. Chandler. This is an amazing place."

He turned, distracted by something, then took my hand and said, "You ladies will have to excuse me. The mayor is motioning me over. Enjoy the evening."

In a surprising move, he kissed the back of my hand. How charming. We watched the dashing man stroll toward a group of important-looking people and slap Mayor Hendrix on the back.

Jill's mouth dropped open dramatically. "I can't believe we just met Alex Chandler! My Mom will just die when I tell her. She's had a crush on him for years. I should have taken a selfie with him. No, that wouldn't have been cool. Maybe I can still get a shot of him."

She fumbled around with her phone, trying to get a good shot, while I replayed his comments in my head. I turned to Jill, "Was it my imagination, or did he act as if he liked Larry?"

Jill dipped and stretched, aiming the phone camera at Chandler, then gave up trying to get a picture and stuffed her phone in her purse. "He probably got him mixed up with another Larry. A guy like Chandler wouldn't have a weekly lunch with your Larry."

"Eew. He's not *my* Larry." Just then, I spotted Victoria's red dress again. With renewed confidence, I said, "Hey, I'm gonna go talk to the newest suspects. Be right back."

Holding my head high, I straightened my dress and carefully wove through the guests. I tried to compose a classy opening line in my head as I walked. "How funny to run into you guys" – too informal. "My, my, don't you two clean up well?" – way too familiar. I finally decided on a friendly, "What a coincidence seeing you both here."

Just as I got within earshot, I overheard Jett say, "He won't evict you. You've paid him most of the money, right?"

Victoria shrugged, then scrunched her lips into a big Shirley Temple pout.

I slunk behind a man who had to be a customer at the Big and Tall shop. His large girth could have hidden two of me. At least on this surveillance, there was no chance of being speared by a yucca spike. Casually sipping my wine, I strained to hear Jett and Victoria amidst the polite chatter of the guests. I realized my glass was almost empty, so had to pretend to drink. You can't look nonchalant standing alone with an empty glass.

I peeked around at the couple, finding it hard to believe they weren't Hollywood A-listers on the set of a James Bond movie. Jett in a sleek tuxedo, Victoria in a clinging red dress, their attire accentuated their beautifully proportioned bodies. After noticing her perfectly toned arms, I glance down at my own, which weren't flabby but certainly didn't have the contours of hers. Where do people go to get in that kind of shape?

She purred to Jett, "You'll make sure he lets me stay in Out of the Box, right? I just have to stay near my Jett ski."

Jett ski? Jeez. Victoria stood on the tips of her red high-heeled shoes and kissed him, then whispered something into his ear.

He responded with a sincere look. "Victoria, let me help you get a loan."

She dipped her head in a poor me fashion and said, "That's OK. You've done enough for me."

I was interested in how he would reply, but a deep friendly voice interrupted my surveillance, "Well, hello there."

I looked up, way up, to the large man talking to me. "Oh, Hi."

"I'm John Wickersham. This is my wife Mary."

I smiled at him, then at a woman, who was at least a head taller than me. Great. Instead of *pretending* to mingle, I had to mingle for real and couldn't spy anymore. I said, politely, "Nice to meet you. I'm Maria Olson."

I shot a glance at my targets who were still talking.

Jett: "Only 8 of us left."

Before I could think of what Jett was talking about, John said, "We own Tall John's Tires."

Now, that impressed me. I'd seen their ads for years and should have recognized the big guy from the commercials. "I love your commercials. I should…"

I was distracted by a shrill voice. Victoria: "But they're all a bunch of losers."

It was hard to pay attention to two conversations at once. Who was Victoria referring to? I saw the raised eyebrows of the nice couple, waiting for me to finish my sentence. I spoke up, "Uh…I should probably stop by your shop. The tires on my truck are questionable."

I wished Jill was here to help me listen, but when I glanced back at her she was talking to a woman.. I gave my full attention to the couple and smiled. "I'm starting my own business, a shop called Upcycled, in the new Out of the Box shopping center."

Now, that seemed to impress the two, for their eyes lit up. I was happy someone would be excited about my store.

The woman said with an eager nod, "That's where the murder happened, right?"

My heart sank. This was a new reality. All we were known for was a murder and we hadn't even started our businesses yet. "Um yes, but we open on Saturday and I hope you'll plan to stop by to see our unique offerings."

The semi-famous tire man said, "We will do that. Can I get you another glass of wine, Maria?"

I wanted to stay near my suspects to hear more so I smiled and said, "That would be nice, John. I'd like white this time, please."

He took my nearly empty glass and walked away. I moved over a smidge to remain hidden from Jett and Victoria. The wife's eyes sparkled at me. Why did the topic of murder excite people?

Jett: "Just try to be nice. They are good people."

I wondered who "they" were, then realized Mary had said something else to me, so I said, "Pardon?"

She repeated. "Was the man who died a friend of yours?"

At least she had enough empathy to consider the deceased. I said, "Mr. Harrison was a new acquaintance, but he seemed like a very sweet man."

Victoria: "Well, I can't stand the girl with the rat. Be a dear and burn down her shop, please."

My head jolted towards Victoria. How dare she? Tall John walked up and handed us fresh glasses of wine. I desperately wanted to hear whether Jett would stand up for me or agree with Victoria, but when I looked, they were both laughing. My new friends kept the murder conversation going so that I couldn't hear the other two at all.

Finally, I excused myself, making a nod toward Jett and Victoria, "I need to go talk to someone. It was so nice to meet you, John and Mary…and thank you for the wine."

John handed me a card and said, "Stop by anytime. We'll take good care of your truck."

I took the card from the gentleman and smiled. When I turned around, I was eye to eye with Victoria. She sneered at me. I ignored the gesture, gave a little wave, and took a step forward ready to say my rehearsed line. But she rolled her eyes and pulled Jett away without him noticing me.

Feeling foolish for being rejected so easily, my face flushed. I made a bee-line back toward Jill. As I fled, Mr. Chandler spoke into the microphone asking everyone to be seated since dinner would be served soon. I was relieved to rejoin Jill, who visited with an older man at our table. I felt lightheaded from the humiliation.

All the other guests at our table were from New Mexico Bank and Trust. After polite introductions, I felt more comfortable and relaxed a bit. Jill kicked her tight shoes off under the table cloth. That wasn't a bad idea, but I opted to keep my shoes on.

Jill's big blue eyes stared at me. "So…what happened? Did they murder the old man?"

I looked at my wacky friend in disbelief, "Sure, they just came up to me and confessed to the whole thing." I sighed. "No. I didn't even get to talk to them because as soon as Victoria saw me, she rolled her eyes and walked away. That was after I heard her say she wanted to burn down my shop!"

Jill shook her head slowly in disgust. "That b…" Jill glanced around at the high-class company and rethought her word choice, "woman." She shook her head.

"Hopefully, Victoria was just kidding." I tried to calm Jill down by saying, "I did, however, meet Tall John from Tall John's Tires."

"Well, that's something. Was he as tall as he seems on TV?"

"Taller I think. And his wife is up there too. They are so nice."

Jill started telling me about some former customers she visited with, but before she could finish her story, a waiter lay down a gorgeous salad in front of her, effectively shutting the redhead up.

We were served a wonderful three-course meal and waiters refilled wine glasses every time they were emptied. Feeling just a bit tipsy, I put my napkin on top of my glass and said to Jill, "I hope this stops them from pouring more."

She nodded. "Not to worry. I'll be driving us home. Who would ever have thought I would ever be a designated driver?"

I chuckled at that. She had always been the wild one.

After dinner, a live auction spiced things up. Prizes included famous local artwork, turquoise jewelry, hot air balloon rides, and weeklong cabin rentals. I wished I could bid on something since the evening was a fundraiser for the local Roadrunner Foodbank.

I turned to Jill and whispered, "Do you think I'll ever be able to afford to bid on something like that?"

"Sure," Jill encouraged, "Your shop will be a hit. You'll pay off your student loans and your house, then you'll probably be a regular at this kind of affair." She winked. "And I'll be your plus one."

"Sounds good, but it's more likely that nobody will go to Out of the Box at all, now that we're only known for a murder."

She gave me a sympathetic look. Since I hate being pitied, I bucked up and said, "But, even though I can't afford to bid on anything now, I can and will make a small donation directly to the food bank this week. It's the least I can do for this fabulous food."

Jill smiled with an 'atta girl' look and said, "Me too."

I had lost sight of Jett and wondered where they were sitting. During a boisterous bidding war over season tickets to the Santa Fe Opera, I caught sight of Victoria making her way to their table. My view was clear as I followed her red dress gliding across the room like a graceful cardinal. I watched her laugh and visit with Jett at their table. He didn't seem as moody or aggravated as he had earlier.

When Jett moved his head, I was shocked and thrilled to see Joey sitting on his right side. His blonde hair was slicked back and he looked amazing. I sure wasn't expecting him to be here. Wow! The guy had been transformed from a rugged outdoorsman to a prince. Even from that distance, his grin made me smile. I willed him to stand so I could see him all gussied up in a tuxedo.

When he didn't hear my silent plea, I pictured myself sitting with the handsome man, enjoying a glass of wine. Of course, in my scenario, we were not at the table with Jett and Victoria, but alone in a romantic setting. I took a deep breath as I watched Joey.

He turned his head the other way and much to my dismay, there was a pretty brunette sitting beside him. She laughed at something he said and patted him on the back in a familiar way.

"What's wrong? You look like you saw a ghost." Jill said.

I sighed. "No. No ghost this time. Just Joey with a woman." I was surprised at how disappointed I sounded. It wasn't like we were dating.

"Where?"

I pointed them out to her.

She craned her neck to see. "She's cute and has a nice smile."

I frowned at Jill. "Thanks. I know."

Catching on, she backtracked, "Maybe they're just friends. And if not, it's okay. There are lots of good-looking men around here, probably richer than him. Let's check them out."

I certainly wasn't in the mood to look at other guys, and being wealthy was never my goal. I sighed, "I don't know. I think I'm ready to leave." What had gotten into me? I was never a whiner.

"Okay, if you're sure. Let me get my purse."

I stood and tried to look inconspicuous leaving early, but waited while Jill tried to put her heels on. In her enlarged awkward state, she lost her balance, and grabbed the tablecloth. Unfortunately, she was no magician whipping the cloth off and keeping the setting in place. Plates crashed and wine glasses dumped onto the other guests. The squeals were deafening.

Flustered, I straighten the tablecloth, righted the vase, and apologized profusely to the bankers and their spouses. Jill asked a nearby waiter for napkins. I looked up to see a woman sporting red splotches on her beautiful yellow gown. Her spoiled dress and horrified face made her look like she'd been shot.

I grabbed Jill's hand and hid my face with my purse as we left the event in humiliation.

CHAPTER 14

After a restless night of bad dreams, where I was caught in embarrassing situations, I awoke to remember I had endured a doozy for real. I could only hope that the woman's dress wasn't permanently damaged and that Jett and Joey hadn't seen us in our mortifying attempt to leave early.

To redeem me as a decent human being, I dressed in a black skirt and nice top to attend Pops' funeral. I ate cereal and drove to my shop with Zia in tow.

The store looked good. I straightened some picture frames on shelves. There were only a few things to do before opening in 25 hours: I still needed to get a receipt book. Luckily, Square, PayPal, and Venmo had their own accounting and receipt services, so I just needed to keep track of checks and cash without the computer.

Just thinking of how soon the store would open, my heart beat faster and opening day jitters came a day early. Calm down, Maria. What's the worst that could happen? Nobody would show up? To help ease my mind, I planned to get a pad of receipts at Walmart. I also needed bags, but figured, if someone did buy something, they could carry their purchase out in some recycled bags. After all, it would fit with my theme of repurposing.

I turned to my pup. "Zia, you did such a good job watching the house last night, would you keep an eye on it while I'm at the funeral?"

She crawled into her bed, clearly ready to attack any intruder who may appear - not.

Arriving at the Methodist church twenty minutes early, I saw Milly walk up the sidewalk flanked by who I assumed were nieces and nephews. I held back so as not to intrude on the family and followed them slowly to the door. Milly was dressed in a beautiful black skirt and jacket. She held the arm of a teenage boy, and was steadied on her other side by a cane. I noticed neither Carl nor Flick were in the group.

An older couple stopped the crew to give the widow a hug. When they left, Milly caught my eye and motioned me over.

I walked to the elderly woman and said, "Hello, Milly. This must be a difficult day for you."

She nodded and said in a clear voice, "Maria dear, why don't you sit beside me?" She took hold of my forearm and practically pulled me forward.

I was surprised since I had no claim to sit with the family. Furthermore, I had only met the woman once. I shook my head. "Milly, I barely knew Pops. Those seats are reserved for family."

"But, you would be doing me a favor as my new friend, to sit with me." She glanced at her entourage. "The children all have somebody to keep them company."

Indeed, the youngsters weren't even looking at Milly. They were huddled in their own sort of sibling or cousin cliques. As awkward as it might be for me to sit in the family section, I couldn't refuse the grieving widow. "Well, then…of course."

She took my arm and we slowly processed into the sanctuary. The flowers were abundant and gave the air a sweet aroma. The lighting was stunning. Along the aisles, candles were lit and the stained-glass window glowed with the reflection of the sun.

As we continued to the front, Milly nodded politely to mourners as she passed. I fidgeted with my skirt, sensing the stares of people who probably wondered who I was. An usher handed us each a program as we reached the front row appropriately roped off for immediate family.

Once seated, I was hit with the familiar pang of melancholy, having been in this position too many times already in my life

Beside the casket, an enlarged framed photo of Pops stood on an easel. His warm smile sent an overwhelming wave of anguish through me. I couldn't shake the image of his lifeless face and started to tremble.

I closed my eyes and took a few deep breaths which helped calm myself a bit. To distract from my thoughts, I studied the details of the beautiful stained-glass window. It was truly a work of art. I wondered how difficult stained glass would be to make. I thought of my bicycle rim idea and wondered how I could attach glass to the rims. Silicone would probably be best since it would be weatherproof. I looked forward to starting that project.

Scanning the sanctuary further, I focused on the vases of white lilies around the pulpit. There were so many flowers at the gala last night which were probably just tossed out. Too bad they couldn't have been moved here to save Milly money. I knew from experience how expensive funerals were.

Calming organ music covered the polite murmurs of the congregation as they filled the pews behind us. As I looked around for Flick, I was surprised to see Sgt. Barnes across the aisle, dressed in his signature wrinkled suit. Hmm. He didn't seem the type to be here. Maybe he planned to badger the family with rude questions. I hoped not.

I finally spotted Flick sitting alone a few rows behind us. How odd that he wasn't sitting with his children and grandchildren. I flinched when I caught sight of Carl, lumbering down the opposite aisle wearing an ill-fitting suit with a crooked tie. His hair was still greasy and hanging in his eyes. He passed his father and sat at the other end of our row. Even though I looked away, I could see through my peripheral vision that he stared at me. His eerie attention gave me the willies.

Milly also noticed him and leaned in and whispered a little too loud, "I just heard that Carl has a big crush on you."

What? I looked at her in surprise, then glanced at the man. His eyes bored into me with contempt. How those actions could translate to anything besides disgust, I didn't know. I looked at Milly and said, "Are you sure? He seems to dislike me very much."

"Oh, he has an odd way of doing everything. But, he told me himself, that he thinks you are the most beautiful woman he's ever seen." She pulled a handkerchief from her purse and added, "Then he said something about books, but I didn't hear him as I was busy writing Pops' obituary."

She sighed at the mention of her husband's name. Tears fill her eyes and I patted her hand wishing there was more I could do but I knew there wasn't.

What had Carl said to her about the books? Before I could give it much thought, the minister stepped up to the pulpit and asked everyone to stand.

The service was beautiful. A few grand-nephews spoke about their Uncle Pops. I learned that he was quite a jokester and everyone in the congregation laughed at the stories told about him. I wish I'd gotten to know him. Out of habit, I gave the sign of the cross at the end of the prayer.

During a hymn, I felt my iWatch buzz. I was instantly glad I had put my phone on silent, but who was calling me? Probably Jill. I tried to ignore it, but a few minutes later, my wrist vibrated again. What if it was something important? Worried, I held my phone under my hymnal and since my face couldn't be scanned, I had to type in my code to open the phone. I glanced at it discreetly and saw it was a call from Walgreens, probably saying my prescription was ready.

As I started to put the phone away, it buzzed with a notification from my new camera app, saying movement had been captured in my shop.

I started to panic but remembered Zia was there. She must have triggered the camera by jumping on something. I sighed and continued singing.

Once we sat down again, the minister went into a lengthy sermon about the Hereafter. I tried to concentrate on his message, but I thought about the topic. Were my parents now welcoming Pops into heaven? Though I hadn't known him well, after Milly's stories, I was pretty sure Dad would think he was a hoot. Mom would love his antics. With my whole immediate family on the other side, I wanted to believe there was a heaven and that they were there waiting for me. But what was it like? Was my sister still 12 years old? Would I recognize them? I've pondered these questions for years and apparently would never know until I got there myself.

My phone, carefully hidden beneath my hymnal, buzzed again, bringing me back to the here and now. I carefully shielded the phone from view by Milly and opened my camera app, hoping she wouldn't notice my disrespectful behavior.

I expected to see Zia up on the counter prancing around. What I didn't anticipate, was seeing Larry in my shop, rifling through papers on my counter searching for something. He looked under my pink notebook, lifted the stapler, then looked inside boxes. He disappeared from view, possibly to look in my storage area, which was behind the camera. My eyes strained to make sense of the scene and my pulse began to race as I viewed the live transmission.

What the heck was he doing there? I scanned my tiny screen for little Zia but couldn't see her from the camera's vantage point. I hoped that Larry hadn't hurt my baby. My first reaction was to jump up and leave, but I couldn't do that. I was stuck in my seat until the service ended. Maybe I could get a note to the sergeant to tell him about it but passing notes during a funeral would be disrespectful. All I could do was watch and wait.

We stood for a prayer, which I hoped meant the funeral was coming to an end, but then we sang yet another hymn. While everyone was distracted with singing, I watched as Larry popped up again on my phone. This time he did an awkward dance. I looked down and there was my sweet Zia with her teeth sunk into his jeans. He tried to shake the dog loose. I almost screamed, "Don't hurt her!" but contained myself as I watched the scene unfold. The poor dog was just flying to and fro, causing my heart to pound and eyes to fill with tears.

I felt a tug at my sleeve. Milly said, "Dear, the hymn is over. You can sit down." I looked around and noticed I was the only one still standing. How embarrassing. I sat and put my phone in my pocket for the rest of the service but was restless, dying to know what was happening.

When we were finally released, the usher slowly helped Milly down the aisle with me inching close behind. I was eager to get away from the church but had to be patient.

In the lobby, people approached Milly to pay their respects. Before she got into a long conversation with someone, I leaned forward and hugged her. "Please let me know if there is anything I can do for you."

"I will," she said with a grateful nod.

Just as I was ready to scoot out the door, Carl walked my way with his watery eyes fixed on me. I just couldn't. Not now. I dove into the crowd and wound my way through mourners until I exited the church. As I headed to the parking lot, I spotted Barnes getting in his car and ran to him. I said in a relieved rush, "Sergeant Barnes! I'm so glad I caught you."

He turned around, frowned, and said, "Olson, you do get around."

I wasn't sure what he meant by that, but I spurted, "My landlord Larry was in my shop without permission." I pulled up the video and showed it to him, relieved to show someone else the break-in.

"Your landlord? He has a key, right?"

I said, "Yes?" excited he took an interest.

But, he just shrugged his rumpled shoulders and said, "Don't talk to me. Ask him about it." The detective got in his car and started the engine, leaving me in disbelief.

I fumed at the gall of that man as I hurried to my car. My heart was still racing as I arrived at my shop.

Although I was pretty sure Larry was long gone, I slowly opened my door, half expecting to see the place ransacked, but everything was in order. I saw Zia's black figure lying still in her yellow bed.

I slapped my hand over my mouth and practically tripped over my own feet in a desperate attempt to get to her. Was she breathing? I cautiously put my hand on her tiny body and she looked up at me and yawned. Whew! I was so relieved I made the sign of the cross again, this time in thanks.

I scooped the pup up in my arms and said, "What in the world happened, Zia? Did a mean man come in the store?" I checked her little body over, happy that she seemed to be unharmed. "I sure wish you could explain that crazy scene to me."

I sat on my tractor seat cradling the dog like a baby. Why had Larry been here? What was he looking for? Was he involved in the murder? I mean, he was the reason there were no lights by my building. Could that have been on purpose? He certainly had access to my shop and could have erased the video as Jill had suggested. Come to think of it, hadn't he walked in while we were watching it? And…he sure did seem to think the murder's publicity would be good for business.

My list of suspects was growing; Flick, Carl, and now Larry. But with Victoria's implication of taking out the old antique, I had to add Victoria and Jett.

My blood boiled the more I thought about Larry snooping in my shop and touching my dog. I got the courage to confront the creep at his little hole of an office. I opened my door only to find Jill standing on my porch, reaching for the door handle.

"Jill! What are you doing here?"

She rolled her blue eyes and said, "Dad won't let me work anymore. The baby's room is ready and I'm bored sick. Kelly had to work. He said I should come to help you, as long as I don't do anything strenuous or spill wine on anyone." She covered her eyes in mock embarrassment. "Can you believe I did that last night?"

"Kind of," I said and hugged my huge friend. She entered the shop and made herself at home on the Ford car seat bench that she had claimed as her own. I was about to tell her my horror story, but she interrupted my thoughts.

"I've had a stomachache all morning. Got anything to eat?"

"Just Goldfish and grapes." This girl was always hungry. I went to my little pantry and grabbed a box of the fish-shaped crackers and a bag of grapes and handed them to her along with a napkin.

With a mouth full of grapes, she asked, "So, was the funeral really sad?"

"Yes. So sad. The stories told made Pops sound like a great guy." With much more animation, I said, "But, guess what?" I shook my head, still shocked at what had just happened. Squinting in interest, she popped some goldfish in her mouth.

"While I was there, I caught my first and hopefully last intruder on film with the camera you gave me.

She spit orange cracker crumbs all over the floor in surprise. "What?"

I pulled up the video which was saved automatically in the cloud for 24 hours. I handed her my phone and told her about the incident while she watched.

Her mouth dropped open. "Larry! I knew he was a jerk." She switched into her baby voice as she watched. "Oh my! Zia! Look at you fly!" Jill picked up the dog and snuggled her, saying, "You have some tough teeth, girlie. I'm sure glad you weren't hurt with that acrobatic act of yours." She snuggled the dog to her chin. "Aren't you just the cutest guard dog ever?"

Looking up at me, Jill asked, "Hey, Maria, you should send me that video, in case you need it later and it mysteriously disappears."

"Good idea."

She clicked some buttons on my phone as I watched over her shoulder. "You can save the day brief on your phone by clicking this down arrow. I know because we have one and some of the clips of our animals are hilarious."

"I'll bet. Thanks." I shook my head. "I still find it hard to believe Alex Chandler is friends with this Larry." I took my phone from Jill and sat back on my stool.

"I know. Are you going to call the police about him being in your shop?"

I made a face at my friend, "Been there done that with little response. I'm going to confront Larry myself in a minute. I was heading there when you showed up."

"Want me to go as your back-up?"

I thought about this. But, in case the confrontation escalated, I wouldn't want to get Jill involved and said, "Nah, that's OK. I'll go after a while."

"I'm sorry but do you have something to drink? This is a great snack, but you know crackers. Now I'm thirsty." Her pathetic pout was unbelievable.

"Gee, you sure are needy today," I said, kidding, and went back to my fridge for a bottle of Yerba Mate tea. When I came back, Jill stood staring at the floor where a puddle had formed by her flip flops.

"Did you just pee on my floor?" Then my eyes widened, "Is that? Your water broke?"

Jill held her stomach and winced, apparently in extreme pain. I ran and got a towel.

The poor girl fanned herself and sighed as the pain subsided. She took a few big breaths. "Holy Moly! That hurt. Guess I should start counting between contractions."

She pulled off her wet underwear from beneath her skirt and dried herself off and immediately doubled over again in pain.

I watched my friend with worry and said, "That was quick," When she relaxed again, I made her lie down on the short, cushioned car bench then grabbed a pillow from a basket and put it under her head.

"I'm sorry, Maria," she said. Then her face wrenched in agony.

I said, "Sorry? It's ok, silly girl." I kissed the top of her head and said, "I'll call 9-1-1 to see if I should take you to the hospital." I made my plan aloud. "Then, I'll call Kelly and your doctor. Everything is going to be fine." I sure hoped this was true.

I fumbled for my phone, dialed the emergency number, and said as calmly as I could, "My friend's water just broke. Should I drive her to the hospital?" I listened as I watched Jill contort her face in pain. "Her contractions? They seem practically constant."

The dispatcher said, "Better not move her. I'll send an ambulance. Make her as comfortable as you can and don't panic."

I gave the address and hung up just as Jill made a loud grunt. When I called Kelly, he said he was across town, but would come immediately and would call the doctor as he drove.

I took a deep breath and tried to soothe Jill by talking to her, but the pain was so intense she didn't want to hear anything. Not being well versed in midwifery, I felt helpless and started to tear up, then remembered Joey may be at his pub. He had more medical training than I did so I called him.

I moved behind my curtain so she didn't hear me. "Joey, it's Maria. Can you come over right now? Jill's in labor in my shop. I've called her husband and also 9-1-1, but everything seems to be moving so fast. I'm kind of worried."

He waited for a beat then responded, "Sure. I'll do what I can."

I wet a paper towel from the bathroom sink and wiped Jill's forehead as we waited through her agony. Zia jumped up to see what was going on. I couldn't handle her at this point and said a little too gruffly, "Zia, go to your bed."

My little girl toddled over to her yellow bed and climbed in obediently. I sat by Jill and held her hand through some super strong contractions. She said, "Just take me to the hospital."

"I'm sorry, but they said not to move you. I called Joey and he's coming to help."

Between puffs of air, Jill said, "What does a brewery owner know about labor pains?"

"I don't know. He seems to know stuff?" I felt so stupid for calling him but didn't have any other options.

With her typical sense of humor, Jill said, "Well, he is handsome. Maybe he'll distract me from this." Her face tightened and turned red.

Just then, Joey rushed through the door carrying assorted supplies in a bag. He assessed the situation and said, "She needs to be on the floor, so nobody falls from the bench. Do you have towels or blankets to lay down?"

I ran to my display of quilts, thinking about the word "nobody". Oh my. It wasn't only Jill we needed to worry about, but the baby. Joey calmly said, "Jill, don't forget to breathe."

With a grimace, she panted. After scooting a few baskets out of the way to make room, I lay the quilt made from jeans on the floor to cover up the goldfish crackers she had spit and anything else unsanitary. Then I lay a quilt made of sweaters and finally the t-shirt quilt on top since it was the softest. Joey and I helped Jill to the new semi-padded area and placed a pillow under her head.

She continued with pants mixed with screams - all of which made me nervous. Where was that ambulance?

"Nobody said it would hurt this much," Jill said mid-groan. I worried that something was wrong and wiped her brow as Joey looked under her skirt.

"Looks like someone is ready to come out. The head is already crowning."

Astonished, I asked, "Is childbirth supposed to be this quick? Her water just broke like ten minutes ago." I was baffled by the whole thing.

Joey, careful not to upset the mother-to-be, said, "I've heard of this happening. I can't remember the name, but it's a thing." He put on gloves and in a few seconds brightened as he remembered the name. "Oh yeah. It's called precipitate delivery. It's not common, but sometimes babies just pop out."

How in the world did he know that? I stared at him with a little more confidence. At any rate, he knew more than I did about labor.

Jill cried out, "No! Kelly has to be here when Sophia arrives."

Just then, as if summoned out of her anguish, Kelly rushed through the door wearing his police uniform. He ran to Jill, kneeled beside her, and said, "Are you OK?" He took her hands in his.

Jill's face relaxed when he arrived. She answered him with a pouty lip, but within seconds she screamed again.

Kelly looked terrified at the change in his wife, and his face turned as white as hers.

Joey said to the very soon-to-be father, "I think everything is OK." He looked at me and gave an 'I sure hope I didn't lie' shrug.

Kelly turned to me and asked, "Where's the ambulance?"

I shrugged. "We called a while ago. I'll call again." I gave my spot to Kelly and stepped away, to redial 9-1-1.

Kelly leaned over Jill and cooed, "I'm here now Bumblebee. Squeeze my hand as hard as you want and focus just like we learned in birthing classes. Looks like it's showtime."

I reveled in his sweet demeanor and take-charge attitude. He was just what Jill needed.

When the dispatcher answered, I said, "I called for an ambulance to come to 555 Franco Street and it's not here yet. Can you tell them to hurry?"

The dispatcher said, "They are on their way." I hung up and repeated the news.

Kelly said calmly to Jill. "I called Dr. Brown and he'll meet us at the hospital.".

Joey took a deep breath and said to Kelly, "I know it seems scary, but she's going to have the baby here and now." He turned to me with sweat on his brow. "Maria, can you get more clean towels, blankets, and lots of paper towels? We need anything you can get your hands on."

I ran to get what I could and handed them to him without stepping on the quilt, then steadied myself against the counter and watched the incredible scene. My best friend was delivering a baby on my floor. Her loving husband was by her side and my crush was playing doctor. How surreal.

CHAPTER 15

Jill screamed, "I have to push."

Joey said gently, "If you feel the urge, do it." He sat between her legs; hands splayed as if ready to catch a football. Her face reddened as she bore down.

Jill stopped pushing to catch her breath. Kelly kissed her on the head and held her hand as she took another deep breath. This time, she pushed as hard as she could. The pained expressions on both mom and dad-to-be were hard to watch. For the third time that day, I gave the sign of the cross. Not a devout Catholic, but with so much happening, I felt comforted by the motion. After the exertion, Jill stopped again, apparently exhausted.

"That's it!" Joey didn't take his eyes off the baby's head and said encouragingly, "She's almost here. Push again."

"I can't," she said, tears streaming down her face.

Knowing Jill's predisposition to quit anything she deemed difficult, Kelly encouraged her. "You're doing great, Jilly! Our sweet Sophia is just about here."

She took a few more deep breaths, and let out a primal sound as she pushed again. From my angle, I saw a small round head, full of wet dark hair, emerge. I was in awe. Joey placed his gloved hand under the baby's head. I didn't know how he knew what to do, but he carefully stroked downwards on the tiny nose and mouth, wiping away fluid from the airway. It was the most amazing thing I'd ever witnessed.

Jill panted out of pure exhaustion.

Joey said with a relieved smile, "Jill, you did it. You've done the hardest part. Believe me. One more push and she's all yours."

Kelly held both of her hands as she gave one final push.

The tiny, beautiful, Sophia slid right out and into Joey's large hands. It was amazing. Jill's looked as if she'd run a marathon. Her hair was wet and she was out of breath.

Joey said, "She's beautiful." He turned the baby over and massaged the tiny back.

Jill croaked in a hoarse voice, "Let me see her."

Kelly helped lift Jill's head, so she could see their baby. Joey held the newest Standing Bear up slightly for the new parents to see. Both of them sobbed, unable to contain their emotions at the miracle.

What a beautiful sight. I wiped my face and realized I too was crying with happiness. I wanted to revel in the joyous event but remembered Jill wanted the birth recorded. How did I forget to document this momentous occasion? I grabbed my phone and took a few shots of the new parents getting their first looks at her, then some of Joey drying Sophia with a soft towel. I moved around and got some close-up shots of the tiny newcomer, still attached to her mother by the umbilical cord.

I studied the baby through my lens, blurry as it was, with my tears. She had her father's dark hair and her mother's fair skin. I wondered if she would have Jill's green eyes, but when I got closer to the baby, I saw her dark curious eyes soaking up her new surroundings. Amazing. What a blessing to experience someone's first moments in life. She made a tiny cry, like a weak kitten mewing.

Jill said with a cry/laugh, "Listen! She's so sweet and quiet."

Kelly said with a chuckle, "If she is anything like you, she'll be working those lungs and vocal cords soon."

Joey's voice cracked when he said, "I'll let the EMTs cut the cord."

"If they ever show up," I said. What in the world was taking them so long? From my observation, everything looked fine, but it would be nice to have confirmation from professionals.

Joey said, "Kelly, can you lift Jill's top so I can lay the baby on her stomach?"

He did so, and soon the baby lay on her mother, skin to skin.

Jill looked into the tiny face and said, "There you are, Sophia. I've been waiting to meet you, little pumpkin." This choked me up even more.

I took a few more photos of Jill and Kelly as they watched their beautiful dark-haired baby.

Joey covered mom and baby with one of my embroidered cotton blankets, giving the scene a vintage feel, and I snapped more photos.

A siren wailed causing us all to laugh at the irony. When the ambulance finally arrived, I ran to the door for the paramedics.

Jill croaked to the first one to reach her, "Did you take the scenic route around the mountain?"

The tall man, wearing all white, shrugged, "Not on purpose. Somehow, we got the wrong address and ended up in the Northeast Heights." He shook his head as he looked her over. "I'm so sorry."

Well, at least that explained it. At any rate, I was sure thankful that Dr. Joey had been available. I leaned over Jill and said, "I'm sure I gave the right address."

"Maria, I know. That's a mistake I would make — not you. Thankfully, you called the beermaker, or I'm not sure what would have happened."

That thought scared me. "No joke. I don't know how he knew what to do."

Within moments, the calm atmosphere was energized with paramedics cutting the umbilical cord and taking the blood pressure of two special people. I was relieved when both baby and mother were deemed healthy.

I leaned in to Jill and whispered, "I'm so proud of you."

She gave a relieved smile. "Thanks, Maria. I did it!"

"Yes, you did and she's perfect. Do you need anything?"

"I have to call Mom. Can you get my phone?"

I was glad she felt good enough to make a call. When I got her phone from her purse, I airdropped the photos to her phone.

As I stood watching Jill's animated description of the birth on the phone, Kelly handed the tightly wrapped bundle to me. I felt the warmth of Sophia's small body through the thin cotton blanket. She was so sweet and tiny but had the longest dark eyelashes I'd ever seen. Ha! Jill would be thrilled and probably jealous of that.

I said softly to the sleeping baby, "Hello, Miss Sophia. I'm your Aunt Maria." Her eyes opened and locked onto mine. I felt an instant connection with the little one and kissed her soft cheek.

After a beat, I looked up and said, "She's amazing, Kelly." I handed her back to the dad who couldn't control his smile.

While Jill was moved onto a stretcher, Joey talked to the EMT and Kelly stood mesmerized by the new baby in his arms. I carried Zia over to my bestie, "You've always wanted to ride in an ambulance, so you can check that off your list tonight."

She gave a relaxed smile, apparently in no pain at all anymore, and said, "And having a baby in a store was another big goal of mine. Thanks for letting me use your shop as my delivery room."

I laughed and waved my hand at her, "Eh...No problem. Anytime!"

"Nope. Never again. If I have anything to say about it, Sophia will be our final offspring. That hurt like Hell."

I knew she wasn't lying about the pain but highly doubted this would be the last Standing Bear to join their family. Jill always planned to have a full house like she did while growing up.

She added, "Please tell your boyfriend thank you for saving the day."

"First of all, he's not my boyfriend and second of all he's not my boyfriend. And he's right there. You tell him.".

Jill smiled, "He seems like a keeper." She winked. "You better come see us in the hospital as soon as you can."

I leaned down to kiss Jill's forehead just as the paramedic pushed her away and said, "I'll be there tonight."

I wiped a happy tear from my cheek as the new family left. It was the second time in a week Joey and I watched an ambulance leave my shop. This time was much better than the last.

He said, "That was amazing." Without thinking, I turned and collapsed in his arms, being careful not to squish the dog I held. At that moment, I didn't care if Joey did have a girlfriend. I just needed to hug him for all he did. Plus, I was exhausted. He hugged me back, then took my hand and led me to the steps of my shop where we sat in silence.

After a few moments, I asked, "How did you know how to deliver a baby?" I looked up at his beautiful turquoise eyes and saw that they looked tired. "Had you done that before?"

He shrugged. 'Yes, twice, but under different circumstances and in a hospital with all the modern equipment. This was much more stressful." He sighed. "I'm so glad everything went well."

I questioned him with my eyes. He cleared his throat when he realized I needed the rest of the story. He looked at me. "I planned to become a doctor and spent four years in med school."

I was shocked. "Really?" I wondered what could have happened to change his path from becoming a doctor to making beer. "Why did you stop?"

He rubbed his forehead. "It was purely selfish. I mean the job itself was awesome and I felt I could do well in the medical field. The problem for me was that being a doctor is such a demanding profession. So many of the surgeons had no life outside of the hospital and got burnt out quickly. I was young and wanted to explore the real world rather than be tied to a sterile environment, so I quit before my residency."

I was blown away at the thought he gave all that up, but said, "I'm glad you got to use some of your education here today."

He shook his head, "Yeah, on days like this, I regret my decision. I mean, I could have made a difference in people's lives."

His eyes were fixed on something beyond me. Joey was a really good man. No doubt about it. I grabbed his arm and hugged it. "You sure did today."

He leaned his head on mine and I felt a sense of comfort I hadn't had for a long time. "By the way, Jill told me to thank you."

He scoffed. "Yeah, she told me. I was just worried I'd drop the slippery baby."

I had to laugh at that, but he was probably serious. "Speaking of which, I've got some cleaning up to do before tomorrow morning." I stood, took his hands, and helped him up from the low steps. "Thanks so much for being here, Joey. I could not have handled that alone."

"Oh, I think you could." His blue eyes pierced through me, "I mean...anyone who can do a disappearing act after practically tipping a table over, can do anything."

My face immediately turned red. "You saw that?"

"Uh-huh." He nodded. "Hard to miss." He stifled a laugh, then became serious. "I also saw that you were the most beautiful woman in the entire room."

As much as I wanted to kiss him for saying that, the moment felt awkward. Was the girl at the gala his date or just a friend? Why couldn't I just ask him? But no, I fell into my regular habit of fleeing when faced with uncomfortable relationship moments. I stuttered, "umm…thanks?" I gave a quick smile and kissed him on the cheek then said, "Good luck on opening day tomorrow." I went inside.

Just before I shut the door, I looked back at Joey. He wore a slight frown and his eyes were downturned. I hated to see the dejection on his sweet face, but I was confused and tired. Why didn't I just ask him about the girl?

After putting the towels and quilts in large trash bags to wash at home, I mopped the floor and scrubbed the bench. I'm so glad I didn't have carpet. That would have been worse.

I shuddered, realizing Jill's water could actually have broken last night at the fancy hotel. I sat on the clean bench and sighed. At least we dodged that bullet and didn't owe Alex Chandler a cleaning fee, but I cringed remembering the lady's yellow dress.

Chandler…Invitation…Larry! Since we had an impromptu baby delivery, I hadn't confronted the creepy landlord. I got my mojo back and locked my door. Zia toddled alongside me as I marched to Larry's office, situated just behind the center's community restrooms. I knocked hard, but there was no answer, so I knocked again. I looked up his number on my phone and called but got no answer there either. Frustrated, I picked up Zia and started back across the parking lot.

I heard a car behind me and moved to the side, glancing over my shoulder to watch it pass, but the engine roared, causing me to scoot further to the right. The driver accelerated far too quickly to be safe in a parking lot. Rather than zipping past me, the gray sedan swerved towards me! Blood rushed in my ears. Terrified, I jumped onto the steps of the coffee shop, clutching Zia to my chest as she squirmed, probably scared too. Just as the car was about to clip the steps, it veered back to center and sped past the bakery.

I swayed on the spot, adrenaline pumping. What had just happened? Was that deliberate? I was furious and wished I'd seen the license plate, but the only way out of the shopping center was behind me—so the car would have to circle around to exit. I sprinted after the car, hoping to see the tag number. When I rounded the corner, I found the plain gray car parked at the antique store with the driver still inside. How odd that someone involved in a near hit and run would just park. Maybe the driver experienced a medical episode that caused the car to swerve towards me.

I stormed over to the vehicle, ready to either help the injured person or kick some butt, depending on the scenario. I knocked on the tinted window. When the door started to open, a rush of dread ran over me and I regretted my action since it could easily be a madman. I stepped back, hoping the maniac didn't have a gun.

I shook my head in disbelief when I saw familiar strings of long greasy hair. Carl emerged and straightened slightly. A quick glance at his hands confirmed that they were devoid of guns.

"Carl! What in the world were you doing? Were you trying to kill me with your car?"

I waited for a response, getting more exasperated by the second. Thankfully, he answered before I had time to put my hands around his neck.

"I wasn't going to hurt y y you. I just wanted to sc scare you." He looked as if he would start crying. "It's your fault that m m my uncle died."

Again, with the accusation. I threw my hands in the air. "How? I need to know why you keep blaming me." I burned with outrage and my voice rose in pitch and volume, sounding frantic.

Carl pushed his greasy hair out of his face and said with spittle coming out of his mouth, "M m my dad and P P P Pops were fighting about some b b books that Pops sold."

OK, so just as I thought, the brothers had been fighting about the books.

He took a shaky breath and continued, "Then, I saw y y you with the b b books. If y y you hadn't b b b bought them, h h he would still be alive!" His red eyes connected with mine for a beat then flicked away.

I didn't know what to say. My blood pressure modulated from the terror of being nearly killed to anger, to anxiety over being accused of someone's death. Although Carl's reasoning for me being at fault didn't make sense, I tried to formulate questions for the childlike man. I took a breath and asked in a calmer tone, "Do you know why your dad was upset about Pops selling the books?"

He shook his head, which was again facing the ground. Eye contact was apparently difficult for him. The guy truly looked distraught. I tried to think of how to ask the other bigger question and just came out with it, "Carl, do you think Flick, I mean your dad, was angry enough to hurt Pops?"

He shrugged, then wobbled his head, which could have been either an affirmative or negative gesture. "B b but *you* made them fight." He held balled fists by his sides, still agitated.

Although I felt slightly calmer myself, I needed to make him understand I had nothing to do with his uncle's death. I dipped my head down to look into his eyes, used my hands to help get the point across, and explained in a calm but pleading voice, "Carl, I didn't know Pops wasn't supposed to sell the books. And I doubt he knew either. Please don't blame me. Besides, I don't even know where the books are now. Do you understand?"

He blinked, looking slightly confused, and nodded.

I sighed, hoping I'd cleared up any misunderstanding and added, "Do you know where the books are now?"

His gaze fixed on his hand as he considered the question, then with a shake of his greasy head, he said, "The nice detective already asked m m me about them."

'Nice' detective? That's what Milly had called him. Was I living in an alternate universe where Barnes was only offensive to me? And furthermore, why did the sergeant ask about books that he didn't believe existed?

I shook off that thought and asked, "Carl, did you happen to hear or see anything the night you…" I was careful not to say anything to upset him further, "um…found your uncle?"

Tears started to well up in his eyes and he said, "I m m m miss my Pops."

I sighed, realizing I was getting nowhere. Carl probably wouldn't answer, but surprisingly, he spoke up. With his typical detached words, he said with a scratchy voice, "I dumped the trash from the antique store and found Pops. I tried to move him to the antique store, b b b but I hid when I s s s saw you coming"

So that's how the body got moved. "Why did you hide?"

He shook a little, then answered, "I didn't want to get in trouble with J J Joey."

I wondered why he worried about that but remembered he had just been fired and was probably still upset from that confrontation. I nodded. "Did you see anyone else while you were there?"

Silently, he shook his head.

Call it a hunch, but from his attitude, I believed him. He had simply taken out the trash and wasn't involved in his uncle's death.

However, he had nearly run me down and I needed to address that. Flick's car was parked on the other side of the store and so I said, "We need to talk to your dad about what you did with your car."

His face sank as if he was going to get a spanking, but I couldn't just let the horrific incident slide. He followed me as I stepped up to the antique store and knocked.

A gravelly voice bellowed, "Come in!"

Carl followed Me into the musty, dim store.

The old man sat at his desk in the back. Sunlight from the open door glinted off something long and metal he held in his hand. A shiver ran down my spine. Was it a knife? I opted to leave the door open in case a quick escape was warranted. As I slowly neared Flick, I saw the item shiny was actually a screwdriver. When I noticed an old clock in his other hand, my shoulders relaxed a bit.

I repositioned Zia in my arms and said confidently, "Hello Mr. Harrison, I'm Maria from across the way?"

If I'd expected him to stand, nod, smile, or even look up, I would have been very disappointed. When he eventually lifted his head and looked at me, he showed no hint of recognition. He said in an eerie flat tone, "What do you want?" He went back to working on the clock.

How should I tell him that his youngest son had almost killed me? I took a deep breath and started. "I thought you should know that a few minutes ago, I was walking across the parking lot and your son, Carl, drove so recklessly he almost hit me with his car."

"Nope. Not my boy."

Other than his lips moving slightly, this statement came with no other facial change. I might expect a father to defend his kid, but a complete denial was weird. Weirder yet, he didn't even look up at us.

With even more force, I said, "Um…Actually, it *is* true, Sir. I was shaken." My voice began to rise again. "Carl even admitted to me that he tried to frighten me. I could have been killed."

Flick kept working on his clock. I turned to Carl. "Please tell your father what you did."

Unbelievably, Carl cleared his throat and said with a little wobble in his voice, "I was mad at her and I wanted to scare her."

Flick's eyes slowly lifted from his work to his son. He put down the clock but continued to hold the long screwdriver as he pushed himself up from the table to a standing position.

I suddenly regretted entering the shop at all. The fear of being hit by the car was one thing, but this man terrified me. I stepped back, pushing Carl with me, not knowing what the old man might do.

With a red face, he shouted, "Leave us!"

I wasn't about to leave Carl alone with this madman. It seemed crazy that ten minutes earlier, it was Carl who was the madman. I squared my shoulders and said, "No, sir. I won't leave him here alone with you in this state."

Flick's white eyebrows moved together, nearly touching as he squinted at me. Was I now the new target of his ire?

"Then, both of you leave. Now!"

I jumped at his bark but at least felt reassured for the moment that he wouldn't harm either of us. I turned, grabbing Carl's arm and headed for the exit.

Once outside, the heat of the sunshine felt like a warm rush of relief on my skin. Flick was a horrible man. Nothing I'd seen of him could change that impression. I turned and studied the impassive face of the strange guy standing on the porch. Wasn't he rattled by Flick's eruption?

"Carl, does your father scare you as he does me?"

He shrugged slowly. "Sometimes."

How odd that I now commiserated with this former suspect. Had the world turned upside down?

Suddenly, I was exhausted. "You know, Carl, I'm still shaken from what you did, and now by your father's outburst…" I didn't know what else to say and just let the statement dissipate.

In an unprecedented action, Carl patted my shoulder awkwardly and said, "I'm sorry I scared you." Then he put his arms down by his side.

I took a big breath, feeling oddly comforted by his statement. "Thanks, Carl." The guy was probably 10 years older than me but he seemed little more than an overgrown boy. I felt sorry for him and asked, "Do you live with your father?"

His hair covered his eyes as he nodded.

"Could you go stay with your Aunt Milly tonight?... Just until your dad calms down?"

He looked at the sky, considering the question, and nodded again.

"I think that might be best. Look, I have to go now. Take care of yourself and don't EVER EVER scare someone like that again."

CHAPTER 16

I walked to my shop after the unsettling experience with Carl and Flick. Zia didn't seem upset at all, prancing along beside me.

I edited my list of suspects on my phone while the dog did her long-awaited business by my building. The first change I made was to delete Carl's name. He had a temper for sure but didn't seem like he would hurt his beloved uncle. Flick and Larry were moved to the top spots. Was there a connection between the two? I'd have to figure that out without asking the old man.

As I put my key in my door, I heard laughing coming from the brewery and looked up to see the same pretty woman from the gala, climbing the steps to greet Joey in a hug. As they entered the pub, disappointment again washed over me.

In an exhausted and confused state, I made sure my shop was back in order after the surprise birth. Then, Zia accompanied me home, where I left her to go visit the new family.

Jill's colorful hospital room was brightly lit. The windowsill was already filled with flowers and balloons and the bed was covered with a bright handmade quilt. She sat up in bed holding her baby with Kelly standing beside her. I stood in the doorway watching the natural scene, then said, "Is there anything sweeter than this?" I gave Kelly a hug and leaned over to kiss mom and baby. "Sorry I'm so late. I've had a very eventful day."

Jill said, "It's about time you showed up." With a wink, she held Sophia out to me and I carefully took the tiny bundle in my arms, amazed by the fact that a human could be so small. I gently eased myself down in the blue vinyl armchair next to the bed and breathed in the sweet baby powder scent as I studied the tiny face with wonder.

Sophia's shock of hair, which had looked so dark at birth, was now clean and dry and shimmered with a reddish tint under the bright lights. I smiled that Jill's Irish heritage was alive in this new generation, but the baby's smooth, lightly tanned skin was obviously sun-kissed by the Standing Bear genes. Wrapped tightly like a cocoon, I couldn't see her arms or fingers, but what was visible was perfect. I willed her to open her eyes again, but she was out cold.

After being mesmerized by the teensy sleeping baby for who knows how long, I heard Jill say, "I think she's sleeping."

Without looking up, I answered with a smile, "Oh, she is, just like a baby should be."

Jill chuckled. "I meant you, Maria. Sitting so still and quiet, I hardly recognize you."

"But, she's just so beautiful. Look at that tiny nose. I can't stop staring."

"Well, you'll have to, because the nurse kinda needs to take her for screenings."

I looked up. Sure enough, a tall woman dressed in white stood at the foot of the bed tapping her white Sketchers. She reached out and snatched the baby from my arms. The nurse swept her out of the room as if it was an emergency.

Still stunned by the quick disappearing act, I said, "Gee, that lady means business."

Jill nodded. "Yep. There's no wasting time in here. Maria, I still can't believe I had my baby in your shop. I hope you can clean everything up before your big day tomorrow," she said, with a slight frown.

Tomorrow. Hearing the word hit me pretty hard. My shop was opening in 13 hours! My to-do list whirred in my head, but I snapped back to answer her question. "I already took care of it. Just have to do a few loads of laundry tonight, but it's all good." I looked at her bedside table where a tray of food lay. Not a crumb was left. "So, are they taking good care of you here?".

"Yeah. They are sure feeding me well. By the way, I think we saved a lot of money by having her at your place. Well…except for the cost of the ambulance."

Kelly said, "But, it was worth it. I would have been a wreck taking you to the hospital."

I nodded. "Oh, you have to hear what happened after you guys left."

She sat up taller in her bed. "Did you ask Larry why he was in your shop?"

"No. But, I almost got hit by a car…on purpose."

Both sets of eyes were wide as I started to tell my friends the story of Carl. Kelly wore a concerned policeman face, then said, "You should file a report, Maria. That's not normal."

"I don't know. I think he was just confused."

Kelly said, "And even after that experience, you don't think he had anything to do with the murder?

"Either Carl is innocent or the best actor I've ever seen, and I highly doubt that. But Flick frightened me more than the car scare. He's awful. And, my sights are also set on Larry, the trespasser."

After a few minutes, I excused myself so we could all get some sleep, but promised to see them again the next night. Jill said with a twinkle, "You need to go relax in front of your TV." She winked.

That was a weird statement to wink about. Once home, I did turn on the TV and listened while washing and drying my prized quilts on gentle cycles. I felt a little bad about trying to sell the quilts since they were used in the delivery. But I knew they would be as good as before when clean. And it wasn't as if someone had died on them. That thought made me cringe.

When I finally collapsed in exhaustion after a full, crazy day, Zia licked my face relentlessly. She was apparently glad to have me home to pay attention to her. I tightened her body under my arm so her tongue couldn't reach my chin and within seconds she was so still I had to look to see if I'd squeezed her to death. But her sweet black eyes stared adoringly into mine. She seemed very comfortable in the confined space.

At the end of the news, the anchor started her "Heartwarming Moments" segment. It's usually an uplifting story, so I paid attention, hoping for something sweet to send me off to sleep. Suddenly, a photo of the exterior of my shop appeared on the screen causing me to sit up straight. The woman said, "Just days ago, a murder took place outside this quaint shop in the new Out of the Box shopping center."

That didn't seem heartwarming at all and I heckled the TV, "Just keep rubbing it in, lady. And why did you show my place?"

The reporter continued, "But today, the tables quickly turned as this "Upcycled" shop, filled with repurposed items and owned by Maria Olson, was christened with an emergency birth."

The picture changed from the front of my shop to an inside shot of Jill on my floor, holding the baby with Kelly looking over her shoulder. I stood up and stared at the photo.

"Maria's best friend, Jill Standing Bear, was visiting and went into labor. With no time to get to the hospital, the baby was born on the floor, amid handmade quilts and pillows. The unsuspecting "doctor" was the co-owner of the newest brewpub in town, The Rusty Railroad Brewery, located only steps away from Upcycled."

To my surprise, they showed a photo of Joey holding up the baby, then one of the parents holding Sophia. All were photos I had taken. I just couldn't believe this.

The newswoman continued, "Although Upcycled doesn't open until tomorrow, I believe Ms. Olson had her best day of the year with the arrival of her new Godchild."

The last photo was of me kissing the baby on the cheek. I didn't even know that photo was taken. Tears of joy came to my eyes as the title sunk in. Godchild?

That Jill! She must have sent the pictures and shared the story to Channel 4 all from her room in the hospital. That's why she told me to watch TV tonight. I shook my head in wonder.

The woman said, "The new, greatly anticipated Out of the Box shopping center opens tomorrow..." The anchor went on to tell the hours of operation, the address, and named all the businesses in our center. She ended with a wink. "I hear they may have some Grand Opening sales too."

I grinned uncontrollably, amazed that my best friend had thought of this incredible publicity stunt for our shopping center.

Before going to sleep, I texted Jill with, "Godchild?" followed by a whole row of hearts.

The big day arrived with no clouds in the sky and the air was crisp and clean. It was a great day to open my store. After letting the dog out, I snacked on my last piece of cinnamon bread and flipped through my boring mail. Suddenly, I heard a horrible screeching sound. What in the world? I jumped up as the sound came again. It came from my courtyard. I raced out the door praying Zia wasn't being attacked by a coyote. When I rounded the corner, my little dog stood there so low to the ground, looking up at the wall. The sound coming out of her tiny mouth was hideous, but she didn't look hurt. I followed her glare and saw a quizzical roadrunner blinking his eyes at us.

"Zia, stop that annoying noise. It's just my friend, Rudy."

She made a little growl, more ferocious than I imagined could come from the tiny dog. I lifted her up so she could see Rudy better. "See, it's just a bird." She sniffed and snorted, then lost interest once she saw what it was. How in the world did she not know a roadrunner? Maybe she had come from some other part of the country where the big birds didn't stop by regularly.

After feeding Rudy his breakfast on the wall, I gathered my stuff, got in the car, and said, "You have a very loud and obnoxious bark if that's what that noise was."

I drove to the shop in nervous anticipation, glancing across the parking lot to make sure Flick wasn't there. I found a note on my door ordering me to meet in the parking lot with the rest of the shop owners at 8:15. It was signed, 'Louise'. Although I was glad she had left the reminder, I was a bit worried that if I didn't stay in my shop, I wouldn't be ready to open in time.

I quickly put the newly cleaned quilts and pillows in their spots and remembered I still hadn't gotten a receipt book. Oh well, I would just write receipts for purchases by cash or check on notebook paper if need be. It was entirely possible that I wouldn't sell anything anyway. *Calm down. Calm down.*

I sighed while looking around the place, pleased that it looked pretty good. Just as I closed my eyes and took in a deep breath to compose myself, I heard voices outside. I opened the door and walked across the parking lot to join the quirky but familiar group.

Louise, bedazzled as usual, stood front and center holding a bag with a comical drawing of her face printed on the side. She barked, "Can I have everyone's attention?" as if she was addressing a crowd of a hundred rather than the six of us present.

She walked around the group and handed each of us a book, then pinned a button on our shirts. I smiled when I recognized the familiar paperback as a copy of the first mystery in the Boxcar Children series. I had loved these books as a child. I looked down at the button and read upside down, The Boxcar Adults.

With a wave of her hands, Louise announced loudly, "I hereby dub us, 'The Boxcar Adults'. You are part of an elite club that begins today."

We smiled and gave an animated but silly cheer. She continued. "May we all be as productive as Maria was yesterday." Louise gave a comical wink.

The group chuckled as they looked at me. Joey smirked but didn't look my way. Victoria, who didn't pay attention to anyone but Jett, cooed something in his ear. He turned his head the other way in an obvious attempt to ignore her.

In a childish fit, Victoria took off the button, and threw it along with the book on the ground before stomping off to her shop. The bakery boys' eyes widened at me and we all shrugged. She probably wasn't familiar with the book or more likely was just rude.

Louise said, "Looks like the barista hasn't had her coffee yet."

The remaining group snickered at the quip and made small talk. As the group dispersed, I picked up Victoria's book from the ground and handed it to Louise. "Thanks so much. What an adorable idea. I hope you sell a ton of books today."

"We'll find out in about twenty minutes when the gate to the parking lot opens. Good luck to you too, darlin.'" She straightened her Boxcar Adult button. I wondered if anyone would even see the pin amid all the sequins on her star-spangled shirt.

I took a big breath and walked across the lot to my shop. I set out the large placard that read; 'Making marvelous out of the discarded,' and placed it outside my door.

At promptly nine o'clock, I heard the rumble of a train. But, when I looked out my window, the noise turned out to be a stream of cars entering the parking lot. Oh my! What would I do with an actual crowd? Without counting Zia, I was the only one on duty in my store. I was so nervous that I actually wrung my hands in anticipation.

Within seconds, my new xylophone chime jingled. In walked two women, one older and one younger.

I took a big breath and said, "Welcome to Upcycled!" with what I hoped to be a pleasant, but not pushy tone.

The younger woman said with a big grin, "Is this where the baby was born yesterday?"

I was taken aback, but answered while nodding to the side, "Yes, right there on the floor."

"Oh my, how exciting." The ladies walked around and made flattering comments about my products as a few other people arrived. Within moments, the tiny shop was filled with shoppers. The first woman came up and asked, "Is this the quilt the baby was born on? I think I saw it on TV."

I hesitated, worrying that it would turn her off if I admitted it, but said, "Yes?" Then I quickly added, "But, of course, it's been laundered."

I hoped she wouldn't tell me how rude I was to try to sell it, but instead, she said, "I have to buy it for my daughter. We just found out she's expecting. I think it will bring her good luck."

Baffled, but pleased, I rang up the purchase on my antique register, wrote out a receipt on a sheet of notebook paper, and folded the quilt. "I'm sorry I don't have bags yet. Will you be OK carrying it like this?"

"Sure. Then I can show off that I got the quilt that was featured on the news last night."

OK. That was weird, but a sale was a sale. Within 30 minutes, I had sold earrings, two teapot sewing kits, some shelves, and even a globe lamp.

A young girl, probably in her twenties, walked up to me and said, "Do the wine bottles outside actually work in watering the plants? I'm just terrible at remembering to water. And can you use them inside or just outside?"

"I believe you can use them for any plants, potted or in the ground. I have some more over here if you want to look at them." I pointed to a shelf where I had placed my newest glass products. She picked out three and said, "And you hand-painted them?"

"Yes, I did. Just yesterday."

Without blinking at the price, (which I thought might be too high), she handed me her card, which I quickly swiped on the Square attachment on my phone. I wrapped them each in newspaper, feeling a bit giddy that my spur-of-the-moment idea had worked. I put them in a grocery store plastic bag.

The rest of the morning was busier than I could have dreamed. With no computer, I documented purchases in my notebook and hand-wrote many receipts. I hoped to get my computer back soon because as much as I loved sales, analog receipts weren't fun.

"That is the tiniest dog I've ever seen." This statement came from a woman buying a set of windchimes made with keys. I winced a little at the sale because I didn't know where I would ever find enough keys to make another windchime to replace this. Maybe I should have marked the price higher. Oh well. Too late now.

I responded, "I actually found her. You should see the before pictures of her. She was a matted mess."

The woman gave a pout, "Poor little baby. She was sure lucky to find you." She picked Zia up and let the dog kiss her face as I started to wrap up her purchase. I may not have had bags, but I had tons of newspapers handy. I remembered what Louise had said and kept my eye on the woman holding my dog. I didn't want anybody walking off with the little squirt.

As I ripped a piece from the local section of the Albuquerque Journal, I saw a small article that caused me to freeze. The headline read, 'Valuable Books Stolen from Wealthy Entrepreneur'. Needing to read more, I looked up to see if the windchime customer was ready, but she was debating another purchase with her husband.

Since they were busy and no others were in the store, I quickly read on. The entrepreneur was Alex Chandler! The four books, all rare first editions, were taken last week from his mansion in the foothills. One book was mentioned by name: Huckleberry Finn!

I slapped my hand across my mouth. They had to be the books I'd bought. I finally had a way to connect Larry to illicit activity. He probably had access to Chandler's home and lifted the books while there. He may have taken them to the antique store to sell. It was all coming together.

"Dear, can you add this to my ticket? I just have to have it."

I tore my eyes away from the paper to see the woman holding the pillow I'd used underneath Jill's head the day before.

She snuggled the pillow, nearly squashing Zia who was also in her arms. "I just love that it was made from an old apron."

Her husband rolled his eyes but pulled his wallet from the pocket of his Dockers.

I carefully slid the section of the paper with the article behind my counter, and smiled. "It was one of my grandmother's aprons. It had a hole in it and I decided to make a pillow…just for you." I taped the last of the windchime bundle and stood fully to take care of her transaction.

The woman reluctantly handed Zia over to me and beamed as her husband carried the purchases out of the store. I sighed, relieved to have a moment to breathe and get my thoughts together.

What luck to find the article. I grabbed my sandwich from the fridge and started eating while debating what to do. I figured I should call Sgt. Barnes about the article, and did so while watching the door.

He answered in his typical way, "Barnes."

"Maria Olson here. I think I have a significant clue to the missing books and maybe murder."

"Uh-huh."

"I saw in the paper that Alex Chandler had rare, first edition books stolen last week. I think they are the ones I bought from the antique store. And Larry, my landlord works for Chandler."

His statement was bland. "There's no proof there ever were any books."

"But I held them! Carl saw them too. He even told me you asked him about them." Haha. I had him there. "And what about the video where Pops returned the books?" Then I remembered he hadn't seen it before it had mysteriously disappeared.

He was silent on the other end.

"Sergeant Barnes?"

"I'm busy, Olson. I'm trying to solve a murder. Get back to peddling your salvaged stuff."

I stammered, "Well...I just thought it might be helpful information." Why did he always fluster me? I hung up, embarrassed again. He was mad when I didn't tell him something, then mad if I did. There was absolutely no winning with that man.

Frustrated, I carried my sandwich outside with me and let Zia out for a break. As I chewed, I watched people visiting all the businesses. My irritation with Barnes started to subside as I marveled at the successful first day. A group of four women approached my shop, carrying bags from the bakery. I quickly put my trash in my lunch bag, called the dog, and stepped back inside to welcome them.

The first lady, dressed in a bright sundress, entered the shop and chirped, "Is this where the baby was born?"

I smiled and started telling the story for the umpteenth time. At least people were asking about the birth rather than the death.

She and the other women became animated, eyes growing wide and oohing and ahhing with each new bit of information. I half expected them to cry or clap when I finished the story. You would think I'd be annoyed being pumped me for details, but most people bought something, so I didn't really mind. Jill wouldn't have sent the story to the news if she wasn't comfortable with people knowing about the birth. I made sure not to get too personal with the details though.

After the group left, there was a steady stream of customers until closing time at eight o'clock. My body felt limp by the time I shut the door. I was dehydrated as well as physically and mentally exhausted. Why did I think I could handle the whole first day alone? Realistically, I knew the crowd was there because the center was new. Business would undoubtedly drop off next week. Despite the long hours, I hoped I could handle it alone for a while.

I collapsed on Jill's car seat bench, which had been sold but not yet taken, and looked around at the nearly empty shelves. Those people practically wiped out my inventory. I'd have to upcycle more products pronto, or the store would have to shut down. At least we weren't open on Mondays so I'd have that full day to work on projects. There was always tomorrow to worry about.

I gathered my store's trash and carried the bag out to the dumpster. As I approached, something wooden sticking out of the top caught my eye. I stood on my tiptoes to look over the side of the giant metal container and found a beautiful large, antique mirror leaning against a few black garbage bags. It looked to be in great shape. There was no way to get leverage to retrieve it, so I ran inside and got my step stool. I climbed up, leaned over the side of the rusty dumpster, and tugged on the wood. I froze when a hand grabbed my leg.

CHAPTER 17

My breath caught and I slowly turned to find Jett standing with a steely expression locked on me. My heart skipped a beat when his hand tightened around my calf.

His smooth deep voice said, "Need some help getting in there?"

Was he going to push me over the edge and into the dumpster? I gulped for several reasons:

1. I'd never been alone with this man.

2. He was on my shortlist of suspects

3. I'd tattled that he was MIA during the murder.

4. Victoria wanted me out of the way.

I turned back around so he couldn't see my fear and sputtered, "Um…I'm just trying to get this big thing out of here." I closed my eyes waiting for a blow to the back of my head, but instead, Jett released my leg and looked over the edge.

"That? The old mirror? I just took that old mirror out of Victoria's shop a few days ago. She said it was an eyesore. She has another one too, but I said forget it."

His mood was so light all of a sudden. He didn't seem like he was going to kill me.

I sighed and said, "But it's so beautiful." Then it hit me. The phrase "took out the old antique" must have been the mirror Jett had "taken out?" What a fool I'd been. A flood of relief washed over me. It wasn't the old man they were talking about at all. I hadn't even considered that Victoria might have spoken literally about an old antique. I berated myself. Why did I make everything so dramatic? This guy hadn't killed anyone. I rolled my eyes at my own paranoid conspiracy theory.

Jett held out his hand, "Here, let me get it for you." He helped me off my stool and climbed up. In one swift movement, he heaved the frame over the side of the dumpster and placed it into my arms.

The old wood was heavy, but even in the dim light of dusk, I could tell it was amazing. "I can't believe Victoria just dumped this."

"Yeah, well, there's no telling what goes through her mind. She made me get it from her apartment, bring it here and dump it in the bin. I thought the antique store could sell it, but she refused to take it there." He threw his trash bag into the dumpster as well as mine, then took the heavy mirror from my hands and hauled it to my shop as I carried my stool.

He said, "I didn't mean to startle you, but I was afraid you would fall from that stool."

"Oh. Thanks, but I'm pretty used to dumpster diving. Jill and I could medal in it if it was an Olympic sport, we've done it so much." I laughed then changed the topic as we reached my steps. "I saw you at the gala. Did you have a nice time?"

He shrugged. "It was OK. Would have been better if I hadn't gone with Victoria." He shook his head, "That's over now."

"Oh. That's too bad." I tried to sound concerned but felt pretty relieved for him.

He shook his head. "Not for me. I'm glad to be out of that toxic relationship."

"Not a perfect match, huh?" I probed, hoping for more information.

"She's too clingy. I need to be on my own for a while anyway to ...figure things out." He lifted his shoulders lightly and said with a waggle of his head, "and find me." He gave a small smirk. I noticed that his face was much more relaxed than in the past week.

I held the door open for him. "I guess we'll put the mirror in my storage room in the back if you don't mind?"

"Sure." He looked around as he entered. It was the first time he'd been inside since the day we met. "So, is this where Dr. Joe delivered the baby?"

"Uh-huh. Right there on the floor." I pointed down in front of him and picked up Zia who toddled over to greet us. "He did a great job, especially for his first time being a midwife."

"Yep. Joey can do just about anything." He rolled his eyes and added, "Your place looks great."

"Well, I sold so much today, it looks bare to me."

I led him to the storage area where he leaned the mirror on my little refrigerator. "I'm glad you had a good day." He walked back by my counter. "You didn't sell the trombone light?"

I was surprised he remembered the lamp, "I'm keeping it." I pointed to the 'Not for Sale' label I'd placed beneath it.

When he smiled, his dark green eyes bore into mine, causing my stomach to flutter. This guy was unbelievably handsome. He rubbed his hand through his black hair like a model in a shampoo ad. "Hey, if you need any design work for logos, etc., let me know. I love doing that."

I turned away from his mesmerizing gaze but managed to nod and say, "I could definitely pick your brain on that. And Jett, thanks so much for hauling the mirror...twice." I turned back to him again. "Oh! I forgot to ask. How was business at the brewery today?"

"Great! We actually have a huge crowd in there now and I'll be in deep sh...um... trouble if I don't get back. We're open for another two hours." He started to walk to the door then looked back and nodded with a wink, "Later," and left my shop.

Well, my mind was just blown. How could two brothers be so different and both so charming? The thought that the dark-haired beauty was so attentive to me was just too much. It felt like I was being disloyal to Joey, but that was ridiculous especially since he might be in a relationship. Guess we'll just see where things go. Of course, they both could just be big players. Calm down, Maria. Forget boys. Concentrate on your new business.

In any case, I was happy to check Jett and Victoria off my list of suspects. Time to focus fully on Larry and Flick. I took Zia outside before going home. The air was unusually muggy. Even though it wasn't quite dark, a light glowed through the window of the Antique store. Maybe Flick was there getting ready to open on Monday. Hopefully, he was in a better mood than yesterday. It would be nice to talk to him in person and see what he knew about the books. I needed a concrete link between him and Larry. I put Zia inside my shop and headed that way.

When I reached his door, I knocked but there wasn't any resistance and the door pushed open and slowly moved away from my hand. I called into the shop, "Mr. Harrison?"

Remembering the man was old and most likely hard of hearing, I upped my game and shouted louder, "Mr. Harrison, are you here? It's Maria from across the lot."

With no answer, I pushed the door open further and stepped inside. The shop was dark with no lights except a small lamp on the desk where he sat the day before. I didn't want to flip on any more lights and draw attention to my trespassing, so I reached in my pocket for my phone's flashlight but apparently, I'd left it at my shop. I shuffled my feet as I inched through the dark building.

A chill went through me as I wondered if something was amiss. After all, I'd found his brother dead less than a week ago. I scanned all areas as I moved toward the dim light, hoping and praying I wouldn't find another Harrison lying somewhere.

When I made it to the back wall and found nobody, I let out a big sigh. I didn't realize I'd been holding my breath the whole walk. I took a cleansing breath and looked around, hoping to find some clue or a connection to Larry.

I figured the desk would be a good place to start, especially since it was the only area lit enough to see. The surface was covered with papers, clock parts, and old radios as if the antique store had been open for years. Without touching anything, I looked over the cluttered top. There was an ancient black rotary dial phone which Flick was probably talking on when I overheard his half of the conversation. Next to the phone, a slip of paper caught my eye. It had a local 505 phone number and 'Books?' written in pen.

I searched the desk but found nothing else of interest. I decided to try calling the number on the paper. Since I'd left my iPhone in my shop, I picked up the landline and started the slow process of dialing on the rotary dial phone. A sound startled me, and I looked up, but it was just a clock chiming the half-hour. With the distraction, I accidentally dialed a two instead of a three and had to start all over. I thought of how fast we can make calls these days. A quick tap and the phone rang. This method took forever, especially if you dialed a lot of zeros.

Finally, the phone started to ring. Was it a mistake to use the store's phone? Before I could think about it further, a familiar and irritating voice answered with a loud friendly, "Flick, you old buzzard, you! I'm looking at the books so that's good, but I think you still owe me a check. You finally gonna cough it up?"

It was Larry! He waited for a response. As much as I wanted to confront him, this was not the time and definitely not the phone from which to start an argument. Flustered, I hung up.

At least I had connected Larry to Flick and both of them to the books. So Larry had them and was waiting for his check. Did that mean he had killed Pops? At any rate, it sure sounded incriminating for Larry and maybe even Flick. On a personal note, I was also perturbed that Larry wouldn't take my calls but answered one coming from Flick's shop.

Excited with my information, but not wanting to be discovered, it was time to vamoose. I made it to the front of the shop without incident except for hitting my shin on the same piano stool I'd sat on just a few days earlier. I hopped around trying not to cry. Now I'd have a bruised shin to go along with my skinned knees and palms. Luckily, my yelp didn't elicit a response from anyone.

I made it to the door but froze when I heard tires on gravel. I peeked through the door which was still ajar, and saw a big red truck pulling into the space out front! When the driver opened the door, the light shone on Larry. He was probably checking on Flick to see why he hung up so fast.

Dang! I should have handled that better. Now I was going to be caught. I quickly glanced around the shop and figured I could hide behind the Victrola. I hobbled over and crouched down behind the large wooden phonograph cabinet, hoping not to be seen. Admonishing myself, I figured I couldn't really get onto Larry for intruding in my shop when I was doing the same thing at another. I closed my eyes, imagining the headline, 'New Shop Owner Trespasses in Dead Man's Shop.'

Squatting in the tight space, I was glad I wasn't trying to maneuver with Zia in tow. And heaven forbid she'd do her obnoxious screechy bark.

The door creaked open further and Larry hollered, "Flick?". He flipped on the lights and said, "What the heck?" I could see him sauntering to the back, looking for the old man. When he reached the desk, he scratched his head.

He shrugged and stepped out through the back door. I thought about making a run for it but kept completely still. Good thing I didn't go because he came right back in shaking his head.

Larry made his way back through the shop. I held my breath and almost choked when he stopped mere inches from my hiding place. He said, "Stress getting to you, old man? Leaving the door unlocked." He shook his head and continued to the front door, turning off the lights. As he shut the door the porch light lit up his bewildered expression.

This time my sigh was huge and audible. With all the holding of breath I'd been doing lately, my lungs were going to be strong enough to swim a mile underwater.

He hadn't turned off the small lamp, so I was able to find my way back to the desk. Since I didn't have a rag, I used my shirt to wipe down the receiver and destroy my fingerprints. Assured that I'd erased any trace of my visit, I slipped out the back door. I hugged the outside corrugated wall of the building just in case Larry hadn't driven off yet.

The sky was void of stars and had turned black, probably due to the smoky haze of the Jemez fire. Since I wore fairly dark clothes, I hoped I wasn't visible while inching along. I tried to keep from crunching the gravel beneath my feet.

Before I saw him, I smelled smoke that wasn't from the forest fire. I peeked around the corner and watched my creepy and possibly murderous landlord lean against his truck, puffing away. I thought about his actions tonight. He had simply looked for Mr. Harrison. There was nothing, besides mentioning the books and breaking into my shop, to tie him to murder, but I had to know for sure.

The moonlight reflected on a cell phone held up to his ear. He stuffed it in his back pocket and said, "Damn, Flick. Where are you?" He threw the cigarette on the gravel and ground it out with his boot. He hopped in his truck, started it, and did a U-turn, heading out of the center's lot.

Once in the clear, I ran to my shop and grabbed Zia along with my bag, then got in my truck to follow Larry.

I couldn't see his truck when I pulled up to the stop sign exiting Out of the Box. Dang! Which way had he turned onto Montgomery Blvd? While I sat deciding whether to turn right or left, bright lights shone in my rearview mirror. Probably someone leaving the brewery. I had to make a quick choice to get out of their way. I turned right, eyes peeled on the road as I drove, hoping to see any sign of Larry's red truck.

When the car behind me changed lanes, I was relieved because the glare from its headlights killed my eyes. Miraculously, as if fate intervened, the guy driving the vehicle passing on my left was Larry. Ha! He must have stopped by his office for something and ended up behind me. Full of excitement, I changed lanes and slipped behind his Dodge Ram and tailed him, ready to catch him in some illicit activity to prove his guilt. Adrenaline pumping, I gripped the steering wheel, all set for a high-speed chase. "Hold On, Zia!"

I wished Jill was with me. Years ago, she coerced me to go on surveillance of her boyfriend who she thought was cheating on her. It turned out to be a big misunderstanding and the teen had just driven his cousin home. When we were caught, his parents never let him speak to Jill again.

But, this time, alone, I was nervous about what I was getting myself into. After all, I was following a possible thief, trespasser, and even murderer.

Surprisingly Larry didn't exceed the speed limit, so there was no high-speed anything. He just drove along and followed all the traffic rules. At this rate, Jill would have been bored stiff.

When Larry turned on his signal, my heart picked up the pace, but he just pulled into the drive-thru at Blake's Lotaburger. I only had a second to decide what to do and followed him into the narrow drive. When opening my window, I could hear his whiny voice say, "I'll take a green chile cheeseburger and fries with spicy ketchup, please."

Wow. This suspect is so polite. The thought of the burger made my mouth water, so when it was my turn at the speaker, I ordered the same thing. Larry took his food and turned onto the street. At the window, I grabbed my food, handed the girl five dollars cash, and feeling anxious said, "Keep the change." It was only 32 cents anyway.

I found Larry's truck with no problem and followed, trying to focus on my mission, but the smell of food in the passenger's seat was intoxicating. I needed to be alert, so left it there with Zia sniffing the bag. She was probably just as famished as me.

His next stop was equally unexciting—Walgreens. I sat in an inconspicuous spot in the dark lot, grabbed my burger, and took a bite. I gave Zia a French fry. It felt just like I was on a stakeout in a police movie, but instead of having an irritating partner, I had a tiny dog as my squad. I ducked down when the store's automatic door slid open and Larry emerged carrying a small bag.

I threw my food back in the white paper sack and crept behind him. This was kinda fun!

After following him a few more miles, Larry pulled into the parking lot of the popular New Mexican restaurant, El Pinto, where he parked his car. I shook my head. Larry had just eaten at Lotaburger. Why did he need to eat again?

I glanced at the beautiful well-lit entrance covered in vines and spotted a recognizable shock of gray/white hair. There was the tall, distinguished, Alex Chandler standing beside the hanging ristras. In his sleek suit, and casual pose, framed by the strings of red chiles, he looked like a model for Esquire magazine. Mötley Crüe

I watched as Larry, dressed in a Motely Crue t-shirt, worn jeans, and cowboy boots, ambled to Chandler and shook his hand. The millionaire patted his back and they stood talking. I found their relationship extremely bizarre and hard to believe.

I pulled around and found a parking spot, while summoning courage to tell Alex Chandler that his "good friend," Larry, might be the one who stole his rare books. As I unbuckled my seatbelt, I watched the two and saw a few more well-dressed men join them. They all shook hands before entering the restaurant. I slumped back against my seat. I couldn't confront them with other people around.

I was far too tired to wait for them to finish eating, drinking, and meeting, so turned around and drove the six miles back to my home. Apparently, I wasn't a true detective if I didn't have the stamina to wait. But, in my defense, the day had been long and eventful.

Once ready for bed, I called Jill, apologizing for the late hour and for not making it to the hospital. I relaxed while hearing stories of the baby, then told her about my exhausting day.

"That's awesome that you sold so much. But, if you are going to play Sherlock without your Dr. Watson, be careful." The sound was muffled, then she said. "Oh, Kelly wants to talk to you."

His deep voice came through the receiver loud and clear. "I stopped by the PD today. Barnes is upset that they still haven't found your missing video."

I scoffed. "Me too. I need my computer back. At least he's interested. Every time I talk to him, he acts like I'm an idiot and my information is useless."

"Yeah, I know. Now, he's obsessed with finding what scraped Mr. Harrison's face that night."

"Can't help him there. At this point, I wouldn't even want to try."

We hung up and I fell into a deep sleep.

Thankfully, since it was Sunday, the center would only be open from 10 to 6. I grabbed a few surplus items that might sell and loaded them up along with Zia and drove to Out of the Box.

I stopped by Mike and Pat's to get one of the scones my customers had raved about. When I entered, the door jingled. I turned to see an adorable chime made of spoons. Cute. I'd made one like that a long time ago. I should make more since I had so much silverware.

I could see the bakers bustling about in the kitchen and hollered, "Hey guys, how was your first day?"

Pat came around the counter wiping his floury hands on his apron. "Well, we were depleted by noon and had to close down." He raised his eyebrows confirming this was good news. "A lot of people said they want to take pastries to work, so we hope to start opening at six a.m. and closing at two. That is if we can ever get hold of Larry to arrange it."

I nodded. "So, you need his approval to open the gates that early?"

Mike appeared at the doorway, drying his hands on a towel. "Since we need to be open early and the brewery will be open late, I'm not sure why we need a gate anyway. I mean...what's the big deal? It's not like there is any crime here."

My stomach tightened at the comment. There was an awkward silence until Mike sheepishly added, "Well, except a murder."

Pat leaned his floury hands on the counter and said, "Have you heard anything yet about who was responsible?"

Not ready to spread gossip, I said, "Oh, I've got my suspicions, but nothing certain. I'll tell you when I know something concrete."

Mike said, "It's a little nerve-wracking to think someone around here might have been involved." He gave a little shiver.

I looked at the hulking man and figured it would be pretty difficult to overpower him. "I think you'll be ok, Mike."

I bought a blueberry scone and went to my shop to get ready for the day.

Only a few customers showed up early, but I expected a larger crowd once churches let out. During the lull, when I should have been making more products, I couldn't help but focus my attention on the clues and suspects. Pink notebook out, I sat on my tractor stool and went over my collected information. I scratched through Jett and Victoria on my list and circled Flick and Larry.

At about 11:00, a group of three teenage boys entered. They looked around the shop awkwardly. This was not at all the clientele I expected. The tallest and most confident-looking kid was eating a donut. He asked bluntly, "Where did that dude get whacked?" He wiped his sugary fingers on his jeans.

I was taken aback by his crude question. The store turned eerily silent as an older couple looking at jewelry froze. Not sure of the protocol for answering such a direct question, I said calmly, "Well, I found the body outside of my shop."

A freckled boy with a Star Wars t-shirt brightened. He asked in a voice that straddled two registers, "You found the body? Cool."

Finding a body was anything but cool and I felt the need to tell them that. "Um. It wasn't cool. Death is nothing to celebrate. Besides, Mr. Harrison was a very kind man."

He dipped his head down and his face turned pink. "Oh yeah. Sorry."

I felt a little bad reprimanding him and was going to say something, but the third boy, wearing glasses that kept slipping down his nose, said, "Hey Michael, look at this. It's a bank made from a retro Nintendo console." He gestured at one of my only tech-related pieces that had 'Video Game Fund. Donations accepted' printed on the front.

Michael, the tall donut-eating boy, and apparently the cool kid, nodded and said, "Nice."

That was just enough encouragement for the guy with glasses to say to me with bright eyes, "Can you hold this for me for a few dasy?" He walked over with it and said quietly, "I have to pull some weeds at my neighbor's yard to get enough money."

"Of course. This bank was meant for you." I gave a wink and placed the bank behind my counter along with his name.

I noticed the Star Wars kid fingering a keyring made from a bicycle chain. He pulled out a ten from his pocket and bought it, saying, "Sorry if I was rude."

I smiled and said, "You're fine. I might have done the same thing at your age," causing him to loosen up a bit.

The three boys left, attention focused on finding blood or some other gruesome sign of the murder outside. I could hear their animated voices discussing it as they left. Unbelievably, a murder had actually brought paying customers into the store. You can't make up this stuff.

CHAPTER 18

A bit later, when the shop was empty, I stepped outside to let Zia go potty, and marveled at so many unfamiliar cars.

I took a deep breath and exhaled, happy with the early success of Out of the Box. When I looked at the deserted antique store, it looked so lonely. Had I actually hidden in the store last night? Maybe I could get more information from Flick once he opened. I took out my phone and made a note to call and check on my new friend, Milly.

Even though I couldn't see the book store and only the corner of the coffee shop was visible from here, I hoped all the Boxcar Adults were having a good second day.

Since I couldn't solve a murder today, I went back inside and started making a list of projects for my day off. I would have to choose easy-to-make items to fill in the empty spots quickly.

I heard a strange scraping sound on my window. I looked out the window but saw nothing. There were no trees nearby, so it wasn't limbs blowing in the wind. Within minutes the same sound came from the other window. The hairs on the nape of my neck stood up. Was somebody watching me? Then, the sound moved and the scrape was heard slowly moving around the periphery of the whole container. Goosebumps covered my arms as I crept to the door to look.

Just as I reached the doorknob, a tall woman stormed in, practically knocking me down. The impeccably dressed lady said, "I came to look at charms."

Confused with her abrasiveness and still uneasy from the mysterious scraping sound, I said, "Um…sure…right this way," and led her to the remaining jewelry items. "I'll be restocking soon."

She said in a brusque manner, "Well, I would hope so."

I opted not to explain that I had been wiped out of inventory yesterday. No need to even debate with a bully. I politely pointed out some other jewelry hanging on a rack nearby. She frowned, and walked around the shop with a scowl.

I took a chance and asked, "Did you happen to see anybody walking around my container?"

She looked at me as if I was crazy to ask her that, then she said, "I wasn't aware that I was supposed to be guarding your place."

Dumbfounded, I shook my head in disbelief. I knew only one other person who talked to me like that and wondered for a second if this woman might be Victoria's mother. I studied her face. No real similarities except they wore the same disdainful sneer.

I backed away and sat at my tractor stool, deciding the scraping sound was all in my imagination. Thinking of Victoria and charms, I checked my phone case and saw that the tiny spoon was there-stuck in tight. I should probably return it to her, even though I didn't owe the Barista any favors.

The woman wrinkled her nose at everything she passed. Why was she still here? As she lingered, I pried the case off of my phone and then with a pair of jewelry pliers, grabbed the spoon charm and put it in a tiny plastic bag meant for rings. I slipped it into my pocket just in time to answer a few more questions for the insulting woman. It's fine that she never bought anything, but I just never dealt with this kind of customer in my online shop. I guess I'll get all types now. When a big group of women arrived, she left.

The afternoon was as busy as the first day. About an hour before closing, I was surveying my nearly empty shop when Louise entered, causing the chimes to tinkle.

"Where is that delightful sound coming from?" She looked on the other side of the door and said, "Let me guess. You made that?" She shook her head. "Isn't it just the cutest thing ever? I'll bet my little granddaughter, Lisa, would be tickled pink to have one of these in her room."

I smiled and said, "I hadn't even thought of making them to sell, but I'll start looking for more old xylophones when I'm out. So, Louise, how were your first two days?"

She wobbled her head. "Better than a roll in the hay."

This woman had the weirdest sayings. I raised an eyebrow. "Oh, really?"

"Not that I actually remember much about that. Golly gee, it's been years since my Hank bought the farm. He was one sexy man, I tell you." She gave a mournful sigh, then perked up. "So, yeah. People scooped up all my used books and they seemed to like the full-priced ones too. How about you?"

"Very good. Who knew babies and murders would attract customers? I'll have a lot of work replenishing tomorrow. Glad we have a day off. So, have you closed already today?"

"Nope, still open. My daughter stopped by and I told her to hold down the fort for a while." She fingered a few necklaces as she wandered around without saying anything.

"Nice. So, did you need something?"

She bonked her head with the heel of her hand. "Duh. If I didn't have my head attached, I'd just leave it in a corner along with my old shoes. I came by to tell you that we're having a rally Tuesday morning - 8:00 at the bakery to gear up for the new week and see how everyone's doing."

"OK. I'll be there." I wondered if this was going to be a weekly thing. If so, that might be kind of nice.

She came in close and looked around as if there were people in my store. She whispered, "The Barista might not make it much longer. I heard the down-payment check for her container bounced." Her eyebrows lifted, and she shook her head.

I wasn't sure how to react to her gossip, but it confirmed some of what I had heard at the gala. I just said, "Well, that's interesting."

She bellowed, "Keep up the good work, my little Norwexican." The funny lady sashayed out the door and barged toward the bakery, although I doubted they were still open.

I had a few more sales and I stayed late to paint more wine bottles and price necklaces. Zia toddled over and jumped up on my ankle, stretching her tiny body out with a yawn.

"Are you ready to go home?"

I packed up a few things. I figured I'd stop by the house, grab something to eat, then go to the hospital for a quick visit.

I walked outside, relieved to know I had a relaxing evening and day off ahead of me. I put my stuff in the truck, but when I leaned down to pick up Zia, she was trotting across the parking lot past the bakery. Not again. This time I worried that she would be hit by one of the cars leaving the brewery. I called to her. "Zia!" She kept going. "Zia. Come!"

That dog! From now on, I'd just have to put her on a leash. I couldn't keep chasing her around the center. Annoyed, I followed as she ran toward The Barista. She hopped up on the first step, the same place we'd almost been hit the day before.

Sounds of a lively crowd drifted through the brewery's open windows. I smiled, happy that it was becoming a hopping place. The coffee shop sign read closed, but the lights were on. I started to grab the dog as I neared, but nearby voices caused me to stop.

Instead, I slipped beneath the window. I had no interest in running into Victoria. I patted my legs, hoping Zia would run to me.

Victoria's shrill voice said, "Are you threatening me, Larry?"

I perked up. Larry! I had finally found the jerk and now he was harassing Victoria. Should I get help?

Larry replied in a voice so quiet I couldn't hear the words.

I started to reach for Zia, but a couple walked by me, arm in arm, on their way to the Rusty Railroad. If they hadn't looked so enthralled with each other, I might have asked them for help. I leaned casually against the window looking at my phone until they moved on to the pub.

In a screechy voice, Victoria said, "It creeps me out the way you always hang around here."

I knew that feeling myself but listened for something more concrete to implicate Larry.

She continued in her snotty voice, "Want me to call Jett? He'll beat you to a pulp if you don't leave."

I started feeling anxious and texted Barnes, 'Larry, the landlord, seems to be threatening Victoria Yates. I think he was involved in the murder. I may have to defend her.' I pushed send, then made sure my phone was on silent in case he called back.

The only weapon I had with me was my set of car keys. I quickly poked them between my fingers in preparation to fend off Larry if need be.

Larry whined, "Me? I didn't do anything except what you wanted me to. Come on, Vicky, you promised me we could go out. I just want to know when we get to finally have our date."

Wait. That didn't sound very murderous.

Victoria said, "Not gonna happen. You're weak. You're skinny, and for God's sake, you smell."

There was silence after her beratement. Then Larry whimpered, "But, I did everything you told me to do. I took you to Chandler's place so you could see his pretty house. Then, I checked on Maria as you asked. You said I did good work when I told you she was watching a video." He stammered, "Then when you lost your keys, I loaned you mine."

The information started to soak in. So, Larry loaned Victoria his master keys? Could Victoria have gone into my shop to erase the video? The turn of events baffled me.

Larry continued, his voice cracking as though he would cry, "I even gave you tickets to the gala, and what about yesterday? I hunted everywhere for your stupid charm. What more was I supposed to do for you?"

I tried to process the wealth of information I'd just heard. Victoria had accessed everything through Larry. It was all coming together. She had probably stolen the books from Chandler's and maybe even erased my tape.

A male voice interrupted my intense thoughts, "You OK?"

I turned to fine two young men staring at me. I must have looked odd hunkering down under the window. "Oh. I'm fine. I just got something in my shoe." I leaned down and realized I was wearing flip-flops. I took one off and shook it anyway.

The two chuckled and walked away, speaking Spanish. They probably wouldn't have said what they did, if they knew I was fluent in the language.

Zia sniffed at the side of Victoria's door. I tiptoed towards her to pick her up, but when there was rustling inside, I hopped back to my spot in case they opened the door. What had I missed during the interruption? Why Victoria was so desperate to find the charm? I patted my pocket, confirming that the tiny bag was still there.

As I tried to come up with a motive for Victoria to commit murder, she spoke again, her voice changing from brash to sickeningly sweet. "You're right, Larry. You did everything I asked."

She sure went overboard buttering him up. Maybe she realized he had a lot on her. She crooned, "How about we go out next week? I'm sorry for what I said. I really do owe you."

Larry's voice instantly lifted into his smarmy tone, "I'll take you somewhere real nice. Don't you worry, Vicky. How about Thursday? I'll pick you up here and we'll paint the town."

Gee, he got snowed over easily. I should have known he wasn't smart enough to plan a murder.

She answered, "Yeah, whatever. You choose where to go."

I could tell she had no intention of going anywhere with the poor sap and I felt a bit sorry for Larry. I started a new text to Sergeant Barnes. 'Maria here. Forget Larry. I think the murderer was Victoria Yates…'

When the door opened, I jumped back and hid in the shadows. Why hadn't I grabbed Zia? Stupid, stupid me. I hoped the two wouldn't notice the tiny dark body standing to the side of the porch. I pushed send on my phone then peeked around the corner in time to see Larry lean in to give Victoria a kiss on the mouth, but she turned her head quickly, causing his lips to land on her ear.

A soft rumble, almost like thunder, started in the distance. But, since it was a clear night and monsoon season was over, the sound had to be the northbound 8:00 train.

Larry practically skipped down the steps and said, "See you Thursday, Barista Baby."

As soon as he got in his car, Victoria said quietly, "Over my dead body." When she turned to go inside, that little scoundrel, Zia, scooted past her through the door and followed her inside.

I raced up the steps after my dog and opened the door to see Victoria walk past her cappuccino machine, unaware of the two uninvited visitors in her shop. Why had Zia gone inside? I couldn't see her but saw something else. The very books in question sat on the counter behind the register. I gasped.

Victoria heard me and turned. Her nostrils flared. "What the hell?"

The train got louder as it approached. I sputtered an excuse, "Um… my dog came in and I…sorry…" I called the dog, "Zia!", but she was behind the counter somewhere.

The books caught my eye again and I couldn't help but spit, "So, *you* have the books."

Without saying a word, her eyes narrowed. The menacing look matched the eerie train noise. She leaned down and I feared she would come up with a gun, but what she had was much worse. She stood up holding Zia.

I froze as Victoria, dog in hand, bolted past me to the door. She warned in a voice reminiscent of the wicked witch of the west, "Follow me, and this dog is toast!"

Unbelievably, she ran out the door with my pup. My heart faltered and I froze in shock. I frantically considered what to do. What kind of evil person was Victoria to take Ziu? I dashed to the door and saw her sprint across the parking lot, past my shop and ran along the train tracks. Where in the world was she going?

Despite her ominous warning not to follow, I ran to my truck, started it and sped past the cars of the bar customers, and drove out our entrance, praying I wouldn't hit anyone in my haste. My heart raced along with my truck as I made a bee-line to the nearby Railrunner station, in case that was her destination.

Even though it was only a few blocks away, I was stalled by a stupid red light. I beat my hands on the steering wheel, urging the light to change. Surely she wouldn't hurt an innocent little dog. My mouth was dry and my pulse quickened.

Finally, the light changed. I pulled forward and turned into the station parking lot just in time to see Victoria board the train. I shivered when I saw the tiny black ears and nose of my dog poking out from her arms. By the time I parked and opened my door, the train had pulled away. Shoot!

In a frenzy, I jumped back in the truck and turned onto Montaño. Obviously unable to drive on the tracks to follow, I tried to remember where the next station was. I thought it was just a few miles away by Plant World on El Pueblo and started that way.

I quickly dialed Barnes as I drove. Come on. Answer the phone! Of course, he didn't. When I heard the beep, I barely recognized my distraught voice leaving the message. "Officer Barnes, Maria here. Victoria Yates has taken my dog hostage and is on a Railrunner heading North from Montaño." I continued in my frantic voice. "I saw the stolen books in her shop and I think she murdered Pops. I'm following her and hope to board the train at the Los Ranchos station." A big lump filled my throat and I sobbed without meaning to, "Please help me get my dog back."

The short drive seemed to take an hour with long traffic lights, but somehow I beat the train. I slung my purse strap over my shoulder, locked my door, and ran to the platform, arriving just as the train pulled up.

I climbed aboard the steps of the 4th car with no real plan in mind except to get my Zia back.

Familiar with the Railrunner after riding it to Santa Fe for a month-long class at a glass studio, I knew each train had five cars. The last one was deemed the "quiet car" for commuters to work or sleep as they rode, and I checked that one first. At this time of night, there were only a few people riding and none were Victoria. I poked my head past the bathroom to the left and saw that the next car was pretty lively. I cautiously made my way down the aisle, my heart beating so hard I was sure the passengers could hear it. I scanned the seats, getting shuffled sideways by train movement while inching along, but there was no sign of Victoria.

As I picked up the pace, my stomach twisted with worry. I entered the third car, knowing I had to be getting close. Zia better not be hurt. Why would Victoria take my dog on the train?

A woman stared at me as I passed by, probably wondering why I hadn't found a seat when there were so many open. For once, I didn't engage but kept on my mission through the next car.

When my hunt through the second car was a bust, I continued to the last one, the first in line. I held my breath as I approached and was surprised to see only two people. On my right, was the back of a teenage boy's head. He held a skateboard upright on his lap with familiar white iPhone earbuds in his ears. Across the aisle and facing me, I recognized the dark blunt haircut belonging to Victoria. My emotions ran from fright to hatred. Victoria's head was bent down apparently fiddling with her/my contraband dog. She didn't see me approach, but a tiny head popped up from her lap and reacted to seeing me by squirming to get out of her captor's hold. Tears of relief welled in my eyes when I saw Zia was safe.

I moved forward as smoothly as I could while trying to gain the courage to speak. Victoria looked up, mouth dropping open when she spotted me. She said with eyes boring into me, "I told you not to…"

Before she had a chance to finish, I squared my shoulders and said firmly, "Give me my dog."

Her lip curled up on the right, transforming her mouth into an evil grin. She looked at the open window and cackled. Then as if in slow motion, she lifted my tiny dog in one hand and held her outside the open window. My heart jumped, then I jumped forward, and yelled, "No!"

Victoria gave a haunting laugh reminiscent of a Disney villain as she held the dog firmly in the night air. I watched in horror as Zia's ears flapped and her tag fluttered in the wind.

She hissed, "Step back or I'll drop it."

I gulped, thinking Victoria couldn't do something so horrible as to drop my precious dog out the window of a moving train. But then again, if she was involved in a murder, she probably could. I felt as though I would suffocate and stepped backward trying to deescalate the horrific scene.

My brain was so muddled I could barely think. I caught movement from the corner of my eye and saw the teenager slowly lift his phone up by his skateboard. Was he recording the moment? I quickly turned back to watch my terrified dog struggling to get back in. Her little legs ran through the night air in vain. I prayed, 'Please, please, please, don't drop her.'

My mind reeled with questions about this disturbed woman. What was going through her mind? Would she come after me next? How could I prevent this disaster?

There had to be something I could do to get my dog back safely. I closed my eyes trying to concentrate but was distracted by the loud thumping of my heart. Then I remembered the charm that Victoria seemed to want so desperately. It was in my pocket. If nothing else it could be a distraction.

I opened my eyes and slowly pulled out the tiny clear bag and held it up. With caution, I said, "Victoria, did you lose something the night Mr. Harrison died?"

Victoria's gaze flitted from my face to the charm. She lit up when she recognized it and her free hand flew to her chest. As her confidence faltered, mine increased. I didn't know why the charm meant so much to her, but this was my chance to get Zia back.

I continued, breathing slightly more regularly, and said, "I found this charm beside my shop."

Her eyes bulged and she lunged forward trying to grab the charm but I was too far away for her to make contact. Thankfully, by reaching out to me, she had inadvertently brought Zia back into the train car. I gave a shaky sigh of relief and stepped back even further. I had to choose my words carefully or Zia could be out the window again.

"Give it to me!" she shrieked and stood up holding the pup awkwardly.

I said with a glimmer of hope, "I'll trade it for my dog?"

She looked down at Zia and scoffed, "This rat isn't worth anything, but I'm not giving it back to you."

I was disheartened that didn't work, but I stayed focused. "The books you stole from Mr. Chandler were valuable, right?" I paused, to watch the woman's reaction. Her face was hard to read as she kept her eye on the charm. "But, were they worth murder?"

CHAPTER 19

My dramatic pause leading into the big question had been somewhat effective. She sat down with Zia on her lap, but kept a finger through the tiny collar. She scowled as her eyes bore into me.

I continued, "I've contacted the police so they know about the books and your involvement in the demise of Mr. Harrison. So, you really have no reason to harm my dog unless you want to add a charge of cruelty to an animal." I looked at her with pleading eyes. "It's time to stop."

Something I said, must have hit home and she shook her head, causing her perfect hair to swing side to side. She said something under her breath.

"What? I couldn't hear you." I made a step forward.

Victoria answered in an oddly loud and defensive way, "He lost his balance and fell!"

So, she *was* there when he died. I was on the right track for once but she needed the chance to explain. I said calmly, "Why don't you start from the beginning, Victoria?" Despite my despair over my dog, I faked a casual pose, and leaned against the seat across from the boy, forcing myself to breathe and listen.

Victoria dipped her head down. As if trying to convince herself, she said seriously, "It was an accident." She raised her head to me and started explaining her defense. "The dumb coffee shop used up all my cash. I only started the business to be near Jett. When Larry took me to see Chandler's house, I saw all these books, rare books. He had so many of them." She shrugged. "So, I took a few, figuring he'd never miss them."

There was proof she'd stolen Chandler's books. I ventured, "Then you gave them to the antique store to sell?"

"No!" Her face scrunched up. "The old man was just going to appraise them for me and if they were valuable I would find a buyer and pay off my debts. But, his idiot brother sold them to you for next to nothing!" This comment came complete with spittle and a glare, the ~~latter~~ former hitting me in the eye.

I flinched but kept a careful watch on Victoria in case she loosened her grip on Zia. "Did either of the Harrisons know the books were stolen?"

She rolled her eyes. "Well, why would I tell them that?"

I nodded, finding it hard to believe she was actually telling me what happened. "So, you went after Pops because he sold the books?"

"No!" Her look was incredulous. "I was beside your shop looking for the bracelet I'd dropped earlier when Jett and I took an old mirror to the dumpster." She stared out the window with a wistful expression at the mention of his name.

I interrupted her story to ask, "Was Jett there? Was he involved in Mr. Harrison's death?" I crossed my fingers that the answer would be another resounding no. I wasn't disappointed.

"Of course not. He's a big boy scout." She rolled her head around on her shoulders. "Jett was very anxious that night about his ex and the new brewery, but I had my own problems and couldn't coddle him. So I gave him something to settle him down."

My mouth dropped at the thought. "You drugged him?"

The surprise must have shown on my face for Victoria waved her hand, "Oh, he was fine. I just put a few muscle relaxers in his decaf coffee." She said this as if it was just creamer. "He slept on my shop's couch while I went to look for my charm bracelet."

She continued, "Anyway, I found the bracelet glistening in the moonlight and had just put it on when the old man came out of your shop. I was surprised to see him holding the books and demanded he give them to me. But the stupid old man couldn't hear me because a train was passing by. I had to repeat myself several times, telling him to Give Me the Books!"

Victoria was so animated it was as if she relived the confrontation. "But, he refused to do it." Shaking her head in disbelief she said, "He said he had to give them to his brother."

I nodded. So, it had been Victoria's voice we heard arguing on the video recording. I could hardly believe the details of the event I'd been trying to decipher were unfolding right in front of me.

She frowned. "You probably think I should have let the old man keep the books, but he was so stubborn he made me mad!"

She was right. If she *had* just let Pops go with the books, Flick would have appraised the volumes and Victoria could have gotten them back without hurting anyone. Unbelievable.

Shaking my head, I said, "And that's when you killed him?"

Her eyes flared as she yelled maniacally, "I said it was an accident!" She closed her eyes and composed herself again, then continued, "He lost his balance and fell."

I found it hard to believe he just fell down on his own. I was now witnessing her wild temper and could imagine it being even worse when Mr. Harrison refused to give her the books. "And how did he lose his balance? Did you hit him with something?"

A look of guilt flashed across her face before she answered. "I grabbed one of the books from him, but he had a good grip on the others." She scoffed, "I barely even tapped him on the head, hoping he'd release the other two, but instead, he fell and hit his head on the ground."

So, she had hit a defenseless old man. My stomach did a little flip thinking of poor Mr. Harrison falling to the ground. Poor guy. I looked at the charm still grasped in my fingers and gasped in revelation. I cocked my head and fished, "Did the bracelet scrape his face?"

She stayed silent and looked down in an admission of guilt if there ever was one.

I held up the charm as if presenting an exhibit in court, "So, on this spoon charm we may find your DNA as well as that of Mr. Harrison?" I shook my head.

Victoria changed the topic by continuing her defense, "What was I to do? I knelt down and felt his neck, but there was no pulse. That's when I heard you coming and hid behind your building."

So, it was her shadow I had seen.

The teen who was recording looked at me with huge round eyes. We said in unison, "What happened next?"

Victoria was so wrapped up in her story she didn't notice the boy's involvement and continued, "When you left, I grabbed the books. I had to leave quickly because that loser janitor from the pub showed up with his trash."

"Carl?"

She waved me off with her free hand. "After I ran across the parking lot, I watched him come around the other side of the shop to find the old man. He sobbed like a big baby." She rolled her eyes. "Then he tried to drag the body towards the Antique store. God knows why? I took off after that."

In contrast to her callous reaction, my heart broke to hear the description of Carl finding his uncle.

The train made a jerk as it began to slow down for the Bernalillo station, the last stop before the hour-long trip to Santa Fe. All I wanted to do was get my dog and go home. I looked at the tiny bag in my hand and said, "Why are you so frantic to get the charm?"

She paused before answering. "When I got back to my shop, I noticed blood on my bracelet. Maybe it scraped his face when I hit him...I mean *tapped* him with the book. I washed it off but realized one charm was missing." She held her hand out abruptly. "Give it back to me." Her tone was so condescending, that I didn't want to oblige, but then again I wanted my dog back.

I lowered my hands and said in confusion, "Victoria, if it was an accident why didn't you call an ambulance? Or why didn't you tell me when I showed up? Maybe he could have been saved." I was baffled by this.

She stayed silent as I considered her odd behavior. Then, I deduced aloud, "Was it all just because of the stolen books?"

She lifted her mouth in a creepy smile and locked squinty eyes on me. "He was already dead. I figured the police would think he died naturally." Her lips turned down. "But, then you had to come along and see the books, making everything complicated." She closed her eyes and fumed.

I couldn't believe she was blaming me. I watched as the woman opened her eyes and growled, "It's all your word against mine, Maria. But if you even try to tell the police about any of this, not only is your dog toast, but I'll come after you."

I shuddered in fear. Nobody had ever threatened my life before and my hands started to sweat. I let out an uneven breath, realizing too that it wasn't necessarily my word against hers. The boy was still there, recording and it should show her admission of guilt. I sure hoped he realized that too.

The train jolted to a complete stop, making me lose my balance. I fell forward holding my hands out, hoping to catch myself. My hands flew right past Victoria's head and I grabbed her seatback. I tried to right myself, but Victoria took hold of my loose hair and yanked it, twisting me around in some sort of practiced self-defense move. Her arm skillfully locked around my neck so tight I couldn't move. I heard a jingle of keys and then felt something cold and sharp below my chin. I froze and forgot about everything except how to save myself.

"Where Is My Charm?" she hissed in my ear.

I could hardly breathe, much less answer. I tried to reposition myself, but one leg was stretched awkwardly out on the ground and the other was wedged against the seatback in front of me.

"Give...It...To...Me!" With each word, the key dug further into my throat, making it impossible to swallow or move. I thought about where the charm could be after being tossed forward. One of my hands was twisted behind my back and the other was propping my body up on the seat, but I could tell both hands were empty.

I opened my mouth but all that came out was a raspy sound. I squeaked, "I dropped it when I fell," but my voice was so quiet even I could barely hear it. From my vantage point, I couldn't see the floor of the aisle to hunt for it, but I could see the boy sitting wide-eyed and still recording. Why didn't he help me?

In a sudden burst, Victoria wailed, "Ow!" and simultaneously lowered the keys so they were no longer jabbing my throat. Before I could consider what caused her to yell, I saw a blur of black from the corner of my eye and heard ferocious growling. Oh Wow! Zia was protecting me! Although Victoria still had a strong grip on me, I could finally breathe. Thank you, pup!

Then the worst happened. In apparent punishment for being bitten, the evil woman grabbed my tiny dog and tossed her. My stomach dropped as I watched my sweet little Zia fly out through the open window. With my voice fully restored, I screamed.

I struggled frantically to get up and pushed on the seat in front of me, but my leg was numb and didn't seem to work. Helpless, I croaked, "You, Monster!"

Victoria tightened her hold on me, practically crushing my windpipe with her forearm. Just as I thought I might black out, there was a surge of commotion. Voices shouted, people rushed in, and there stood Sergeant Barnes with a gun aimed at Victoria.

He said forcefully, "Hands in the air!"

She paused, then finally lifted her hands. When she released me, I lunged forward and landed in the aisle. I held my throat and coughed. My heart, which had been pounding ever since I'd left Out of the Box, was now a jackhammer in my chest. I scrambled to my wobbly feet and without a word, limped frantically through the door on the platform of the train. Even with the lights above the platform and red flashes from the police car, I couldn't see a black dog on the concrete anywhere. Had she been thrown before the train even stopped? I cringed at the thought and figured I'd have to backtrack to find her body.

I noticed a patch of grass with a dark spot in the middle and hobbled down the steps. As I rushed that way, I could see it was my little black dog lying there, still as could be. My heart gave an extra beat prompting me to run, crying uncontrollably. I touched her motionless back gently. "Zia! Oh, Zia!

Tears streamed down my face as I picked up her lifeless body carefully. I sat cross-legged on the grass and held her up against my shoulder and patted her back while sobbing. I rocked, hugged, and patted while telling her, "I'm so sorry, baby." How could I love Zia so much after only knowing her a week?

After a few minutes, I felt a twitch. I held her away from me, watching a miracle unfold. Her little muscles seemed to come to life and she opened her eyes. I squealed when she turned her head and stuck out her tiny tongue trying to reach my face. I laughed in relief.

Either my patting had served as CPR or she had just been stunned by the fall. No matter what, she seemed fine and squirmed to be closer to me. She licked my face with such fervor, my sobs turned to giggles. The happy pup buried her little body in my arms. My relief was overwhelming. I stood and held her close to my body and climbed the steps to the train car, elated.

When I re-joined the activity, a young officer had control of a handcuffed and fuming Victoria. She stared at me then glared at Zia. It was at that time I noticed the bloody marks on the barista's arm. Had Zia bitten her? My baby really did protect me. I squeezed her a little tighter in thanks, but that bite must have been the catalyst for being thrown out the window. I felt like biting Victoria myself or at least punching the woman for everything she had done. But, I had to settle for watching her get arrested. I just hoped she got what she deserved in the courts.

I noticed the tiny bag under the seat in front of the policeman and leaned to pick it up. Victoria's eyes followed me as I returned the charm to my pocket. I felt great satisfaction and gave her a waggle of my head, my own version of her smug look.

With the charm safely back in my possession and my face sufficiently washed by Zia, I focused on the drama unfolding in front of me.

Barnes growled, "Victoria Yates, you are under arrest in connection with the murder of Jonathan 'Pops' Harrison, and for kidnapping her pet rat." He motioned back to me.

Seriously? Even in an official arrest, he had to make fun of my dog? At this point, I didn't care. I was just glad to have Zia back and let someone else handle the horrible woman.

The uniformed officer finished the Miranda Warning, then led Victoria down the steps. The train conductor held his hat in one hand and scratched his head with the other as he observed the whole incident. Victoria lowered her head to her chin, probably to hide her face from onlookers. She didn't get sympathy from me.

As Barnes started to leave, I said, "How did you get here so fast?"

"I got your message. And you better be right about her."

I couldn't believe he listened to my message and had actually shown up. I said quickly, "Oh, I am. She confessed everything to me. And this boy recorded it all on his cell phone." I turned, motioning to the boy, but he was gone.

Barnes looked at the empty space where the nonexistent boy sat and nodded slowly. With an eyebrow lifted, he nodded, "Right."

Where was he? Had he slipped away during the hubbub? I ran to the door and looked outside. Flashing lights of the police car lit up the area in rhythm, but there was no sign of the kid. Shoot!

"I'm serious. He was right here." Why had the boy left? Surely, he knew that I needed the information.

Barnes shook his head and walked down the steps to stand by the police car. He spoke to an officer and the train conductor. Stepping off the platform and into the fresh evening air, I took in a deep breath and kissed my dog on her head. "Hey, girl. You must be part cat to survive that fall." I looked back at the open window and the 4-foot patch of grass where I had found her. It was surrounded by concrete. What were the chances?

I walked to the parking lot, looking for my truck, and realized that of course, it wasn't there. Glad to see Barnes and company were still standing by the cruiser, I walked toward the lights. Finally, away from the stuffy moving train full of drama, I felt my exhaustion hit.

The grumpy detective leaned against the driver's door jotting something in a notebook as I approached. "Sgt. Barnes, I left my car at the El Pueblo station. Could you give me a ride back there?"

He said dryly, without looking at me, "Take an Uber."

My face dropped. Uber? Seriously? After the trauma I'd been through today, I wanted to punch the man. My face turned red and I opened my mouth to give him a piece of my mind, but he sighed and said with a frown, "Alright, get in. But you'll have to ride in the back with the perpetrator."

Still hot with irritation and without thanking him, I climbed into the backseat. I was happy to sit down even if it was behind the grill in a police car and next to a murderer. I refused to look at Victoria, and instead studied the interior of the squad car. It looked cleaner than I expected but smelled stale and sweaty. Just how many dirty criminals had sat just where I was?

I reluctantly looked over at the fashionable suspect and she could only be described as rabid. Her scowl was clearly aimed at me. Even though she was handcuffed, I scooted as far away from her as possible and held Zia even farther.

Victoria whispered to me with separated and accented words, "Your dog bit me!"

I faced her and said incredulously, "So? You tried to kill me!"

She scoffed. "I did not," then hissed, "Let…me…have…the …charm!"

Feeling more secure with Zia in my arms, the culprit cuffed and belted, and being surrounded by policemen, I said, "Um…I think they'll need it as evidence." I nodded to the officers just inches away.

She looked frantic, "But that's the charm Jett bought me. It's really special." Again, she spit as she spoke, but this time her saliva actually hit my face.

While wiping my cheek with the back of my hand, I was reminded of Larry's comment about looking for the charm. I asked, "Did you have Larry look for it in my shop yesterday?"

She nodded, "Yeah. I made him look in case you found it and refused to return it to me."

"So, Larry knows you were involved in the death?"

She made a face, "Ha! That bumpkin? He doesn't know anything."

"Then, why would he risk going in Upcycled to look for a charm Jett gave you?"

She laughed as though he was so dumb. "I told him it was given to me by my grandmother and that you said you had found it and it was ok for him to stop by for it. He'll believe anything."

My wheels turned with so many more unanswered questions. "Did *you* erase the video on my computer?"

She shrugged an admission. "Larry saw you watching a security video. I thought you might also have a recording from an outdoor camera. I told him I'd lost my keys and he actually loaned me his whole set. When your truck left with that fat redhead, I went in and found the video on your computer. Even though the video was just from the interior, I erased it just in case."

Grrr. Now, this was all getting even more personal. She'd trespassed in my shop and because of her, I had no computer and almost didn't have a dog! And she called Jill fat? I pursed my lips.

She shrugged, "I'm not admitting anything. Who do you think they'll believe?" She chuckled, "I heard how that Sergeant talked to you." She sat up straighter and looked at me with an air of superiority, which was funny since she was the one handcuffed.

I looked at the beautiful girl through the eyes of the detectives. She may be right. Barnes didn't seem to believe most of what I said. At least I had the smoking gun - the DNA-coated charm.

She leaned over and demanded, "Give me the charm, or I'll…"

Before Victoria could complete her threat, both front doors opened in unison. The policemen entered the front seats, essentially shutting her up. Victoria's eyes blazed at me, but there was nothing she could do to me now. Barnes started the engine.

As we rode in silence, I felt Victoria's wild eyes aimed at me. When the car stopped at my station, I hopped out with Zia safely in my arms. I sighed, so happy to get away from that beastly woman.

Barnes rolled down his window and with a little smirk said, "Now that you've finished your private investigating career, will you please go back to selling junk?"

I shrugged. "Maybe. But, let's see… I do have one more detail to handle before I hang up my badge." I dug the little bag from my shorts pocket and held it up. "You might be interested in the item my assistant detective, Zia here, found. It fell from Victoria's charm bracelet the night of Pops' death." I made a face at the culprit in the back seat as I handed it to him.

She growled as I added, "You may want to check the DNA on it." I turned before he had time to make a smart-aleck remark and strode to my truck. "I believe it scraped Mr. Harrison's cheek."

I turned and walked to my truck. Once in my driver's seat, I took a deep breath, relieved that the whole thing was out of my hands. The murder mystery was solved, even if Victoria wouldn't admit anything. Too bad I had lost the boy with the recording.

I looked at the time on my dashboard and said to Zia, "It's too late for me to go visit the hospital. Let's go home."

Before going to bed, I sent a text telling Jill that I had a crazy, crazy night and the mystery was solved! I told her I'd go to the hospital in the morning.

I heard a ping and read the reply. *Don't leave me in the lurch. Who was it?*

I wrote back, *Victoria!*

OMG! Figures. I never trusted that snob.

I know.

We're getting released from the hospital before noon. Meet us at home after lunch. I have to hear all about it.

A calm Monday morning at home was just what I needed. I pampered Zia with the world's smallest back rub and a bite of my scrambled egg. I was happy to think that Jett, Flick, Carl and even Larry were all in the clear.

I worked on a few projects to replenish my stock and wrapped Sophia's baby gift before heading to Jill and Kelly's house. On the way, I stopped at the store and got a receipt book to start out the new week right.

Kelly met me at the door with his sidekick, Rosco. The kangaroo dog, true to his nickname, jumped so high he nearly touched my nose. I patted the excited black dog and hugged Kelly, then walked into the living room where Jill sat on the couch, nursing Sophia.

She looked up with a smile. "Hey, you! You sure look more relaxed than I thought you would after just opening the shop. So, tell me about the murder!"

I placed my present on the coffee table and sat beside my friend. "Nope. First things first. Let me see my sweet Godchild." I peeked over at the bundle baby nursing silently and half asleep. "Welcome home, little one."

I leaned over and kissed her on the head. "She's so beautiful." I don't know how, but she seemed to have already grown in only one day. I thought about the birth in my shop and all the pain Jill had endured. I stroked Jill's red hair. "How are you, my friend?"

"Me? I'm fine. Pretty sore in certain places, but it was worth it."

"That's good." I smiled and pointed to the gift. "I brought you girls something."

Jill brightened and moved the groggy baby from her breast. She carefully handed the sleeping Sophia to me, then situated herself. With a maniacal glee, she grabbed the wrapped box. I sat on the chair next to her, having a hard time deciding whether to stare at the sweet baby's face or watch Jill open the present.

CHAPTER 20

Jill untied the pink ribbon and ripped off the paper. When she lifted the box lid, Rosco stuck his nose in the tissue paper and snorted with disgust that it wasn't food, and left to curl up in his enormous bed.

Jill parted the tissue and her eyes instantly welled up. "No. Maria. You didn't. You can't."

I said, "Yes I can."

My own eyes filled with tears as I watched her lift out the Norwegian doll she had loved all her life. She held it so gently, even more gently than her baby. Sure, it was porcelain and fragile, but that's not why she held it so carefully. Jill had always treated that doll with special reverence. Her face told me all I needed to know. It was the perfect gift for a perfect person.

"But it's yours. It's your family heirloom."

"No. It has always been your special doll. You deserve it."

"You know, I'm going to put it on the top shelf and the little rascal, Sophia, will never get to touch it, just like we couldn't. I can't believe I'm finally old enough to hold it."

"And I got the blessing of Far Mor. I talked to her a few days ago and she agreed that you should have it since you are our honorary Norwegian."

We both laughed and cried at the same time. Finally, Jill wiped her eyes and put the doll back in the safety of its box, and stood to give me a hug above Sophia's body. "You are the best, Maria."

I said, "Oh, and there is a gift card in the box for you to get diapers or whatever you need."

Kelly said, "Thank you Maria. You didn't need to do that. The doll was plenty."

Jill added, wiping her eyes, "And remember, you decorated her whole room."

I looked at my two best friends and said, "But, you're going to share Sophia with me. I can't do enough to repay you for that."

Jill sat carefully with a contented grin, then popped back up excitedly, "You have to see what Joey brought for Sophia in the hospital on her actual birth-day… He made it himself!"

Kelly motioned for her to sit back down. He walked behind the couch and lifted up a gorgeous rocking horse made of walnut.

I leaned in to see the dark, chocolate-colored horse and with a free hand, rubbed my fingers along its smooth back. I was amazed by the beautiful woodgrain. "It's absolutely gorgeous. But how did he have time to do that with his place opening?"

Jill reached over and petted the horse. "Apparently he made the rocking horse a few months ago as a prototype. He plans to sell these along with some tables at a shop in Nob Hill, but he wanted to give his first horse to the child he helped bring into the world."

I gave a happy pout and felt like crying at the sweet gesture. "That's perfect. Oh, Jill, you would love his tables. They are amazing. I'm sure he won't have a bit of trouble selling either one." That Joey impressed me more and more every day.

Jill lifted her eyebrows. "OK. Enough baby present talk! Tell us all about last night."

I started telling the story of the evening to the captivated audience being careful not to disturb Sophia with my excitement.

Jill opened her mouth and eyes so wide, I thought they would pop. "She kidnapped Zia?"

Nodding, I continued with more details, watching her shocked expression when I told her about the keys digging into my throat.

"You have a bruise on your neck!" I had noticed it in the mirror this morning but didn't think anyone else would see it.

Kelly's face was red with fury. Jill responded with her lip curled, "I never liked that b...barista, but now..."

I said brightly, "It's all OK. I'm fine. Zia's fine. We're safe. She's locked up and all the questions have been answered."

Jill wrinkled her forehead. "Good, but I could have sworn Larry was more involved."

Kelly rubbed the back of his neck and said, "Maria, I meant to tell you I recovered the missing video from your computer, but I doubt that news would have kept you out of trouble."

"Well, you have had more important things on your mind." I nodded to the pink bundle in my arms. Then his statement sunk in. "Did you watch the video? Could you tell who was speaking on the recording?"

He shook his head. "We could only tell it was a woman's voice. The only words we could understand were, 'Give me the books!'"

"Well, now it makes more sense that Barnes met the train." I perked up. "I can only hope this means I'll get my computer back soon."

Jill smiled and said, "Oh, we had an interesting visitor stop by the hospital this morning." She leaned over and got an envelope from the table, handing it to me.

It contained a gift card to Target for $100.

I said, "That's nice."

"Look who it's from," she was bouncing on the couch.

"Steven Barnes?" I shrugged, trying to recall any Stevens that I knew.

"Your favorite person?" Kelly said, urging me to think.

I dropped my jaw. "No. Not our Barnes?" I looked at the envelope again and said, "Well, I'll be." So, the man actually had a heart. He just didn't like me, apparently. "The envelope says Kelly Standing Bear. He got your name right and knew you two were married?"

Jill nodded, "Yep. Go figure. He was pretty nice too when he came to see us."

Kelly walked into the dining room and came back with a reusable Trader Joe's bag with the New Mexico designs. He set the heavy bag next to me. "He asked me to give this to you."

I looked inside the bag. "My computer!" I was so relieved to have it back that I closed my eyes and visualized an easier day in the shop tomorrow and sighed.

Jill said, "So your first two days went well?"

I'd almost forgotten about my store with the crazy ending to yesterday but filled them in on my success. "Now, I need to make a ton more products, because I was wiped out!"

Jill started laughing. "Speaking of making products, while I was posting photos of Sophia online, guess what video has gone viral?"

I had no idea and shrugged. "Baby goats again?"

"No." She did a little drumroll in the air. "Zia, photobombing your tutorial video! It's been shared hundreds of times just today." Her eyes were sparkling as she giggled.

My tutorial video had gone viral? I wondered why the dog's appearance would have gotten such a reaction and asked, "Why?" Just as Jill started to answer, her mom and dad entered the house and I couldn't get to the bottom of it. Instead, I decided to watch it when I got home.

Her mother walked toward me and gave her new granddaughter a kiss and me a hug. Mrs. O'Brien reminded me of Molly Weasley from Harry Potter; short, round, redheaded and absolutely radiating with maternal energy. Actually the whole family was just like the Weasley family. "And how's our adopted daughter and Sophia's Godmother, today?"

This couple had become my surrogate parents after mine died. I couldn't have asked for a more loving family to watch over me, especially during the difficult first six months. I answered, "I'm great and thrilled with this precious family. How are you, *Nana*?" I handed Sophia to her adoring Grandma.

"Never been better!" She cooed at the sleeping child as "Papa" O'Brien looked over her shoulder at the baby.

I stood and said to Jill, "I'd better get movin' and let you all have some family bonding time." I turned to Jill's folks, "June and Jerry, you should stop by my shop sometime."

"You got any manly stuff in there or is it just a bunch of doilies and fruity tooty stuff?" Mr. O'Brien winked. He always made me laugh.

June slapped him playfully on the arm and said, "We will stop by soon. Don't you worry."

That afternoon at home I made a whole crop of new silverware jewelry and another pillow made from an old apron. I thought about making more book safes but that didn't feel right after everything that happened with the last books. And I was scared to cut into any old ones for fear they might be worth a fortune.

I took a break to get a glass of iced tea and look over my computer. I opened the lid of my laptop and saw a sticky note that read, "Good job, junk girl." I smiled at the thought that cranky Barnes actually gave me kudos.

I pushed the power button. Once it booted up, I remembered Jill's comment about Zia, and pulled up my video demonstration on YouTube to see what all the hubbub was about.

I clicked play and there I was explaining how to carefully cut into a book a few pages at a time. I thought I looked pretty good. Then, Zia toddled over and laid down with head on her paws, just as I'd seen her on the table. It was cute, but not that funny.

As I watched myself continue to demonstrate, the tiny dog looked at me, then at the french fries. Shoot, I didn't realize the food was in the frame. With careful steps, Zia snuck over to my plate of fries and took one as slowly and carefully as if she took a block from a Jenga game. She crept back to her spot, flicking her big black eyes to me as she moved. Once seated, she chomped on the fry until it was gone. Then she looked at me while I talk, talk, talked, and as if on tiptoes, she snuck over for another fry. Now I got it. I laughed so hard that I woke my dog up. She looked at me like I was crazy.

"You little rascal."

Wondering if there were any comments on my informative DIY video, I scrolled down and was thrilled to find a long row waiting to be read. I skimmed through them but rolled my eyes when I realized almost all were about the dog rather than my well-thought-out lesson.

I did enjoy reading the clever comments and even replied to a few. One said Blake's Lotaburger should hire that dog for a commercial.

I typed, 'Not only is Zia a little sneak, but she's also part sleuth and even helped to solve a murder just last night.'

When I got to the most recent comments, one startled me so much that I nearly choked on my tea. It read, 'I just saw a crazy video post with a dog that looked just like this one. It was being held outside a window of a train.'

What? Had the boy posted the harrowing experience online? I immediately typed, 'Dog held out a train window.' into the YouTube search bar. Within seconds, there was Victoria's hand holding Zia out the window. I stared at my screen, cringing at the sight, but ecstatic that the boy had posted it. Yay! It wasn't lost. The posted video was short – only two minutes long, so it didn't catch the actual confession, but I knew he had filmed it all, so there was hope I could get the rest of the video if I could just find him.

I rifled through my backpack and found Barnes' card with his e-mail address. After copying the video's link, I forwarded it to him with a note that said, 'In case Victoria isn't cooperating in the interrogation, you might be interested in this. Find this boy and you'll have the whole confession on video - see I didn't imagine the kid.' I signed it "Detective Olson," just to make him growl.

My shoulders relaxed almost instantly. It was all finally over.

Tuesday morning, The Boxcar Adults met in the bakery. The little place bustled with the giddy shop owners, all describing their stellar business on Saturday and Sunday. Jett and Joey talked to Mike and Pat. Jett nodded his head at me when I entered, and Joey glanced my way briefly.

I sat with Louise and ate a delicious blue corn scone. "OK, Louise, you must tell me how to recognize a first edition book when I see it. Did you know I almost sliced into a first edition of Huckleberry Finn last week?"

"Oh. No. You. Did. Not." She said, dramatically blinking with each word.

I nodded, twisting my mouth and shoulders in embarrassment. She lay out a napkin and magically pulled a pen from her bra, and began to draw the markings found on the inside of a first edition book. Just as she finished explaining, the door opened, and a hush came over the tiny crowd. Flick hobbled in followed by his ever-awkward son, Carl.

I stood and approached the two men. "Welcome, Flick… and Carl." I was still somewhat nervous being around Flick after his outbursts. But he patted Carl on the back and pulled him closer to us. The old man's gravelly voice said, "I had a talk with my son. It seems he owes you an apology and I guess I do too.'

He scratched his head, delaying his apology. "Ahem. I was pretty upset about losing my brother and kept forgetting to take my chill pills."

Carl's head was down on his chest as usual, but he flicked his eyes up at me a few times. I didn't know how to respond, but stammered, "Um…thank you, for saying that Mr. Harrison. It's been a tough week all around. Carl and I worked out our differences the other day, and I hope we'll all become friends over time."

Feeling rather uncomfortable, I said in a bright voice, "Have you met the other merchants in Out of the Box?"

Flick said in his gruff manner, "No. Might as well get it over with now."

I gave a nervous laugh and began introducing people. "This fine lady is Louise. She owns the bookstore, called A Likely Story."

Louise stood and said, "How do you do, sirs? Did I hear your name is Flick? Well, I just love that name. You'll have to tell me all about it later." She waltzed over and pinned a button on his shirt before the old man could protest or even know what she had done. "We have a special name for this eclectic group."

Only Louise could get away with touching that man without permission. The woman amazed me.

Louise then turned to Carl and stuck a button on his PacMan t-shirt. "And Carl, you have the loveliest blue eyes. That's right, you can't hide those pretty peepers from me."

Carl blinked and shook his head with the attention, but he didn't run away, so that was good.

I continued with the introductions, "And these two brothers, Jett and Joey, own the Rusty Railroad brewery." Just as I'd said this, I remembered the old man had threatened Jett last week. And then there was the uncomfortable firing scene of Carl I'd witnessed. I bit my thumbnail and held my breath anticipating fireworks.

Jett came over and patted Carl on the back, "Hey Carl, good to see you." Then he leaned over to Flick and shook his hand and said, "We got all the permits squared away and moved my car to the back. I hope that's acceptable to you, sir."

Flick's eyes narrowed and his frown was well pronounced, but after a beat, he gave a nod.

Joey came up next. He said to Carl, "Hey Bud. If you want another try sometime we could sure use you. Last week was stressful for all of us."

Carl spoke up quickly and with his head held a little higher than usual, "I won't have t t t time. My D D Dad wants me to work for him in his st st store."

I was glad to see him show more confidence.

Joey said with a smile, "Good. I'm glad you're happy there." He turned to Flick. "Mr. Harrison, it's very nice to meet you at last. I'm so sorry for the loss of your brother."

The group was quiet at that. I wanted to fill everyone in on the outcome of the investigation but knew it wasn't the time. I finished the introductions by pointing to the two guys in aprons. "And our fabulous baker boys are Mike and Pat. They make the most delicious baked goods you'll ever try."

They waved, a little nervous to meet the crotchety old man. Flick nodded to them, then he surprised me when he said, "Where's that uppity girl who owns the coffee shop? I need to tell her we still haven't found the books that were stolen."

Oh boy...looks like it *was* time to fill everyone in. "Mr. Harrison, I have something to say about that. Would you like to have a seat?" He obliged and followed my lead to a chair at our table, sitting down so slowly it was painful to watch. Carl sat next to him with eyes averted.

I faced the group and cleared my throat. "I had hoped the police would have spoken with you by now, Mr. Harrison." I took a breath and said, "I happen to know that your brother's murder case has been solved." All eyes stared at me. "I'm sorry to announce that the guilty party was Victoria, the owner of the coffee shop."

There was a collective gasp. Louise threw her hand to her mouth but surprisingly kept quiet. Jett's eyes narrowed in disbelief and Flick's mouth dropped open. Dang, why did I have to be the bearer of bad news? My palms started to sweat, so I wiped them on my shorts as I gave my account starting with Zia running to the coffee shop.

Everyone who was still standing found seats and all eyes were affixed to me. I felt self-conscious being the only one standing but there were no seats left in the tiny place. I shifted my weight from foot to foot as I explained the situation.

When I got to Zia being held out the train window, the group simultaneously lifted their eyebrows and leaned in a little. I relieved my audience quickly by saying, "Don't worry. I got Zia back safely." Then I continued with the whole tale. I opted to tell Jett about being drugged later in private.

Once the story ended, the room was unusually silent as all the information sunk in. I was surprised there weren't a lot of questions, but maybe the explanation made sense. People slowly began to fill the void with conversations among themselves.

Mike stood and wove through the chairs. He loomed over me and said, "I can't believe she threw your dog out the window. What a monster!"

It was a bit funny that he focused on the dog incident instead of the murder. I nodded. "It was horrible."

I looked at the bakery clock on the wall, realizing I should go back to get ready to open in 30 minutes. The door under the clock opened. In walked the girl Joey had been with at the gala. Great. What was she doing here?

Not surprisingly, Joey walked over to her with a grin. He announced, "Everybody, I'd like you to meet Julie."

Super. Now I knew her name. I eyed the girl closely for the first time. She had one of those friendly natural smiles; not forced or fake. Dang it, she even had cute dimples.

Jett joined the two and added to the crowd, "Julie's our baby sister and will help us with the books at the pub."

Sister? Did he say sister? A feeling of happiness rushed over me as this information settled. Good grief. I was such a dope. I glanced at sweet Joey and regretted acting awkwardly towards him after Sophia's birth. How awful, especially after all he did for us.

Unable to wipe the smile from my face, I walked to the new girl and said, "Welcome to our team. I'm very happy to meet you. I'm Maria."

A kind smile spread across Julie's face. "I've heard an awful lot about you. The boys said you were pretty and talented. And they are right. You are gorgeous. I need to come to your shop to look around."

I froze with the compliment, but was still so elated about her relationship to Joey, that I said probably too brightly, "Come by anytime!" I looked up at Joey but said to her, "Um… would you excuse us for a sec, please?"

I took Joey's arm and said, "Can I speak to you?"

We stepped outside and I looked into his twinkly eyes. "I owe you a huge apology."

He squinted in interest or possibly because of the morning sun. I gulped and said, "I saw you at Chandler's Gala." I cleared my throat. "When I saw you with her…" I pointed to the door, "well, silly me, I jumped to conclusions. I thought you were on a date with that beautiful woman and to be honest…I was jealous."

Joey's smirk didn't shut me up. As a matter of fact, I spoke faster. "And then I saw her going into your brewery and…well, I wondered why you were still flirting with me when you had a girlfriend." I took a breath and shook my head, beating myself up internally. "And then you were such a hero to bring Sophia into the world, but I was so confused and acted like a dummy. So, you see, I don't have my act together completely."

The corners of his mouth lifted slightly as he took me by both hands. "Besides the fact that it's creepy that you thought I was dating my sister, I'm glad I meant that much to you."

That seemed hopeful and I smiled weakly. "It's been kinda miserable not talking to you."

He looked at me seriously. "I suppose I can forgive you, but it may take some time." He took a deep breath and let it out. "We'll probably have to discuss it at length over say…dinner tonight, if I can get Jett to handle the crowd?" His right eyebrow lifted playfully.

A feeling of relief and possibly lust rushed through me as I stretched up to give him a hug.

A scuffing sound on gravel interrupted the moment. Then came a familiar odor and whiny voice. "Well, lookie at the two lovebirds."

I pushed away from Joey and straightened my shirt, as if guilty of something. It was strange seeing Larry again after all that had happened. It was also odd because he wore a cowboy hat that was much too large for his head. As much as I wanted to wring his neck,

I realized his only real crime may have been that of gullibility. Well, that and invading my shop without my permission.

He turned to me, apparently unaware of all my investigative work of late, and said with a waggle of his head, "I guess you saw that I got the security lights fixed Sunday afternoon. They work like a charm now."

He'd finally fixed the lights? Hmm. I thought back to Sunday. I guess I'd left before it was completely dark and hadn't noticed. Oh! That was probably the scraping sound I heard outside the building that day.

Before I got a chance to say anything he said, "You happy with the new window screen? It was cool of that old policeman to pay for it, huh?"

I closed my eyes and tried to process what he said. A policeman had paid for the repairs in my shop? Kelly? But Kelly is certainly not old. I opened my eyes to find Larry staring at me waiting for a reply. "Um, yes. Wait, Larry. It wasn't a detective named Barnes, was it?"

"Yeah, that sounds right. He just gave me a card and said to take care of it and send him the bill." At that, he waltzed inside the bakery. Before the door shut, we heard him announce, "I have some important news." Joey looked at me, seemingly just as confused as I was, and we followed Larry inside.

Once he had the attention of his audience, Larry leaned his elbows on the glass bakery case as if his hat was too heavy to hold his upper body up. He announced, "Hey ya'll. Sorry I've been out of the loop lately." He stood straight and puffed up his chest. "I have been in the middle of a business deal with Alex Chandler."

I scoffed at the thought, then my smile faded as I remembered his meeting at El Pinto a few nights before. Perhaps the guy was smarter than he seemed.

He continued, "Chandler and a group of investors are working on a deal to expand Out of the Box. Now, I don't know how much it will develop, but at any rate, it should be good for business. Anyhoo, I've got new business cards with my new phone number."

He started handing out the cards explaining, "I changed it last week, which wasn't at all convenient. I hope none of you had any pressing business that you missed."

So, he hadn't avoided my calls, he just had a new number.

I watched as Flick took the card, then reached in his pocket and handed Larry a check, saying, "I'm late on my rent check. My brother always took care of those things." His face turned down more than usual. Aha. The money Larry asked for on the phone was for rent, not for the stolen books. I closed my eyes, silently berating myself for yet another misunderstanding.

When Larry reached me, he held the card and said, "I assume you got my message last week?" He didn't wait for me to respond. "Victoria told me I could enter your shop to look for her stupid charm. I just called to make sure it was OK with you. Man, you sure have a good guard dog there. The tiny thing nearly bit a hole in my jeans."

My mouth dropped open a smidge. The guy had called to ask permission to come into my shop? In all the craziness, I hadn't listened to my messages. Since I was stunned by this revelation and wasn't aware of his call anyway, I opted to comment on the dog instead. "She's got spunk alright."

Larry tapped the card and handed it to me, saying, "I already gave your preggo friend my new number in case The Grass Man company needed a manager." Then, he walked on to Mike and Pat.

I looked at the card, turned to Joey, and said, "Well, I'm relieved about that! We thought Larry wanted a date with a pregnant woman." The card read; Chandler Associates. Growing

Albuquerque One Quality Structure at a Time. Larry Bandersnitch – Property Manager."

Joey said, "I'm not sure I can handle more surprises today." He took my hand and then said, "But, having you back is the best one."

I beamed as I leaned against Joey, half-listening to the wiry, braggadocios Larry ramble on about his new job. He may well be innocent but he was sure still annoying.

In a flourish, Larry said, "Enough about me. I'm not sure if you heard, but our barista is out of commission." He put his hand up to his mouth in a conspiratorial way and said, "And never paid her rent or hardly anything towards her building." I saw a glint of sadness cross his face, but then he brightened and said, "But…with Out of the Box being such a hot new market here in the Duke City, there has been a waiting list to get in…"

The door opened, interrupting his speech, and a young girl with hot pink hair peeked in with wide brown eyes and a perky smile. Larry motioned to her to come on in and she stepped through the door wearing mismatched socks, a short skirt, and blue suspenders.

Larry said with glee, "Well, now that's what I call perfect timing! Everyone, this is Isabella. She'll be opening Bueno Beans, the new coffee shop featuring Mexican and New Mexican coffee here in Out of the Box."

I smiled at the new girl, and with the hand that wasn't attached to Joey, I gave a little wave. Louise stepped up and said in her booming voice, "Welcome to the Boxcar Adults!"

THE END

About the Author

Martha Kemm Landes is a former Oklahoma public school music teacher. Besides writing musicals for her students, she is known for writing the Oklahoma State Children's Song, <u>Oklahoma, My Native Land</u>. After moving to New Mexico, she began her transition from composer to author. She enjoys writing fun mysteries and is a member of Southwest Writers.

Martha lives with her screenwriter husband and three adopted dogs in Rio Rancho, New Mexico, a suburb of Albuquerque. They enjoy spending time at their log cabin in the nearby Jemez Mountains.

Besides writing, Martha quilts, knits, and volunteers by delivering Meals on Wheels. She loves to be outdoors and finds the weather perfect in New Mexico for hiking, gardening, and hosting summer movies at their large backyard movie theater.

Scan for a quick link to the website

Author's note on the real dog, Zia.

Several years ago, while driving to our cabin, a strange little creature crossed the highway in front of me. Worrying it would be hit by traffic, I stopped. Still not sure if it was a rat or a dog, I patted my legs, and surprisingly, the critter ran to me. Upon closer inspection, I could tell the stinky animal with horribly matted fur was a dog, albeit an itty bitty one.

I asked around to find the owner, but people said, "Dogs are dumped here all the time – just take it." In order to save its life, I did, with plans to take the tiny dog to a shelter.

A clinic confirmed it was a female teacup poodle weighing 3 ½ lbs. After being shaved and bathed, my husband and I fell in love and named her Zia. When a vet removed her rotten teeth, leaving her toothless, we worried she couldn't eat, but he said, "This dog is so smart, she'll be ordering her own pizza." And indeed, the smartie nearly doubled her weight since adopting us.

Zia has become an integral member of our family. She pretty much rules the roost and even bosses around our 75-lb sheepdog.

Before

After

9 781956 912067